COMMANDO

COMMANDO
WINNING THE GREEN BERET

HUGH McMANNERS

Network Books

Based on Folio Productions' TV series *COMMANDO,*
made for Westcountry Television, produced and
directed by Charles Thompson.

Network Books is an imprint of BBC Books,
a division of BBC Enterprises Limited,
Woodlands, 80 Wood Lane,
LONDON W12 0TT

First published 1994

© Hugh McManners, 1994

The moral right of the author has been asserted

ISBN 0 563 36981 7

Typeset by Selwood Systems, Midsomer Norton
Printed and bound in Great Britain by Clays Ltd, St Ives Plc
Jacket printed in Great Britain by Belmont Press Ltd, Northampton

(*Frontispiece*) Marine Wilson, 45 Commando, Arbroath, 1993.

CONTENTS

Introduction
7

CHAPTER ONE
All Arms, Volunteer Commandos
13

CHAPTER TWO
Dawn Assault
44

CHAPTER THREE
Ambush
66

CHAPTER FOUR
638 Troop – Dartmoor
82

CHAPTER FIVE
The Reckoning
101

CHAPTER SIX
638 Troop – Commando Tests
133

CHAPTER SEVEN
The End of the Road
160

Epilogue
186

Index
190

ACKNOWLEDGEMENTS

This book arises from the television series of the same name made by Folio Productions for Westcountry Television. My thanks therefore must not only go to Her Majesty's Royal Marines and to those who assisted in the book's publication, but also to the television production team and those who commissioned the series.

Charles Thompson and I devised the series, which from over 40 hours of footage, became five television programmes – and this book. Within the MOD, Major Bill MacLennan was a prime mover, his enthusiasm was shared by successor Captain Simon Haselock, who coordinated the additional photography and information needed for the book; and by PO (Phot) Cowpe. DPR (Navy) Captain Chris Esplin-Jones and Colonel John Meardon made sure things happened, and Major General Andy Keeling provided firm backing in 'high places'.

CTC's then Commandant Colonel Mike Taffinder not only opened every door to us during filming, but also waded through my manuscript making many sensitive, intelligent comments which greatly enhanced my text. (I claim sole credit for any errors that might remain.) Major Jon Lear and Captain Leo Williams helped gather documents and photos, and with Lieutenant Archie Gillies and his training team read chapters relevant to them, ensuring the accuracy of the story. I must also mention Captain Rayson Pritchard and Captain Ian Dunn.

Thanks also to the excellent Folio Productions team: Aileen McCracken, David Gasson, Des Seal and Steve Phillips, Barbara Walters (particularly for sleeping bags), but above all to series producer-director Charles Thompson. I also include our excellent liaison officer Lieutenant Jamie Main RM (scaffolder extraordinary) in the 'crew' section.

With inappropriately short 'mentions' my very great thanks to Network Books' enormously efficient, friendly and positive production team: particularly to Editor Julian Flanders, Picture Research Manager Joanna Wiese, and the Joint Head of Editorial Suzanne Webber. I've greatly enjoyed working with you.

Hugh McManners

PICTURE CREDITS

Network Books would like to thank the following for providing photographs and art work and the permission for reproducing them in this book:
Crown Copyright Section, MOD; Folio Productions Ltd; Westcountry Television Ltd.

CTCRM, CPO (Phot) Al Campbell, PO (Phot) Paul Cowpe, Tony Davies, LA (Phot) Jim Gibson, Capt Simon Haselock, CSgt Loraine, LA (Phot) Terry Morgan, Cpl A Sutherland and Sgt I Traynor.

With special thanks to the staff at Folio Productions.

NOTE ON THE TEXT

Today's Commando Tests are exactly the same as those endured by Second World War Commandos, and the distances given for them here are in the original Imperial measurements. However, distances on maps and other measurements for regular manoeuvres are generally metric as modern Commandos think and work in metric. The reader might find the mixture of measures confusing.

INTRODUCTION

British Commando Forces were formed in the darkest days of the Second World War, to strike back at the German occupation of Europe, giving hope to the occupied nations while creating time for the build-up of forces for the eventual D-Day landings. Initially formed using combat-experienced volunteers from Army units, the lightly equipped Commando units were so successful that Hitler declared them outside the protection of the Geneva Conventions. They were 'terrorists' – men whose very existence caused anxiety among his own troops, whose hard-hitting clandestine operations created widespread terror far in excess of their actual numbers. The Führer declared that captured Commandos were not bona fide prisoners of war, and could be tortured and shot. Many were.

The word 'Commando' is Afrikaans meaning a 'quasi-military party called out for military purposes (especially of the Boers) against the natives'. Having seen the Boers in action as a young man, Churchill was clearly impressed enough to borrow their word for his new force. Second World War Commandos were volunteers from other units, preferably those who had already done well in combat. The new force was very particular about who it admitted. All ranks had first to qualify individually as 'Commandos', before being posted into a Commando unit.

The units into which qualified Commandos were posted were also called Commandos, an amalgam of individuals – officers and men from every regiment and corps in the Army, plus the Royal Marines, a good many specialist coxswains and landing craft experts from the

Royal Navy, and a few from the RAF. As the war proceeded, several Royal Marines regiments were converted wholesale into Commandos (it has to be said, accompanied by a touch of consternation from the more traditional Royal Marines of that time).

The initial Commandos were literally bodies of men 'called out for military purposes', to a strength determined by operations. They were however soon rationalized into units roughly equating to an Army battalion – although in terms of numbers, structure, multiplicity of role and range of expertise, the comparison (particularly today) is very superficial.

The military forte of those first Commandos was the amphibious raid. Through what at that time was a truly unique combination of Army and Royal Navy expertise (with a good deal of initial inter-service rivalry), Commando raiding parties darted across the English Channel to hit German coastal garrisons and installations, returning home for well-earned (and rationed) eggs and bacon. With each raid more was learned, not only about the enemy but also about the whole practice of amphibious warfare and Commando operations.

Amphibious expertise accumulated over the years has made the Royal Marines, to whom the flame of Commando operations was entrusted after the War, the foremost amphibious infantry in the world, backed by Army artillery, engineer and service corps units – all wearing the coveted Green Beret. The formidable sum total of this accumulated expertise enabled the Falklands to be recaptured in 1982 from a well-motivated and exceptionally well-supplied Argentine expeditionary force, three times the size of their attackers.

Today, four Royal Marines 'battalions' remain: 40, 42 and 45 Commando, providing the infantry units (the bayonets) for 3 Commando Brigade. In addition, 29 Commando Regiment Royal Artillery provides fire support and naval gunfire control and advance reconnaissance teams, 59 Independent Commando Squadron Royal Engineers sapper support, and the Commando Logistic Regiment all the supply and servicing back-up the Brigade needs. As with each of the Commandos, their range of capability, capacity and flexibility and of these other units are unique within the British Armed Forces. They are simply not comparable with other Army units.

The Green Beret is the common denominator of 3 Commando Brigade, the basic entry requirement for every volunteer. The three Commandos are manned by the Royal Marines (plus a number of Royal Navy specialists). 29 Commando Regiment and 59 Commando Squadron are manned by the Army – specialists in their own right,

(*Right*) The 'Yomping Marine' statue outside the Royal Marine Museum in Southsea, erected in 1992 to commemorate the part played by the Marines in the Falklands campaign.

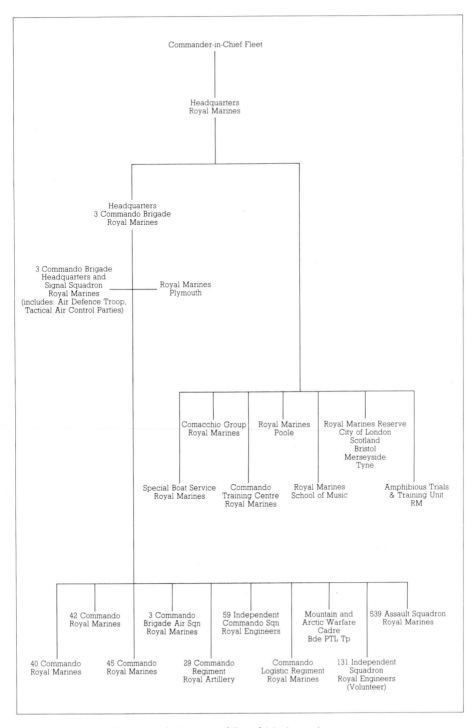

The organization of Commando Forces and Royal Marine units.

who must also pass the All-Arms Commando Course. The Commando Logistic Regiment is a mixture of Royal Marines, Army and Royal Navy. A number of the latter (mostly medics) are not required to pass the Commando Course. Royal Marines do their Commando training at the end and as part of their recruit training, whereas Army, Navy and RAF Commandos must pass the Royal Marines' All Arms Commando Course – both held at the Commando Training Centre, at Lympstone in Devon.

Operation Corporate (the name of the British forces' plan throughout the Falklands War), required 3 Commando Brigade to work at the end of the longest ever supply chain of any past war, 8000 miles with no friendly port – from the top of one hemisphere to the bottom of the other, through the roughest seas in the world. Since the dark days of 1940, the capability of British amphibious operations has developed beyond recognition, but the basics – speed, mobility, surprise and firepower – are still very much the determining factors characterizing Commando operations. For all its scale and complexity, Operation Corporate was a Commando raid, conducted using all the time-honoured factors that must be considered if a Commando raid is to be successful.

Commando soldiers are expected to be able to perform regardless of conditions or circumstances. Being able to do the special Commando Tests when exhausted is therefore very much part of the process. The four Commando Tests, the 9-mile speed march, Tarzan assault course, endurance course and 30-mile forced march (carrying 22 pounds of equipment and weapon), come at the very end of exhausting weeks of testing (mostly living rough on exercise), and a particularly gruelling Final Exercise. By that time, most individuals are carrying some kind of injury. So although intensely physical, the essence of the Commando Tests is actually mental – measuring the ability of each individual to withstand pressure of every kind.

There is however no mystery attached to the Commando course. The standards both on arrival and at the finish are clearly defined, with a strong emphasis on sound preparation. Men must arrive with exactly the right equipment in good order, and are inspected frequently throughout the course. Everything must be correct regardless of circumstances. Being at the right place at the right time with the right equipment is the basis of Commando discipline – and requires the highest standard of personal administration. Individuals who prove unable to keep themselves and their personal equipment in good order, are unlikely to be able to look after vehicles, stores or larger weapon systems under pressure. Many fail simply because of 'poor personal administration'.

Abraham Lincoln's famous remark that: 'By failing to prepare, you're preparing to fail' is a widely held maxim. Despite being muddy and wet for much of the course, military standards are jealously and ruthlessly maintained; kit must always be properly waterproofed, serviceable and in the correct pouches. With the wear and tear, keeping one's equipment in good order is a constant struggle, particularly as detected deficiencies are likely to earn offenders extra parades 6 miles away on the Common, at unsociable hours. Similarly, people are expected always to parade in clean, pressed uniforms – despite knowing that within minutes they will be soaking wet. On exercise, when smartness becomes well nigh impossible, they are expected to keep their kit neat and tidy – and above all ready for action. Penalties for a dirty weapon or rusty bayonet are severe.

Commando training is a million miles away from the popular myth of gung ho, super-fit Captain Hurricanes. The reality is quiet, often tired, but determined bodies of men, working together to overcome adversity. They do have special capabilities and skills which the course teaches them but their most important quality is the ability to keep going until the job is done.

The so-called glamour of the Green Beret is a far cry from the process of actually earning one, which requires a lot of guts and determination. At its most basic, Commandos are infantry soldiers who keep going for that little bit longer than others and in environments that little bit harsher – producing that little bit of extra effort when it really counts . . . which makes all the difference in the world.

But why do these men endure what to the outsider must appear a perversely cold and watery, self-inflicted hell-on-earth? The secret to understanding this lies not in detached observation, but in becoming part of the process, to understand how both trainers and those being trained share the desire to maintain the time-honoured standards of Commando troops. Nobody wants to take short-cuts, to get a Green Beret the 'easy way' – if such a thing were possible. Underneath all the pain and effort, everybody at the Commando Training Centre has but one aim; to match up to the exacting personal standards of the original, wartime Commandos. Boiled down to its essentials, this motivation is incredibly strong – a unique opportunity to match yourself, in the very real world, with the stuff of legends.

We therefore join the 17 survivors of the original 34 starters of All Arms Commando Course 4/92, on the fourth week of their Commando training – learning Commando cliff-climbing drills on Dartmoor. Already trained volunteers from the Army, Royal Navy and Royal Air Force, 4/92 are more akin to the original wartime Commandos than the younger Royal Marines recruits, who undergo Commando training after 27 weeks of fitness and infantry training.

CHAPTER ONE

ALL ARMS, VOLUNTEER COMMANDOS

It's 23 November, and the 17 surviving members of All Arms Commando Course number 4/92 are at the beginning of their fourth week of Commando training.

4/92 have already completed five weeks of physical and military training at the Commando Training Centre Royal Marines, at Lympstone (CTCRM), learning infantry tactics as well as Commando techniques. Even though all the Army students are well versed in basic infantry work, such things are a mystery to most RAF and RN students. Infantry tactics are therefore taught from scratch, which suits the Royal Marines who prefer everybody to do things in the same fashion — their way! Lieutenant Linderman, a slender, mild-looking Royal Navy 'schoolie' (education officer), has gained training team approval through doing exactly what he is told — while maintaining a nicely reflective sense of humour. Flight Lieutenant Taylor, a Tornado navigator referred to as 'Baggage' because he sits in the back seat of the aircraft, is equally compliant. Perhaps the keenest man on the course is Petty Officer Barrel, a cheerful, round-faced stoker who has wanted to be a Commando ever since joining the Navy over ten years ago.

There is an inevitable element of Army versus Royal Marines on the All Arms Commando Course. In order to get their Green Berets, Army candidates (4/92 started with six Army officers, four Army NCOs and 33 Army other ranks) have to grin and bear it. Army people are referred to by 'Royal' as 'Percy Pongo', or 'Perse' for short (based on the historical observation that 'where the pong goes, the Army goes') — and are assumed not to wash as often as Royal Marines.

All Arms Commando Course 4/92.
1 2Lt Arran, 2 2Lt Maddison, 3 Cpl McLean, 4 Pte Thomas, 5 LCpl Hutcheon,
6 LBdr Gornall, 7 Gnr McDermont, 8 Gnr Robson, 9 Lt Coleman, 10 Sgt
Cameron, 11 WO2 Dobson, 12 Gnr Chapman, 13 LCpl Thompson, 14 LBdr
Barclay, 15 Lt Lewis, 16 Pte Xavier, 17 Lt Heley, 18 Flt Lt Taylor, 19 2Lt
Perkins, 20 Cpl Scotson, 21 Spr Rockey, 22 LCpl Flynn, 23 Pte Dredge,
24 LCpl Bristow, 25 LCpl Hodgson, 26 Lt Kepple Compton, 27 Lt Linder,
28 PO Barrel, 29 Spr Roach, 30 Gnr Hargreaves, 31 KCpl Williams, 32 LCpl
Heaps, 33 Pte Jordon, 34 Spr Khanlarian.
Training Team: 35 Cpl Gorrie, 36 Cpl Parnell, 37 Cpl Lannon, 38 Cpl Archer,
39 Cpt Pritchard OC, 40 Sgt Swayne, 41 Cpl Boorn, 42 Cpl Pelling, 43 Bdr
Booth.

Royal Marines are referred to by their historical nickname of Boot-necks, derived from the days when wearing stiff collars forced them to stand particularly straight.

This healthy inter-service rivalry stems back to the very first days of Commando Forces, when initially Commando units were raised from Navy and Army volunteers with combat experience (Royal Marines included). When a large increase in the numbers of Commando troops was required, Royal Marine naval infantry battalions were 'converted' en masse to the new role – or hi-jacked as some Corps traditionalists saw it at the time. When the Second World War ended, the Army proper lost interest in what it saw as mysteriously maritime, almost renegade Commandos, and responsibility for Commando Forces was handed over to the Royal Marines.

Of the 34 who started course 4/92, only 17 remain. Keeping track of numbers is difficult even for the instructors, as people rejoin at every stage having recovered from injuries sustained on previous courses, at times pushing course numbers up to 60 and more. The steady attrition rate, however, prevents the course becoming too large.

In the first three weeks, unsuitable people are weeded out not only by the various 'criteria tests' (which everybody must pass) and by injury, but also on field training exercises, whose underlying purpose is the testing of motivation and character through sleep deprivation coupled with rigorous insistence on maintaining military standards. In particular, many of the younger soldiers have gone, lacking the preparation and mental maturity necessary for surviving this course.

Injury is the main problem. One of CTC's Medical Officers Surgeon Lieutenant Commander Hughes RN, himself an All Arms graduate:

'Nobody finishes without some kind of injury – which gets better once the phyzz stops. But coping with injuries, which are just as likely to occur in a Commando unit as here, is all part of looking after yourself; frostbite in the Arctic, for example.

'The All Arms is a unique course here – inducing phenomenal pressure. There's no Hunter Troop [CTC's medical rehabilitation unit for Royal Marine recruits]; you either make the grade or you're out. The disgrace of failing and going back to the units is great.'

Royal Marine instructor, the black-moustached Corporal Gorrie:

'We are not here to find people's weaknesses. We don't have their expertise in the Royal Marines, so we need them more than they need us. We're therefore here to put Green Berets on their heads if we possibly can.

'We are not however going to drop the standards, which are the same today as in the Second World War. We could put them through the tests in four days, but over the eight weeks we put them through an awful lot more. In particular, their soldiering skills have got to be up to standard – or they will not pass.'

Royal Marine recruits enjoy the enormous advantage of 27 weeks of the most expert, progressive fitness training before being put to the test. Army candidates have only a two- or three-week 'beat-up' with their parent Commando units, and so must get themselves Commando fit in their spare time. Being fully trained soldiers already, All Arms personnel are usually more generally robust than younger, less experienced Royal Marine recruits. Furthermore, with officers and senior NCOs actually doing the course, the All Arms have a strong rank and command structure, presenting a united course entity – with a backbone that ensures a greater chance of survival for the individuals.

'Character testing' is probably more a feature of the All Arms Commando Course than it ever would, or could be on RM recruits' courses. Having a brace of Army instructors on All Arms Courses helps maintain a balance, although as far as 4/92 are concerned, Corporal Tam Miles of the Royal Engineers and Bombardier Dick Booth of the Royal Artillery are just as fierce as any of their Royal Marine colleagues.

At 32, Sergeant Major Dobson is older than anybody on All Arms 4/92, training team included:

'Some of the guys are not ready for the level of aggravation provided by the training team. Army courses tend to nurture people along – which doesn't happen on the All Arms. The training team push some people until they break. Some guys [on the course] don't realize that the team aren't really bothered whether they fail or not.'

Although the Training Team do not show it, they are in fact trying to get everybody through. It is, however, inevitable that some individuals will not make the grade. For them, the inability to find the resources within themselves to succeed will lead to failure.

Today, however, they are in the hands of the Fleet Air Arm, so life is very much more civilized. 4/92 have travelled in the unexpected luxury of a coach to Royal Naval Air Station Yeovilton to learn Commando helicopter drills, followed by the more alarming-sounding helicopter dunker trainer, and have just filed out of the coach and are standing in three ranks, webbing and helmets on, weapons slung, ready for whatever the Fleet Air Arm requires. A Seaking helicopter lands on the concrete dispersal area beside a large and particularly red fire engine.

The crewman of the Seaking, a naval Petty Officer, gathers them around his aircraft:

'Your weapons are to be made safe [magazines on, but no round in the chamber], with bayonets and radio antennae removed so they don't damage the aircraft. Always approach between ten and two o'clock – so the pilot can see you. With high winds, the blades can swoop as low as three feet above the ground, so duck under the blades, and never approach the tail rotors. They'll take your head off.

'Make sure there's nothing loose on the landing site to get sucked into the turbines or damage the rotors. Do not touch any part painted yellow and black; if you start hanging from these bits, they will break off and the maintenance crew will get very upset with you. Be careful approaching the front wheels. If the green flotation canisters inadvertently go off, they shoot over 100 feet sideways and will seriously injure you.

'Pile your bergens [large military rucksacks] in the centre of the landing site. The helicopter will always approach flying into wind. As it approaches, fall on to the bergens. The down draught is the equivalent of a 90 mph wind, and in the Arctic snow will blow everywhere. The aircraft will land right beside you.

'Two people heave the bergens on board. Lift one bergen between two and give it to me at the door. The rest of you climb on and get seated. The essence of this is speed – for us to get away as fast as possible. But be careful with your weapons, they can puncture the aircraft's aluminium skin.'

They clamber aboard the Seaking, taking seats along the length of the aircraft fuselage. Light comes in from small port holes above their heads, and from the front windscreen beyond the two high-backed crew chairs. There is a strange smell – of fuel, lubricant, and expensive high-tech equipment.

'Get in, fasten the seat belt, then stick your hand up so the crewman can see everybody is ready. The stick leader wears these headphones, and can talk to the crew using the toggle switch. Confirm with the pilot where you want to go.

'Two minutes before landing, you get a warning shown by this red light. The crewman will signal when it is time for you to disembark. Two men stay by the door to hump the bergens, the rest get out, on to the ground.

'If we can't actually land, we'll do a low hover and you'll have to jump.'

Roping is used over trees or on to a hill side. 'Be very careful not to bash your elbows when coming out on the rope.'

Aircraft emergencies must also be prepared for:

'If something goes wrong with the aircraft, you'll get that sinking feeling as we fall out of the sky. Put your weapon under your feet, brace yourself by hanging on to the seat until we impact the ground, then await my instructions.

'If it's been an uncontrollable crash, vacate the aircraft as soon as you can. Pull this ring then punch the window out. Be very careful of moving rotor blades.

'If we go down over water, it's the same routine. On a nice calm day, the aircraft should float. If it rolls over, wait for the rotors to stop and the whole thing to settle. Do not inflate your life-jacket until clear of the aircraft – you will simply not get out.

'Keep your hand on the seat strap, but do not undo it until the aircraft has inverted. If you do, the in-flush of water will knock you around and totally disorientate you. You won't know which way is out, and you will drown. Use your other hand to find the orientation point and hold on to it. There are luminous beta lights around all the windows in case you get confused.'

Lecture over, the aircraft fires up, and for the rest of the morning they practise being picked up and dropped off, doing hover jumps and roping down. In a brisk wind, the Seaking can only get close enough to them by making several hop landings. As these landings are carried out on the flat, mown grass of the airfield – with a marked absence of wind-driven snow – it all seems rather unreal. In any case, most of 4/92 are already familiar with helicopters – RAF Pumas from Army exercises – so novelty value is minimal. It is nevertheless a nice rest from 'phyzz' and the aggravation of CTC.

But although it's a nice easy day, there's the added edge of knowing that after lunch they will be in the dunker trainer, practising ditching in real water, escaping from a helicopter after it has sunk and rolled over. Nobody has seen the dunker yet, but they do know that they have to do it in pitch darkness – an instant cure for claustrophobia.

After lunch, the coach drops them off outside the dunker. They enter, change from their DPMs (Disruptive Pattern Material – i.e. camouflage) into shapeless green overalls, then take seats in the briefing room. The reassuringly massive Chief Petty Officer Diver is in charge, and urges them to get everything clear in their minds right now, before leaving the briefing room: 'The divers will not always understand if you get excited in the pool, so clear up any problems you might have in here, before you enter the pool.'

The lecture starts with a photo of a civilian helicopter that went down into the sea.

'The pilot and crew sitting up front banged their way out. The only others who lived were two old ladies and two children sitting amidships. A large hole appeared in front of them and they got out.

'Everybody else died – not from the impact of the crash, but drowned. At the inquiry, they discovered none of the emergency exits had been used, which led them to conclude that people hadn't been briefed, or didn't know how to use them.

'And that's why you are here today, to learn how to get out of any type of military aircraft. You'll receive a chit that will

authorize you to travel in any military aircraft, at night over
water, provided you do four good runs in the pool today.'
The dunker itself is a 30-foot-deep swimming pool, with a Lynx
fuselage suspended by crane over the water, in a rotating cradle that
rolls over completely under the water. The first batch of six put on
coloured climbing helmets, then dive into the pool and swim out to
the fuselage. The divers help them in, they strap into the web seats
and are hoisted 20 feet up, suspended and swinging. The rest of the
course line the railings overlooking the pool, watching with great
interest.

A motto painted above the pool in bright red letters like a rev-
olutionary slogan urges 'Self Determination Now!' After two practices
with the lights on, all but the emergency lights are turned off, the
pool in semi-darkness. The fuselage is winched out of the water to
hang and drip, before descending, going 12 feet under the water, then
rolling over until upside-down. After 20 seconds or so, the lights snap
back on, and the CPO Diver checks that everybody has escaped.

For the final run, every light in the building is turned off, the
descent, submersion, rolling over and escape accomplished in total
darkness. Despite the presence of safety divers inside the fuselage,
keeping calm is far from easy. Disorientation is as total as the darkness,
the way out of the fuselage indicated only by feeling the guide
rails. People must wait until the men in front have exited – without
panicking. Each run is greeted with cheers from those waiting at the
surface for their turn. There is a measurable degree of apprehension,
as well as relief after the final run for each batch.

The divers inside the fuselage brief each fresh batch of six:
'That's your exit, keep your eyes open at all times, orientate
yourself towards your exit and keep your other hand on your
belt buckle. Try not to swim in the module, you'll only kick
each other. Pull yourselves out. Only release your buckle as you
are about to leave, and wait for the person in front of you to go.
'Ready in the module – Run One!'
At the end of each run, the divers debrief the batch:
'Stay strapped in until you see the others leaving. If you release
your seat strap too soon, you'll float up, get into the others' way
and we'll have to do it again.
'The order in which you escape is very important. As soon as
you can see the way is clear, get out – don't hang around.
There's others waiting behind you.
'Lights off!
'Get it right first time you won't have to do it again.'
It is with evident relief that everybody gets through this low-key but
nevertheless important test. Lieutenant Heley, a King's Own Border
Regiment officer, is doing the Commando course out of interest –

Apprehensive aircrew and All Arms 4/92 Commando candidates entering the dunker trainer at RNAS Yeovilton.

for 'fun': 'The worst moments are when someone gets stuck in the exit leaving five people stuck behind him trying to get out at the same time.'

Back on the coach the acerbic Corporal Tam Miles, a Scotsman with a deadpan sense of humour, presents the dunker certificates in a parody of official prize-giving, officers first. The certificates were very quickly typed up by dunker clerical staff, and several names are spelt wrongly – drawing derisive remarks from Corporal Miles, and many ribald cries from everybody else. As paratrooper Lance Corporal Hutcheon gets his, everybody shouts, 'Airborne!' As Sapper Rockey comes up, somebody shouts, 'Which door was it?' – referring to Rockey having gone the wrong way underwater, causing great confusion.

The All Arms Commando Course is a total of eight weeks in length, including the two-week 'phase one' introduction. In phase one, basic fieldcraft is taught – and tested on two tough exercises – plus weapon training and navigation exercises. The six-week Commando Course proper that follows is a combination of training, arduous exercises to test and confirm that training has been learned, and tests. The actual Commando Tests take place in the final two weeks: the 12-mile load carry, then the Final Exercise on Dartmoor, followed by the endurance course, the 9-mile speed march, the Tarzan assault course and the 30-miler.

However, before even starting phase one, candidates must demonstrate that they meet the 'passing in standards'. As the *Commando Course Preparation Handbook* makes clear: 'Failure to complete any component parts of any tests will result in an immediate return to unit (RTU).'

The basic fitness test requires 50 sit-ups within 2 minutes, 5 pull-ups, then, wearing boots, denims and shirt, running $1\frac{1}{2}$ miles in 15 minutes as a course followed by a best-effort run of the same distance to be completed in less than $11\frac{1}{2}$ minutes. The basic swimming test is clearly vital for amphibious soldiers, consisting of jumping from the high board wearing trunks, swimming 100 metres and treading water for 2 minutes.

The second passing-in requirement is the combat fitness test, which involves marching and running for 8 miles (3 of them cross country) wearing boots, denims, shirt, combat jacket, webbing equipment weighing 22 pounds, and weapon and carrying steel helmet in 150 minutes. Each man must then jump a 5-foot gap, climb unaided into the back of a 4-ton truck, then complete a 100-metre fireman's carry in under 45 seconds.

Before progressing from phase one on to the Commando Course, each man must manage a 4-mile speed march (carrying 22 pounds webbing plus rifle) at the Commando pace of 10 minutes to the mile. Then after one week of the Commando Course proper, each must climb a 30-foot rope carrying 22 pounds webbing plus rifle, complete the assault course in under 5 minutes, complete a 200-metre fireman's carry in less than 90 seconds and carry out a full rope regain. This last exercise involves crawling along a horizontal rope, slipping off to hang suspended by the arms, then 'regaining' the crawling position by hooking one ankle over the rope and performing a much practised pull.

The actual Commando Tests are equally clearly defined: the 12-mile load carry in under 4 hours, the endurance course in under 72 minutes (followed by getting 6 out of 10 shots fired on to a target), the 9-mile speed march in less than 90 minutes, the Tarzan assault course in under 13 minutes and the 30-mile march on Dartmoor in less than 8 hours.

Dartmoor is the most desolate part of the south-west of England, a remote, wet, windswept wilderness, with its own extreme and very special climate. While the surrounding farming country enjoys milder conditions, up on the moor – the highest ground in the south-west, between 1500 and 2000 feet above sea level – things are usually very different. At around 1000 feet normal vegetation stops, a discernible line above which there is nothing but moorland, stone walls, sheep – and Commandos.

The original Second World War Commandos were trained in the equally inhospitable surroundings of Achnacarry, near Spean Bridge in the highlands of Scotland. The original pamphlet issued to potential Commandos before they arrived at this wild and wintry place stressed the importance of being totally used to living rough, and to giving a strong physical dimension to everything: 'Whenever possible, field training exercises should be carried out across newly ploughed fields.' Officers were specifically advised to instruct batmen not to light fires in their bedrooms, and to leave all windows open regardless of the time of year.

Achnacarry created a good deal of mythology during the war years. It was said that men were regularly shot during incredibly realistic live firing exercises. A line of what are reputed to be graves beside the camp gates gave credence to this tale – until one examined the epitaphs, which attributed each death to a failure to carry out some basic drill. Men were no doubt shot accidentally in training; the horrors of Commando training were however much elaborated upon by the time the war ended – which nobody minded as it added to the Commando mystique.

Nobody however needs to exaggerate the problems of training in either the Scottish highlands or on Dartmoor – particularly in winter. Dartmoor's hills have deceptively flat tops, which often conceal deep peat bog, decorated by huge piles of granite boulders precariously balanced on massive tors. There are several dangerously deep bogs, into which animals, people and even tractors have vanished. Compass bearings are vital, and keeping on course while contouring to avoid too much hill climbing is difficult enough without having to steer a careful course around the bogs.

Having survived the dunker and amphibious training at R M Poole, All Arms Commando Course 4/92 are now on Dartmoor, living in the spartan accommodation of Okehampton Camp – rows of Nissen huts on a wind-blasted hill surrounded by barbed wire to keep the sheep out. Half the course are in a nearby quarry learning cliff-climbing skills, while the other half are on the ranges, doing close-quarter battle firing, utilizing their fieldcraft firing live ammunition.

As always the weather is miserable – but not appalling, which is the norm. A bitter wind scythes across the moorland, driving moderate but ice-cold rain before it. Wearing waterproofs while doing any sort of combat drill is not the done thing; they make considerable rustling

All Arms 4/92 parade on Dartmoor wearing woollen cap comforters.

noise, and anyway sweat makes you wet – from the inside. So every-body is wet, combat jackets and trousers almost black on the windward side, but pretending they don't really mind.

A very wet Sergeant Nigel Swayne is taking men through the individual CQB (close-quarter battle): 'You follow the river up, and there are enemy along the way. Any questions? Load. Ready. Safety catch on and continue.'

The first man through is a touch unfamiliar with his weapon, the 5.56 mm Lee Enfield automatic rifle. The route runs up a small stream, which is flowing fast with icy peat water. The targets are hidden behind hummocks and banks, representing men lying in fire positions. For real, survival would depend on spotting them fast, reacting instantly with some kind of fire as you take cover, then killing using accurate, aimed shots.

The stream bed offers the best cover, so after dealing with the first target everybody is soaked at least to the waist. You have to count your rounds as you fire; if you run out, you lose not only firepower but also time in reloading and recocking – which could easily be fatal.

To complicate the exercise, before starting the men were told to load different numbers of rounds into each magazine, forcing them to remember which they are using, making the counting very much harder.

A few words of advice before the start:

'You need to have your index finger on the safety catch ready to flick it off and fire. If you have problems, get into cover and sort it out – don't just stand there.

'Counting the rounds ... it's one mag change, so count the rounds. It's very cold, isn't it? Oh for a summer course, eh? Or warm winters?'

The course OC (Officer Commanding) is Captain Ray Pritchard, tall, moustached and a touch pinched with cold:

'The idea is to get two quick shots and one aimed shot off at each target. The targets are carefully placed so that in following the stream bed, the man is made to think. Live rounds gets the adrenalin pumping quite a bit.

'We're training them rather than assessing – but then we're assessing them all the time!'

Sergeant Swayne:

'With a magazine of 10 rounds, load, ready!

'The tactical picture is as follows: your four-man team was bombursted in a contact, so you have to get back to the RV [rendezvous] up the stream. You are not in contact [with the enemy] so can move with stealth until in contact – when speed is of the essence. Keep within 4 metres of the stream. The enemy moves in teams of four.

'Remember safety – keep your weapon pointing up the range and if the whistle blows or I tap you on the shoulder, apply your safety catch.

'Think about carrying out a magazine change in cover. Head towards that large rock on the horizon ...'

Sleet is now coming down ... He has to go into the river up to his thighs to keep in cover from one of the targets.

'Stop, and unload.'

They each go through twice, the targets in different places for the second run:

'You've corrected the faults from your first time through. Don't be frightened of the weapon. Get two quick shots off, then take another, well aimed from cover. Think about safety too. Make sure the safety catch is applied before carrying out any other drill – and get into cover to do it. Keep to the left of the stream. At one point you'll have to go into the stream ... Fact of life, it's tough at the top.'

Some try to go too quickly: 'Stealth at the beginning, slow it down. If you patrol that fast, you'll miss the enemy.'

Sergeant Swayne wants to see correct drills: 'Dash, down, crawl, observe, sights, fire, then move fast and take one aimed shot, then move again – fast. If there's no more enemy, slow it down and patrol again.'

Counting the rounds is tricky. Sergeant Swayne has to prompt some people: 'Think about it, you've fired nine rounds, and there's one in the chamber. Change magazines and carry on.'

Another debrief, of 'schoolie' Lieutenant Linderman: 'I was expecting you to be quite disastrous, but you were actually quite good! Remember, wherever your head and eyes are, your weapon will be. So you must move around to face the arc [wherever you need to be able to fire].'

RN stoker Petty Officer Barrel is slow and inaccurate, which is hardly surprising as all this is very new to him. Sergeant Swayne has to push him into the river to take up safe fire positions, as well as prompting on weapon drills. Barrel: 'It's all totally new to me – and I suppose it's a challenge! It's certainly not easy.'

The next stage is to do the same thing in pairs, then to work with another pair, four men together, attacking one enemy position.

They start by advancing down the range in pairs, coming under fire, locating then giving fire control orders, firing at the targets, then 'pepper-potting' forward towards the targets, giving covering fire as the other gets up and runs forward – an exhausting process at the best of time, worse when you are soaking wet.

They then go through it as two pairs, with much close instruction from Sergeant Pete Boorn and Bombardier Dick Booth:
'Take cover! Crawl to the bank. What do you see? Get the fire down, two rounds then move your position – safety catch apply! Move!

'Get up here in line, quickly now! Come on, get some fire down there.'

They get up and run forward: 'Come right, come right and get down now! Get up in the aim and get those rounds off – that's better.'

There are weapon stoppages, which have to be sorted out correctly as part of the drills: 'Sort it out, then back in the aim.'

Breathless fumbling in the cold. Stoppage! – sort it out!
'Give him covering fire. Go! Not too far and down! Pairs! Keep level. Close up, Private Thomas. Move, move, move! Keep fighting through . . .

'Stop! Unload.

'Raise your left hand when clear. Ease springs. Stand up. Return to the ammo point. Return any ammo you may have.

'For inspection port arms! As I pass, check the contents of your pouches. Now put your magazines away – don't put them in your pockets. That's why we have pouches.'

Preparing to go through the CQB lane (close quarter battle) with the LSW (light support weapon).

Then the debrief:

> 'You've got to remember what's going on around you, men – if you don't, you can easily end up on your own. Stoppages must be sorted out from cover. At one time, only one of you was firing. But well done, good fire and manoeuvre at the end.'

The other half of the course are learning Commando cliff-climbing skills in a disused quarry. A stiff wind is blowing, on a very cold, dull day, which unusually has so far been relatively dry.

The course are in three groups, each taught by two 'MLs' – Mountain Leaders from the Royal Marines' M & AW Cadre Arctic and Mountain Warfare Training. As with the boat training at Royal Marines Poole, the skills the course will learn today are integral to their future as Commando soldiers – that which sets them apart (as a trained body of men) from other soldiers.

Compared to civilian mountaineering techniques, the skills being taught today seem a touch old-fashioned. There is however a great difference between what Commandos do, and civilian recreational climbing. Civvies climb difficult routes for enjoyment and challenge, whereas the MLs select the easiest route across the obstacle then prepare it for hundreds of heavily laden men to use safely and quickly – invariably at night. If there's a way to walk up using ropes as mere handrails, then the MLs have done a good job. In reality, however, Commando soldiers have got to be able to get themselves and their equipment up whatever routes the MLs have found – using a wide range of climbing methods.

Much of the basic skill is learned at CTC, particularly on the Tarzan course. On Dartmoor, however, with granite rock faces, cold, wet conditions and 100-foot cliffs, it seems very much more realistic. They first climb a wire ladder, having been taught to keep one foot behind the ladder and the other in front as an added safety measure, the insteps of their boots thrust well into the rungs, boot heels preventing feet from slipping off.

At the top of the cliff, they form eight-man 'mule' sections for 'roller haulage' – a means of getting men and equipment to a cliff head quickly and efficiently, particularly heavier equipment. It's potentially dangerous and, with all rope systems, nobody is allowed to step inside the triangle of pulley ropes – 'on pain of giving money to the Restoration of the Palace Fund, press-ups or painting the ML section a picture of the Palace'. (Windsor Castle had been severely damaged by fire the previous weekend.)

The mule team learns the necessary hand signals:
> 'First: "Pick up the rope", "Take the strain", "Take it away and pull" ... do this as fast as I indicate to you.
>
> 'Then "Check" – which means stop! And finally "Walk back" and put down the rope.'

The roller haulage system consists of a metal roller block belayed to long pins hammered into the turf, with a rope running through at 90 degrees to the cliff. A roller at the top of the cliff prevents the rope chafing as it goes over the lip. After a demonstration run, the mule team are told they must pull faster – and watch more carefully for their instructions: 'It is actually dangerous if you do it too slow.'

The men at the bottom are also receiving last-minute instruction: 'You only get one go at this – and I know you'll want more because you'll think it's mega amounts of fun.'

After clipping a loop at the rope end into a carabiner on his climbing harness, each man is pulled up a few feet until he is lying horizontally, legs braced against the cliff. The mule team then runs away pulling the rope, the man at the bottom literally running up the cliff. At the top it's important to let go of the rope, so that when the mules pull you over the lip of the cliff, you don't fall into the roller or get pulled over. 'The trick is to keep your legs stiffly straight. The effect is not unlike jumping off a train while it's still moving.'

First man up is Sergeant Major Dobson, who is grimly determined as he nears the top of the cliff and manages not to fall over. Some men fail to keep their legs stiff and go flying over the top to be pulled by the mules into the ground. Choosing the right moment to let go of the rope is vital too; the roller can clearly act like a finger mangle.

'Lean back, start walking, stiffen the legs . . . Anticipate which leg is going to lead over the top!'

PO Barrel loses his balance and goes flying, falling heavily. Apart from testing nerve, it's also a test of coordination and judgement – particularly in deciding exactly when to let go. Every disaster is spectacular, stimulating much amusement in both mules and instructors.

The shouting of name, rank and unit is a regular feature of the All Arms course, particularly before starting activities that are potentially dangerous. The instructors use this self-identification as a device to divert individuals from their natural feelings of fear, to a more positive determination to succeed, for the sake of themselves as individuals and the honour of their service, regiments and units. Being a corps with tremendous pride and *esprit*, the Royal Marines appreciate individuals from other organizations who display the same self-confidence – particularly as it gives them opportunities for making jokes at their expense.

There is a particularly strong and long-standing rivalry between the Royal Marines and the Parachute Regiment. Of 4/92, PT instructor Lance Corporal Hutcheon has come from 82 Airborne Ordnance Company – and is quietly proud of the fact. He is therefore required to announce himself several times to instructors claiming to be hard of hearing, and is very popular when he messes things up. His presence at the bottom of the roller haulage rope causes great mirth. However, despite the mules being urged to pull extra hard, Hutcheon does it perfectly.

They next do abseiling down the cliff: 'Look down your right arm as you descend, and lean back – looking over your right shoulder . . .'

The next activity is the highlight of the cliff-climbing session, the so-called 'death dive', which the driver of one of the 4-tonners demonstrates, plunging face forwards from the top of the cliff to the bottom, stopped only by last-minute braking by the instructor pulling on the abseil rope. Everybody grins nervously and looks at each other. It looks horrific.

ML Sergeant Furness:

'That technique is a more extreme variation of the forward abseil, last used operationally for evacuation in Aden on inland cliffs as a method of getting off high ground quickly. Since then we've changed the system, changed the ropes, changed the harness, so that old method isn't used any more.

'We found that the old forward abseil was a damn good bottle tester, for finding out whether you've really got the bottle to be a Commando, as opposed to just being an "also-ran".

'So we've modified the new technique slightly to achieve the same effect . . .'

Everybody chuckles.

'. . . and devised our own version of the old system, which is a cross between run-down and sky-diving. But it still provides a very important insight for both you and us, to see whether you've got what it takes.

'There may be a time when you'll be asked to do something which sanely and logically you'll think totally unreasonable, i.e. to get up from cover and advance under fire. By doing things like the death dive, we find out the men who'd stay in cover, who wouldn't carry out the order. And you find out if you have the ability to get up and go for it.

'So you come to the edge and look down, and think, "My God, it looks unreasonable". But you go ahead and do it, because you put your faith and trust in the kit and equipment and the men who are asking you to do it. At the end of the day, wearing the Green Beret, you know everybody else has done the same as you have, so you can rely on them. And when they ask you to do something, you know they would do the same for you . . . and that's what it's all about.'

The death dive entails clipping on to a special karabiner at the top of the cliff, then walking forwards and face downwards off the edge, keeping your body at 90 degrees to the cliff face. The man at the bottom grasps the rope, allowing you to slide downwards at a speed determined by the tension he applies.

'Lean forward and thrust your crutch down towards me. Keep coming down. I'll tell you when to stop – OK, I have you there. Name?'

'Captain Norman.'

'Regiment?'

'First Battalion the Duke of Wellington's Regiment.'

'Jolly good, Sir. Are you ready? One, two, three, go!'

Captain Norman is slightly built, fair-haired, around five foot eight inches tall, fit, and clearly knows exactly what he is doing, coping easily, with a calm sense of humour. He jumps out, away from the face, then, as the tension is released on the rope, falls rapidly to the ground.

'Well done, Sir . . . and run off the rope.'

Sergeant Furness is impressed: 'Not a bad effort. He was very stable.'

(*Left*) The Commando 'death dive' – off granite cliffs on Dartmoor.

Furness addresses himself to the next man at the top of the cliff: 'Both hands pushing forward . . . Shout out your name and regiment. Come on then, "REME". Let's see what you can do. You can certainly breathe – I can hear you from down here! You are in fact smiling. Do a star jump and leap out.'

It's not exactly easy being suspended face downwards at the top of a hundred-foot cliff, then having to do a horizontal star jump out from the cliff face, like a human pendulum.

'Not high enough, no good. Try again.'

Sergeant Major Dobson of the Royal Signals is one of the natural leaders of 4/92 but, being older and a warrant officer, attracts quite a bit of stick from the younger Royal Marine junior NCO instructors. He takes it all good-naturedly in his stride.

'Come down 10 more feet now, Sir. Show confidence that you are not going to fall straight to the bottom. Let's have a nice big star jump . . .

'Oh! Not enough. Come on, a bit more effort . . .'

He jumps again.

'Still not enough – you certainly wouldn't save a penalty . . . Stand by . . . and go!'

At his third attempt, Sergeant Major Dobson jumps high, but to one side. He swings back against the cliff on to his leg and knee, rather than against his two feet. The instructors are concerned – but don't show it: 'Have you hurt your leg? OK, come on down and get checked over by Nursey . . . That's what you get for not doing it correctly, Sergeant Major.'

Sergeant Major Dobson limps off the rope and sits down on a rock. He looks worried. A young Wren nurse helps him undo his boots, then examines the damaged leg: 'I either did it wrong or too hard, bounced against the rocks at an odd sort of angle. Something seems to have happened behind my knee, and I can also feel an old ankle injury which I did last year . . .'

Sergeant Major Dobson, with thinning brown hair and wry smile, is a very highly skilled telecommunications expert, nominated to run 3 Commando Brigade's communications centre – as the Foreman of Signals.

He's had a tough time, until recently being unable to pass the rope climbing, assault course and fireman's carry – the compulsory bottom field pass-in tests or BPT (Battle Physical Training) tests. The training team had expected him to fail – although being a warrant officer, they believed he was unlikely to take himself off the course. He's suffered debilitating chest infections, losing two stones in weight, and until passing the BPT three days ago had felt himself isolated from the course. And now having cracked the BPT, just as he is finding his feet and asserting himself, he takes a nasty knock. As the nurse examines his leg, he believes he's going to be taken off the course, so refuses to go to the ambulance, preferring to 'walk myself around for a while, to see if it loosens up'.

A young, fair-haired artillery officer is next at the top: 'Lieutenant Perkins, don't try to hold the rope, it won't do you any good. I've got you down here. Don't you believe me, Sir?'

The teasing banter ends with Lieutenant Perkins doing an enormous star jump, then being allowed to swoop down to earth so rapidly that he might just as well have fallen. Sergeant Furness tightens the rope, to brake him only four feet from the ground.

Lieutenant Perkins gasps something about needing to change his underpants. When young Private Thomas of the Royal Army Pay Corps does his star jump, he induces much merriment through holding on to his helmet in sheer alarm: 'It's quite an experience! Looking down is the worst bit. You've just got to be confident in the blokes at the bottom, and in the equipment. It is a bit painful, however, in the crutch area.'

PO Barrel has never done anything quite like it during his years in the Navy:

'You feel like a stunt man – the weightlessness, the ground coming floating up towards you ... it's pretty horrific really, particularly walking down the rope to the place where you do the jump. If the guy at the bottom lets go of the rope, you're splattered.

'It's like all these things, once you've done it, they don't seem so bad. I don't think I can describe it – you just do it.'

Once the cliff-climbing tuition is complete, the MLs hand the course back to their team instructors, the stocky Jock Corporal Tam Miles and the tall, dark, well-spoken Corporal Pelling. Despite there being an hour and a half of daylight left, the course are relatively dry – at the end of an unusually easy day. However, it just so happens that there is a deep and excruciatingly cold lake in the far part of the disused quarry.

Although dressed up as an instructional period, despite the lecture beforehand, the not-so-hidden purpose of the next activity is to get the course cold and wet. Corporal Pelling:

'The aim of this next instructional period is to teach you how to carry out a tactical river crossing, and hopefully keep your kit dry – which seems most unlikely in this weather. OK, the map appreciation. First off, local knowledge; for example, are the rivers piranha-infested?'

This question is intended seriously, to get the students thinking themselves into the situation of crossing a tropical river. With sleety rain being blown almost horizontally across their faces as they pretend to take notes, and the prospect of swimming 40 metres in teeth-grindingly cold water, the course are wryly amused.

'OK, you may all laugh and giggle, but working in tropical climates, things to bear in mind – for example, are there hostile fish, so to speak, in the rivers?'

It's moments like this when Army people have deliberately to switch their brains into neutral, and let the Royal Marines do their own thing. The lecture has been taken straight from a training pamphlet – about jungle warfare.

'Is the enemy using bridges, are the bridges blown? Or are the bridges not blown, but are they booby trapped . . . OK?

'. . . does anybody have any questions on map appreciation of river crossings?'

The lecture is almost over. Soon they will have to strip off and pack all their gear into the bergens, which must be sufficiently waterproofed to float across the lake.

'The easy way to do it is simply to put everything into your bivvie bag. Or you can just cross the river as you are . . .

'Or you can do a planned river crossing.

'Things to bear in mind: are there any enemy in the area? You

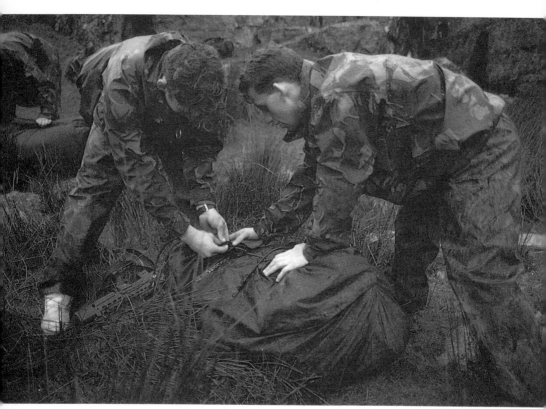

Securing watertight equipment bundles before a very cold river crossing.

need a preparation area under cover to pack your kit. And an emergency RV.'

The corporals demonstrate waterproofing a bergen: first empty the water bottles to help flotation, then wrap the bergen in a poncho, roll the ends up then tie securely with cord. Everybody takes careful note.

'You should all be carrying your 30 metres of comms cord – use it to tie up the poncho. Then tie your weapon on too – but loosely so you could shoot with it.'

The magic moment has arrived:

'You now have 15 minutes to prepare your kit for a river crossing. Remove your gloves and clothes, then put on your waterproof jackets and trousers to give camouflage and some protection from the wind. Take your boots off and get into your plimsolls. Work in your pairs.'

The course fail to organize themselves to work in their pairs but try to sort themselves out individually, some people putting off the evil moment of stripping for as long as they can. Lance Corporal Hutcheon gets warned about his illicit use of a zip-up waterproof bag – 'which I've warned you about before . . .'

'Last 15 seconds, starting now . . . You should be putting your helmets and webbing on, and getting ready to carry your bergens down to the water's edge.'

The last 15 seconds last several minutes, until finally: 'Stop! Stand behind your equipment.' Corporal Pelling's voice sounds like a fog horn. Sergeant Major Dobson has not finished, to both corporals' delight: 'Oh dear, Sergeant Major. We'll just go across with crossed fingers, shall we?'

After his accident on the cliff diving, Dobson is limping and in pain, but at least is still mobile. Corporal Miles is keen on the use of comms cord to tie weapons to bergens. (Being a Royal Engineer, he knows that searching for weapons lost in water is a real waste of time.) He finds several bergens not to his satisfaction: 'You'd better have it sorted, yeah?'

'Aha!' Corporal Pelling spots a field dressing left behind in the rush, and adds: 'Giggle.'

They file awkwardly around to the other side of the 50-metre lake, before the first man enters. Corporal Pelling asks, 'Is everybody happy?' – receiving derisory cries of 'Yeah' to which Corporal Pelling replies 'Lying bastards'. Captain Norman enters the water, his rib cage visibly sucking in with shock as the cold hits him hard:

'Kick with your feet and keep away from that rope. It's there for safety, not for you to use. Hold that weapon properly, on top of the bergen so you can fire it . . . Use a breast stroke kick.'

The irrepressible Lance Corporal Hutcheon is having some problems with his bergen, which rolls round like a barrel.

'Stop laughing and get across.'

'I'm not moving.'

'Probably because you're using that stupid bag ... Where's your weapon, Sir?'

Captain Norman touches bottom at the other end.

'When you get out, get your warm kit back on and start warming yourselves up.'

The bergens are waterlogged and very much heavier than when they went in. Sergeant Major Dobson's is so full he has trouble lifting it:

'Oh dear, how sad, never mind, what a pity ... well done
Sergeant Major, smart thing to be doing at the age of 32 ...
Straight back to the preparation area and put on your dry kit –
you hope.

'Stop playing bumper cars in the middle there – we are not
traffic jamming ... Take charge of your weapon, you!

'Unhook your weapons and get out! This is not a swimming
gala.'

Water cascades out of the bergens and some men can only wait by the rocks for the worst of the water to drain away before being able actually to lift them. A long ball of string has unravelled from Sapper Khanlarian's bergen. Corporal Pelling waits to see if he will notice it. In going back down to the water's edge gathering it up, Khanlarian nearly commits the heinous crime of leaving his weapon behind.

'You leave that weapon behind and you'll be doing press-ups until you're looking like Garth's harder brother.'

Everybody is truly cold, with pinched features, blue limbs and glazed facial expressions. With brains as numbed as their hands, undoing the bergen bundles, getting dried and dressed is taking far too long. The warm, dry corporals offer further advice and 'help':

'Come on then, fast fingers, fast fingers ... Whose kit is
thoroughly soaked? If you'd worked in pairs to start with you'd
have been all right. The system works. I told you three times.
The sergeant major has soaking wet combat trousers. Oh giggle!
Oh joy!'

The first ones finished get to double mark-time on the road, warming up. Captain Norman is made to jog in a circle, arms outstretched, doing finger-extending exercises. Then the Bedford 4-tonner arrives, headlights bright in the gathering gloom. The course pile in the back for the trip back to the nearby Okehampton Camp.

'We'll be back in time for scran [food] ... great!'

The corporals continue to hassle their charges, lest anybody catch cold: 'Get any dry kit you might have on yourselves now! Sort out everything else at the other end.'

The 4-tonner departs, a number of the course waving ironically back at the instructors, who get into Corporal Miles's red Ford Escort. Corporal Pelling:

> 'This was pretty much an inert day for the course – made so much better by the bad weather. They can however dry their kit out at camp now, whereas on the Final Exercise they'll be out in the field for a week with no chance of getting dry.
>
> 'Bad weather makes them switch off a bit, but we treat them like people, being nice to them as well as giving them a hard time. They've got to be encouraged. Anybody can beast or thrash a course through, but if they're not picking it up and doing it correctly, we're getting it wrong. At the end of the day we're instructors.'

However, the main purpose of their harassment is to determine who is suitable for Commando service: 'We're assessing the course right from the beginning, from day one.'

> Corporal Tam Miles: 'The blokes who are messing up stand out quite well from the very beginning. You can normally tell how they'll turn out at the end.'
>
> Corporal Pelling: 'They all have strengths and weaknesses; for example a poor swimmer might struggle doing a river crossing, but still be a good man in the field.
>
> 'We assess them to see what they're made of – which is what it's about at the end of the day.'

Back at CTC 4/92's course sergeant, Nigel Swayne, is standing in the River Exe Club car park with the stocky Sapper Xavier, tall, ginger-haired Lieutenant Kepple Compton and the shorter Lieutenant Lewis, waiting for PTI Sergeant John Morgan. Below them, the bottom field assault course, then the perimeter wire, the single-line railway track to Exmouth and the muddy estuary of the River Exe. A brisk wind is blowing off the river, and the bottom field is particularly water-logged.

Wearing cap comforters, denims and webbing and carrying their rifles, Lieutenants Kepple Compton and Lewis, and Sapper Xavier have failed several previous opportunities to complete the compulsory BPT (Battle Physical Training) tests. Having been kept on the course in the hope that they would pass, this is their last attempt. If they fail they are off, returned to their units – 'RTU'd'. Sergeant Swayne is very straightforward about it: 'If they don't pass this, they've wasted five weeks. Lieutenant Lewis for example knows what the tests are and clearly hasn't prepared for them.'

Sergeant Morgan arrives, complete with muscles, clip board and sardonic turn of phrase, his immaculate white PT vest scant protection from the icy wind. Registered with Equity as a stuntman, he is black, beautiful – and sharp as a knife: 'Hats off, no screw-ups this time. Get it cracked. Your last chance. That way turn . . .'

They do warm-up exercises, then strap rifles to their backs and tackle the first test, climbing the 30-foot rope.

'Power is the game. Get up to the top, shout out your name, then look at the scenery – most people do.'

This being their last chance to pass, course OC Captain Pritchard arrives and, with Sergeant Swayne, urges the men on. Sapper Xavier makes it to the top of the rope, then Lieutenant Kepple Compton – who is referred to as 'KC'. Lieutenant Lewis however seems incapable of making the last six feet. He is blowing, swearing and moaning, with frustration as well as physical pain. His performance does not impress Sergeant Morgan: 'Don't just hang there like a Christmas decoration.'

Lewis loses his grip and slides painfully all the way down, burning his hands. He lies panting on the gravel. Sergeant Morgan shows not one hint of sympathy: 'Nice fireman impersonation ... When you come down the rope, you do so under control – not like Fireman Sam. Get up and move to the assault course.'

Pass time for the assault course is five minutes. They line up behind the water jump and Sergeant Morgan starts them off. They crawl under the low net and the barbed-wire entanglement, running 10 and 20 metres between obstacles, Lieutenant Lewis lagging behind.

'Dry your hands as you approach the monkey bars. Get your thumbs around the bar. Come on, Mr KC!'

Lieutenant Lewis cannot grip the monkey bars and falls repeatedly into the water.

'Out, get out! You are wasting water.'

Lieutenant Lewis abandons that obstacle and chases after the others. They climb over the scaffolding, then up the bars to the rope crawl. Lieutenant KC is knackered, only just getting over the 6-foot bars, and is hard pressed to run up the hill to the tunnels.

'Stop grunting and groaning. Get out of the tunnel quickly and up to the wall. Drive! Push it out! Open your legs up.

'Twenty seconds to go ... and you've done it in 4 minutes 51. Another epic. It's a piece of piss really ... you just make life harder for yourself.'

(*Above*) Sergeant John Morgan. (*Right*) Climbing the 30-foot rope, carrying about 30 pounds of equipment.

Lieutenant Lewis has failed but is nevertheless urged on to complete the course. He is way behind and has given up. The staff continue to give helpful encouragement:

'Don't grab the shackle, you numpty – it'll rip your hand to shreds...'

'Six minutes 35 ... Not the best time in the world. Absolutely no chance.'

Lieutenant Lewis is 'binned' there and then, told to change into dry clothes and report to the course office in 20 minutes. Just Sapper Xavier and Lieutenant KC remain for the penultimate test – the casualty evacuation, jogging 200 metres carrying a fully equipped man and his weapon, to be completed within 2 minutes. KC and Xavier will take turns to carry each other. Sergeant Morgan is a comforting source of wisdom: 'Switch off in the head and use your legs. They will keep you going until you die.'

Lieutenant KC asks to do the first carry, which he claims is 'downhill'. This request is clearly not going to endear him to Sergeant Morgan, particularly as Xavier would have to do the supposedly harder 'uphill' bit. Morgan is not impressed: 'What would you do in the heat of battle? Tell a casualty, "I'm not carrying you because it's uphill"? Don't be silly.'

Sapper Xavier slings Lieutenant KC over his shoulders and does the outward leg, finishing within the two minutes allowed. Lieutenant KC then puts Xavier across his shoulders, carrying both weapons in his free hand. Halfway back across the field, he slows down to an agonized walk, blowing and gasping, his legs failing him. As Sergeant Morgan counts off the seconds, everybody else shouts encouragement, to which KC, legs pumping but slowing, seems oblivious.

'Don't feel sorry for yourself...'

'Relax the shoulders, keep going...'

Eventually he reaches the 200-metre line and unceremoniously dumps Xavier on to the ground. Sergeant Morgan is not impressed:

> 'What's the idea of half killing yourself over 200 metres, then ditching him on the deck? It's like the St John's Ambulance getting you to hospital then kicking seven bells out of you in the carpark ... Quite a waste of time, isn't it, Sir?'
>
> 'Yes, S'arnt.'

There is one more test to go, crawling along the rope of the 'regain tank', slipping off to hang suspended, then attempting a regain back on to the rope. If you can't get back on the rope and crawl to the other side, you drop off into 6 feet of filthy, cold water – and fail. Lieutenant KC looks pretty miserable.

'Stop feeling sorry for yourself, and get your head in gear.'

Lieutenant KC breathes heavily.

'You are still feeling sorry for yourself. Get your kit on, and get sorted out.'

Although KC has failed the fireman's carry, if he passes the regain he will be allowed a re-run. Sapper Xavier crawls across the rope, suspends himself over the water, then by swinging and hooking his leg back over the rope goes through the proper drill and achieves a regain.

'Give yourself a brief congratulation ... a slight hoorah ... only a slight one.'

KC goes next, with some hesitation.

'Come on, KC – you have to pass all the tests on the same day.'

He climbs up the ladder and lies down on the rope.

'Relax one leg and let it hang down. Hook the other one over the rope. Push yourself along with the left leg, keeping the rope down the centre of your body – or you'll fall in.'

KC is not moving well along the rope. Reaching the middle, he is reluctant to swing off, psyching himself up for something that he doesn't seem terribly confident of doing. Then he releases his ankles, and tries immediately to get his legs back up around the rope. He swings but does not seem to be able to coordinate the bending of his arms with the swing, and so fails to hook his ankles back over the rope. His attempts become swiftly less convincing and he falls into the water, swimming to the side.

Xavier has cracked it – passed the BPT. As they line up, KC repeats his complaint about being given 'the uphill' leg on the fireman's carry. Sergeant Morgan says there is no such thing and that he has defeated himself:

'Being defeated by the uphill leg doesn't count for diddly really, does it? It doesn't matter if it's uphill, you still have to do the job. You can't say, "I'm not doing this, I want the downhill leg". You just crack on and do it.

'Thousands of people have come through here, Royal Marines and All Arms, and they've all put up with the uphill leg, with wet ropes, windy days, hot days. You're no different, nothing special. You have to crack it exactly the same as the rest of them. Do I make myself clear?'

'Yes, S'arnt.'

'When you get back to the accommodation, pack ... train.'

Sergeant Morgan turns to Xavier: 'Congratulations. Good effort. You made hard work for yourself ... let's get the next phase done.'

As Lieutenant KC walks away, Captain Pritchard takes him to one side:

'Before you get changed ... you will come back on a future course, but do extra phyzz with the recruits until you've passed BPT. You can rejoin the course for the 6-miler. OK?'

'Yes, thank you, Sir.'

K C doubles wetly up the steps, and away.

Sapper Xavier declares himself to be 'Fucking chuffed to fuck!'

He explains the accumulative effect of physical activity:

'You do so much phyzz that you get up some mornings and you're knackered. This was a good day for me, unlike for your man [Lieutenant K C]. The tests themselves are easy. It's what you do during the weeks before that makes them hard.'

Sergeant Morgan overhears this last comment and makes Xavier dive into the tank 'for saying it's easy'. He sees it somewhat differently:

'The whole principle is that guys can perform when tired. The poo inevitably hits the fan at the end of the task you've been doing, not when you are fresh. There is a wearing down factor in training, which allows us to find the guys who really want to do it. Xavier wanted it, K C didn't. If K C had wanted it enough, he'd have been able to dig deep and come up with the goods.

'I work on the principle of beasting them [pushing them very hard] during the beat-up, so that the test days will be easier. They do twice the work in half the time, so that on the day it seems that they have double the time to do it once.'

Lieutenant K C is packing his bags disconsolately:

'It's a lot of work and I'm gutted. But you've got to achieve the basic standards. The fireman's carry drained my legs, and I couldn't do the rest. I've passed all the tests separately, but you've got to put it all together on the day.'

PO Barrel, the former stoker now at 3 Commando Brigade Air Squadron, arrives from sickbay with the disappointing news that an infection has swollen the back of his hand, preventing him from gripping. It would be impossible for him to attempt the assault or Tarzan courses, so he's been RTU'd for medical reasons. He's dis-appointed, and wants to come back as soon as possible.

'BPT is a lot harder than most people realize. I'll be back . . .'

Sergeant Morgan explains how he sees the difference between Royal Marines recruits and the All Arms:

'It boils down to preparation and the age difference. Some of our recruits come in as young as 16 or 17, whereas these guys are grown men, already trained. Some of them are past their prime fitness-wise. Lieutenant K C is not fit, but he also psyched himself out. Wanting the downhill crack at it I suppose is his prerogative, but real life isn't like that. You just have to take whatever comes.

'Hopefully he'll use this as a lesson to go away and prepare a lot better than he did for this one. The other lieutenant has had five or six goes, and he hasn't yet got to the top of the ropes. There comes a cut off time, when you've got to say, "You're just not going to do it", and get rid of them.

'A lot of them underestimate the course, especially because the All Arms is an intensified version of what the recruits do. Sometimes their pre-course preparation isn't properly planned, either by them or by their units.

'The other thing is motivation. Some of the All Arms course people are nominated, rather than being volunteers like our recruits. If they'd wanted the Green Beret, they'd have joined the Royal Marines in the first place. There's more of the "want factor" with our recruits.'

Despite his apparent lack of sympathy, Sergeant Morgan is not as ruthless as perhaps he seems: 'Behind the hard face, I'm on me veranda in the Caribbean, supping rum!'

'Behind the façade, I'm trying to maintain standards. I'm looking at each individual psychologically; some react to being berated, others to encouragement. You have to decide which type you're dealing with. If you encourage some people, they loll into the "Mommy doesn't love me" routine, whereas if you get on their backs and give them a hard time, they'll lift themselves and produce the goods to prove you wrong. Others will produce the goods in order to stay on your good side.

'You can however push them too hard, over the edge. There are guys who will collapse, or fall off the ropes, who you know instinctively will climb the rope next time round when you shout at them. You've also got to know when to leave them there to regain their composure, or when to get them off to the sickbay.'

The rest of 4/92 are away in their billet sorting out kit for the Final Exercise. As the instructors prepare to walk back up to their office, a Second Lieutenant arrives from sickbay, his arm wrapped tightly in a sling. He dislocated an elbow on the Tarzan course earlier that morning and, with only two weeks to go, is off the course. He reports to Captain Pritchard, before departing CTC.

So as they shape up to the Final Exercise and the Commando Course proper, of the original 34 who started 4/92, only 15 remain. Sergeant Swayne has been supervising this first six weeks, which have been partly introduction to Commando Forces but also an elimination of ill-prepared and unsuitable individuals: 'It weeds out the ones without the right attitude. It's tough. But now we've got a hard core, who are determined to pass.'

CHAPTER **T**WO

DAWN **A**SSAULT

Meanwhile, ninety minutes by road from C T C, eastwards into Dorset, Royal Marines Poole is the centre of amphibious expertise in Commando forces. It provides the basis for combined operations, where naval and land forces work together. Today, this vital form of warfare is maintained here by the Joint Warfare School. Its badge is a large storm anchor topped by an eagle, with a loaded tommy-gun across the bottom – the original Combined Operations 'flash' so proudly worn by Second World War Commandos. Within the barbed wire and steel mesh of the camp perimeter lives the only surviving Combined Operations unit, 148 Commando Forward Observation Battery, a unique unit with both sailors and soldiers serving together, the controllers of naval gunfire, artillery and fighter ground attack aircraft.

Down the hill from camp, outside the wire and across the sand dunes, is the 'Hard', a port in miniature complete with cranes, jetties and boat yards, housing elements of the range of Royal Marines' amphibious boating: from the enormous lorry-carrying LCUs (landing craft utility) down to ultra-fast fibreglass dories (rigid raider assault craft) and the more stable, semi-inflatable RIBSs (rigid inflatable boats). The Hard is constantly busy, on this particular day in early November, with 'bumps and scrapes', landing craft officers learning how to berth LCUs.

We now join 33 Royal Marines recruits, known collectively as 638 Troop, as they learn the basics of amphibious raiding – at the very beginning of their specialist Commando training. They look and sound like Royal Marines, smart and efficient, with all the Corp's banter and unique argot. They cannot however allow themselves to

(*Right*) 638 Troop at the start of training – immediately post-haircut.

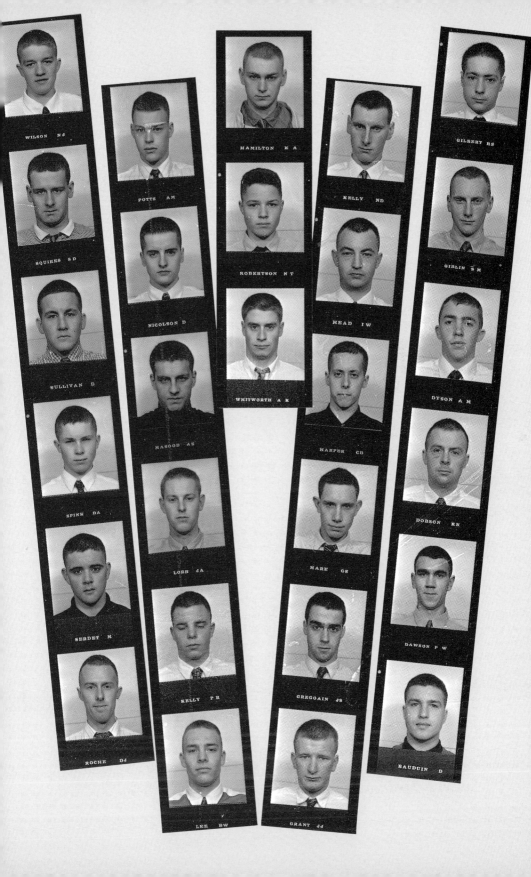

WILSON N J

SQUIRES S D

SULLIVAN D

SPINK D A

SERDET M

ROCHE D J

POTTS A M

NICOLSON D

MASOOD A S

LOBB J A

KELLY P R

LEE B W

HAMILTON K A

ROBERTSON N T

WHITWORTH A K

KELLY N D

MEAD I W

HARPER C D

HARE G S

GREGGAIN J S

GRANT J J

GILBERT R S

GIBLIN S M

DYSON A M

DOBSON R K

DAWSON P W

BAUDUIN D

feel like Royal Marines – at least not yet, even though by anybody's standards they are already very highly trained as infantry soldiers. They've come a long way in 27 weeks since joining the Royal Marines, but as they face the rigours of the Commando Course, the coveted Green Beret seems an eternity away.

Training Staff refer to 638 Troop with affectionate disparagement as 'Nods' (short for Noddys), and their official rank is still 'Recruit'. As Commando trainees, the troop no longer wear dark blue berets, but uncomfortably itchy, woollen 'cap comforters' – as worn by the Second World War Commandos whose boots they aspire to fill – issued to them at the end of their 24th week of training (on completing the 6-mile speed march) as the sign that they are entering the last lap of what is the longest military recruit training of any in the Western World.

638 Troop are on their first military excursion outside the Commando Training Centre Lympstone since joining the Corps in early summer. In two very busy days, the amphibious experts of Landing Craft Company will teach them the basics of Commando boating, then launch them by high-speed raiding craft into a night raid on a naval establishment at Portland, as the start of 'Exercise Highland Anvil' – the recruits' final and most arduous exercise.

Having started in April with 27 people, only 12 of those 'originals' remain. Today the troop is 33 strong, having taken in an unusually large number of 'back-troopers' – those who for many and varied reasons failed to pass out with their original troops. Some of these suffered injuries and, after remedial PT in Hunter Troop (CTC's medical rehabilitation unit), are hoping very much that good fortune will keep further injury at bay.

Others were back-trooped to 638 through lack of progress, mostly for 'poor personal administration' – meaning they couldn't look after themselves well enough to survive Exercise Highland Anvil. Because everybody who starts Royal Marines training has already passed several days of evaluation, testing and mutual familiarization on the potential recruits course, they have each demonstrated the potential to pass out. Nevertheless, some take longer than others to absorb training and information, while also getting used to a very new style of life. Everybody must nevertheless achieve the required standards before being allowed to join a Commando unit, where any weak links in the chain could jeopardise operations and people's lives.

Such potential weak links do not survive the Final Exercise, which only the most determined will finish. On Dartmoor particularly dreadful conditions require tremendous effort simply to keep going. Anybody who loses heart, to the extent of not bothering to do as they have been taught, rapidly becomes a liability – and will be required to do the exercise again. Several of 638's back-troopers have experienced this, and in their desire to succeed this time have the memory of failure very much in the forefront of their minds.

Designed to challenge each man's determination, stamina and sense of humour, the Final Exercise is also a very serious complication to the actual Commando Tests which follow the exercise. Only survivors of 'Final Ex' are permitted to take the four Commando Tests (the endurance course, 9-mile speed march, Tarzan assault course and 30-mile forced march), and earn Green Berets. The troop have already completed practice runs at some of the Commando Tests, and are confident of their ability to pass. They reckon, however, without the debilitating effects of Exercise Highland Anvil, which has an additional purpose of deliberately inducing fatigue (verging on exhaustion) to make the Commando Tests very much harder than they appear on paper to be. Optimism is however a distinct asset in Commando Forces. There is nevertheless an atmosphere of tension and determination as the Troop realize the importance of the next three weeks – and the severe effort that will be required if each is to pass.

It is a bitterly cold, windy day, ice flicking painfully off the surface of an irritable, choppy sea. To one side, away from prying eyes, two Special Boat Squadron NCOs, wearing brightly coloured civilian climbing clothing, are showing a shivering group of potential SBS candidates how to assemble a Klepper canoe. Another two SBS men, lean with shoulder-length hair, wearing jungle light-weights and special canvas and rubber-soled canoeing boots, wait patiently beside the Klepper they have just assembled in a fraction of the time it will take the candidates. After a short portage up the hill to the lake – the candidates struggling to keep up – these two will demonstrate capsizing and other boat drills in its icy water, before 'inviting' the candidates to follow suit. On such a day the prospect of immersion in cold water hangs over everybody like a black cloud.

As 638 Troop shelter in the fuggy warmth of the Hard's automat, they know for certain that before the day is out they too are going to be soaking wet. But getting wet is something to which the 27 long weeks at Lympstone has made them very familiar. After a two-week induction period, their first encounter with the training team took place at low tide on the estuary flats of the River Exe, when to the astonishment of all (except the staff) what was scheduled as a normal PT session developed into a ferocious game of rugby in glutinous, fish-stinking mud. Their fresh-faced troop commander, a young lieutenant who until that moment had seemed a distant and god-like figure, turned the game into a most informal murder ball session. Afterwards, it took ten minutes of fire-hosing before everybody regained their former identities, by which time the ice was well and truly broken between the troop and their instructors.

So, although used to regular soaking in cold water, until the moment comes the troop are making the most of any respite.

'Right, men, on your feet. Pick up your weapons 'n' webbing and get across into the lecture room.'

A Landing Craft Branch NCO brings their unofficial tea break to an end. Webbing and weapons are shouldered, cap comforters adjusted and chairs straightened behind the square formica-topped tables. As the troop file out, the duty student ensures that the room is left tidy, and that nobody has left any kit 'loafing' for gleeful instructors to find.

They walk through a small museum, with diorama models of past Royal Marine amphibious operations: the Dieppe raid, the assault on Limbang in Borneo ... to the lecture room where the OC (Officer Commanding) of Landing Craft Branch, Captain Page, addresses them.

'Good morning, gentlemen. Sit at ease. Sit easy, look this way and pay attention.

'My name's Captain Page and I am the OC of the landing

638 Troop hosing down after their first mud-run.

craft wing down here at Royal Marines Poole. First of all I want to welcome you to Royal Marines Poole and in particular to the Landing Craft Branch down here at the Hard.

'I want you to remember two points: firstly, you're here to learn. You've escaped from the nightmare of Lympstone for a couple of days. The Common isn't outside the door. This is not a testing environment, so you can all relax on that point.

'The second thing is safety. I'm sure that at the moment all of you are really only interested in getting a Green Beret on your head and surviving the Commando Course. However, you're not going to pass out with this troop if you break a leg or an arm – and with boats and the sea that happens. It's real. No blanks out there.

'Two weeks ago on the officers' course, a guy broke his foot. He's now going to have to be put back a course. People injure themselves with monotonous regularity, because they don't pay attention and do as they're told. So listen to what the coxswains tell you, and do it. If you have any questions about anything, don't try and hide at the back of the troop and think you'll get away with it. Stick your hand up and ask. No one's going to bollock you for asking questions here.

'I'm sorry the weather isn't particularly pleasant today but boating and landing craft work is fun, so you should have an enjoyable day.

'I'll put in a quick advert for the Landing Craft Branch, which is the Corps' most important SQ [specialist qualification], the only one that we have as Royal Marines, that no one else does. If you want to be a driver join the RCT, if you want to be a parachutist you can join the Parachute Regiment . . .'

Everybody turns and looks at Hilton, who'd broken his leg as a Parachute Regiment recruit. On recovering, he'd decided to join the Royal Marines.

'The Landing Craft Branch is unique and is the most important period in your training in terms of your uniqueness as Royal Marines – as naval or amphibious infantry. And in just two days we expect you to hoist in all the skills you'll need when you go to a Commando unit.

'I'll give you an example of the difference between you and the Army. It takes the Parachute Regiment four weeks to learn to jump out of an aeroplane. Now that doesn't take the brains of an archbishop. It's a pretty basic thing: there's the door and you fall downwards, all right? And that's their expertise. We expect you to hoist in a whole different variety of skills, and different craft, in only two days.'

Hilton grins as Bailey nudges him.

'Remember, Poole Harbour even in the worst weather is a fairly pleasant place to be. You might be doing this in Norway in January, so use a bit of imagination today, so that when you get to a Commando unit, you won't make complete idiots of yourselves. It's important, and it's far from easy.'

Captain Page leaves the troop in the capable hands of Corporal Boddy, a slight but authoritatively salty figure with a quiet speaking voice, a coxswain instructor of many years' experience.

'The man driving the boat is the coxswain, which in Gemini or Rigid Raiding craft would be a Marine. He is the man in charge, OK? Whatever he tells you to do, you do it. If he tells you to jump in the water there's a reason for it, you do it. You don't argue with him. It doesn't matter what rank is actually in the craft at the time, that Marine will be in charge.

'If he tells you to get in the water – don't worry if any of you are non-swimmers. You will be issued with your Assault Life-Jackets later this morning.'

Before 638 Troop are permitted to do any sort of boat training at Poole, they must learn the very basic safety drills that will undoubtedly save some of their lives in the years to come. These basic rules must always be followed, regardless of the circumstances, and form the basics of all Commando operations.

Corporal Boddy emphasizes that at sea, assault life-jackets (or ALJs) will be their most important piece of personal safety equipment, to be looked after with the same care as their personal weapon. These dark green ALJs are designed to inflate instantly using compressed air from a small cylinder and are strong enough to support a man in the water even when he's fully laden with weapons, webbing and ammunition. Corporal Boddy goes through the drills of putting the ALJ on (you step through the long loop before locating the trailing strap and pulling it up between your legs and securing with the pin), demonstrates the safety whistle and shows them the water-activated light.

Recruit Prater is feeling a touch exposed, standing at the front of the room acting as the model. He follows Corporal Boddy's instructions, demonstrating the correct way to put on an ALJ, how to wear your equipment and weapon, and how it must be looked after. The lecture is clearly building to some kind of climax.

Corporal Boddy takes pains to emphasize the importance of inflating your life-jacket the instant you get into trouble – lest you plummet downwards into the depths of a cold, dark ocean. At the dramatic moment, he steps up to Recruit Prater and pulls the red toggle, so hard that Prater's shoulder is wrenched downwards. Instead of a rush of compressed air instantly transforming the jacket into large red water-wings, nothing happens. Corporal Boddy tries again, several times, but the jacket fails to inflate and Prater is told to sit down.

Recruit Nicolson, a dark-haired, soft-spoken Scot from the Isle of Skye, steps into another ALJ, which despite some equally serious toggle-pulling also fails to inflate. Undefeated and with a flourish, Corporal Boddy produces large red water-wings from under the lectern – 'an ALJ I inflated before we went on air' – to great laughter. Using Nicolson as the model, he demonstrates self-inflation in case of air cylinder failure – pulling the poppers then blowing into the red, self-locking mouthpiece. The troop are paying very close attention, imagining treading water laden with equipment and weapon, trying to use the 'oral inflation device' before sinking. Their laughter has a definite nervousness to it.

Safety drills and lectures over, 638 Troop leave the warmth of the lecture room and parade in biting wind facing a small pebble beach. They've heard about the Royal Marines' 'Rigid Raider' fast assault craft, flat-bottomed, fibreglass dories powered by 140 BHP Suzuki engines, designed to carry eight men (a section) at 40 knots. They've

Rigid raiders in action on Poole Harbour.

also heard about how wet the two men at the front of the boat become, drenched within minutes by spray. While being detailed off into boats by Corporal Boddy, some members of the troop attempt to avoid bow seats, but soon discover that even though the front two men are soaked within seconds, everybody else is drenched shortly after that.

They set off in three Raiders, into the relative calm of Poole Harbour. Even on a calm day, the speed of the craft requires the coxswain to stand braced to his control console amidships, the outboard's propellers digging deep, driving the dory's rigid bottom hard across the tops of the waves, the bow rearing skywards from zero to angles up to 45 degrees. A Rigid Raider has no sides, only a handrail for the express purpose of hanging on grimly, knees bent and straining, trying to absorb the continual shocks while dodging the sheets of incoming salt spray. An inflated sausage of black rubber runs both sides of the craft beside the handrail, without which serious injury to the base of the spine would be inevitable.

Each painfully fast trip past the sights of Poole Harbour (famous for its wading bird population), around Brownsea Island (where the first ever Scout camp was held), ends with the command 'Standby to beach' then 'Action', and disembarkation into waist-deep water, to assault up the beach and lie panting on cold wet sand or shingle.

Forty-knot Commando boating is unlike anything they have ever experienced before. As the boats bounce across the swell, their flat fibreglass bottoms smacking hard into the wave tops, it's as tiring as riding an unpredictably bucking bronco. Recruit Alain Schembri has quite a bit of sailing experience, which he found didn't help very much: 'We don't do 40 knots on a yacht – and I haven't been on speedboats before so it was quite an experience ... very good fun, but wet and cold to say the least.'

Schembri's hands, blue with cold, were covered with blood after the first run: ' 'Cos it was going quite fast and the waves were choppy, I kept on hitting my knuckles on the base of the boat.'

The coxswains indicate formations and changes of direction using hand signals. They swoop smoothly towards Furzey Island, beaching gently out a strip of shingle. Everybody gets off in slow time.

Corporal Teers, the senior coxswain, then uses one boat and its section to teach the others the details of assault landing drills. Although everybody is wet and cold they are all listening carefully, very aware that they are being taught by real experts.

'In good conditions you may well be able to take your lifejackets off before you get to the beach, rolling them up tidily, placing them at the bottom of my steering console. As you get nearer the beach, you'll adopt fire positions; the guy at the front should be an LSW [light support weapon] gunner, and cover to the front. The remainder cover to the sides of the craft.'

As the rigid raider approaches the beach, two men wade carefully ashore, one carrying a line – the painter. The others then disembark in pairs, fanning out to either side, lying down in fire positions.

'As you hit the beach the coxswain turns the engine off, then tells the bowman to get out. You have to get out of this craft keeping low so you don't form too high a silhouette, but so you don't bang the weapon on the side of the craft. Once you go towards the beach, you slide your feet carefully through the water, so you don't make noise.

'Next guy out, go!

'The last guy out is the section commander who then goes in the middle 'cos he's then got overall control, yeah? Once that's been done the bowman looks around, gets the nod from the coxswain, puts the line back in the boat and then takes up the right of arc, so he goes to the extreme right. Everybody happy with that? OK.

'On the beach, in pairs, one of you takes his life-jacket off, then the other, all right? It's the bowman's job to come behind and put them back on the boat. Anybody got any questions?

'Right, split yourselves down into your boats again and we'll go through the drills. Listen to what you've got to do, and do what the coxswains tell you.'

After the demo they practise these drills, slowly walking through each stage several times until the whole process is perfect.

Getting out of the boats into knee-deep, icy-cold water without splashing or making noise is harder than it looks. With small, cold waves washing on to feet, ankles and knees as they lie in the shallows, it's uncomfortable – and the men make mistakes. Each section should form a straight line on the beach facing inland, but repeatedly they form a crescent shape. They are also too far apart; for real, this will be done at night, when the only way of keeping together is by each man placing an ankle over the next man's – as they have already been taught for night ambushes and patrol rendezvous.

Having sorted out the drills for landing, they practise paddling the raiders silently into the shore, at least 300 metres being essential to escape detection. With three paddles to each side, this is a slow, laborious and rather miserable process, particularly now the men are soaked to the skin.

In the middle of Poole Harbour the wind has whipped up, and salt spray is sheeting across their craft. They practise transferring from the raiders to LCVPs (landing craft vehicle personnel, carrying 30 men or a Land Rover and trailer) while moving. With the two boats touching most of the time, care must be taken when climbing up and over the high sides of the LCVP lest fingers and hands be trapped. It's easy to slip and fall on the wet metal decks.

Despite sitting crammed together in the LCVP, everybody is shivering with cold. As the craft turns into the waves, water buckets across the bows, catching the unlucky ones at the back with the force of a back-hand blow to the face. The men are huddling back into their life-jackets, taking any shelter they can, laughing with each fresh deluge – on the grounds that there's nothing else to do. It's like being sprayed by a salt water fire hose, which gets into their eyes. 'At least it's not raining,' says one wag. In their immersion suits, the coxswains can afford to enjoy it.

They next practise beach assaults and re-embarkations at troop strength from the LCVP, piling out as sections to lie in lines on the beach, then pulling back to the LCVP, covering each other the whole way. Being so wet and cold, they find the learning process becoming harder and harder. They do several beach assaults, screaming as they disembark – which, apart from any other benefit, gets the blood circulating again. As they approach the beach for yet another assault, the coxswains shout instructions: 'Prepare to beach – which means sort yourselves out, not move!'

The coxswain's mate releases the bow ramp's safety pins, also putting up the bulletproof screen, blinding the helmsman. The troop move towards the bow, ready to assault.

'Stand by to beach . . . Action!'

The bow ramp crashes down and the men pound forward and off the craft, through the water and on to the beach, forming their tight defensive perimeter. Coming back on is done equally tactically: two men return to the craft to give cover, then the first section embarks, taking up fire positions along the sides of the LCVP. The others withdraw giving cover, moving under the orders of the troop commander. When the last man is aboard, the ramp is raised and the LCVP reverses away from the shore.

Recruit Lyons was troop commander during the amphibious drills, finding it wet but educational, and good fun. Although they're trained only as basic marines, learning to take responsibility is very important: 'Being in charge made me feel a bit panicky; I know what to do, but it's difficult knowing when to do it. It's more enjoyable however to be in charge – more interesting.'

The two days of basic Commando boating at Poole culminate in a full-scale night raid using Rigid Raiders, on a fort at the end of the breakwater at Portland naval base. This raid is also the start of the dreaded Final Exercise, used by training staff to weed out the individuals they feel do not yet deserve to become Royal Marines.

The troop know what to expect, and after all the hard work of the past 27 weeks just want to get on with it. Recruit Snazel is on his first attempt, but tasted failure earlier aged 16, on his initial potential

Amphibious training at RM Poole:
(*Above*) Storming ashore from
LCVPs. (*Right*) A totally soaked
Recruit Dobson marches an
equally wet 638 Troop off to hot
showers and 'scran'.

recruits course at CTC. He waited three years, then returned and
passed, being inducted into 638 Troop in June: 'The Green Beret is
everything, because it's possibly the hardest training of any. We hear
rumours about the Final Exercise, but we're not going to worry about
it – we're just going to get on with it.'

Recruit Michael Holmes is aged 17, and hurt himself during the
landings when he smashed his forearm against a rock while taking up
a fire position with the LSW (light support weapon – the section
machine-gun). Despite this, with all the adrenalin and shouting, he
found learning the drills exciting:

'I joined the Marines because there wasn't much going on in
Civvie Street. I find it fairly difficult but I'm optimistic of
passing.

'The first 15 weeks were mainly fitness, but now with all the
tactics it's more interesting. I'm really looking forward to the
Final Exercise, and feeling confident about the Commando Tests
particularly as we've already done timed runs over the courses.
They've said however that you've really got to dig in to pass –
like if you walk on the endurance course you will fail . . .'

Alain Schembri:

'It was always my ambition, from a small boy, to be a Marine. I joined up on Feb 3, 1992 but was injured, went to Hunter Troop [the remedial PT unit], then joined this troop.

'The first 15 weeks of training were strange – moving into a military environment, being away from home for the first time. It was very hard adjusting, getting over homesickness and getting used to the military way of life.

'It was nothing like I expected it to be. I don't think anyone's got a real idea of what it's going to be like ... whereas the actual reality of everything is completely different – it's a bit shocking in a way ... hard ... it's very hard really.

'There's mental pressure all the time. Your uniform must always be immaculate. You're picked up all the time on inspections. You have inspections every day. Your locker has to be immaculate all the time ... like for six months everything has to be on the ball all the time. You can't relax ... every day ... late at night – as well as the physical pressures. So you can finish a day very tired, but you know you've got the training team on your back too. There's a lot of mental pressure as well.

'There are beastings too, but the instructors are not horrible people or anything. I'm sure they're nice people, but they're paid to do a job.'

This is, however, the beginning of the last lap, the Final Exercise, the Commando Tests, then passing-out and off to a real Commando unit. Schembri seems confident of succeeding, but deep down seems actually to be just as uncertain as he was back in those first strange weeks:

'... we've been training for six months now so physically we should be up to the standards ... however, I think everyone will find it hard – nothing's easy. The exercise will be one of those things where you just have to grit your teeth for five days and get on with it, making sure you survive ...

'Of the tests, I'm dreading the endurance course and the 9-mile speed march more than anything else. It's quite a long way to run, carrying a lot of equipment, in a short space of time. I don't like running a long way with kit.'

Schembri has a knee injury, which he has to be careful not to make worse if he is to survive. Getting a Green Beret is important, 'a way of proving something to yourself', an end in itself, after which he will take stock of life and prospects in the Royal Marines, and the enormous variety of trades and specializations they offer. 'Everyone just wants to, like, get through training, then decide what they want to do. I might be going into Anti-Tanks [using Milan Missiles] ... I'm not sure yet.'

638 Troop are loading ammunition for the exercise under the watchful eye of senior instructor Sergeant Nick Barnett:

'Everybody's got four magazines, yeah? Each section commander and 2IC will also grab four thunderflashes. Make sure you've got a striker. Also each section commander to carry one smoke grenade. Any questions? Good.

'One section grab the ammunition off the Land Rover, the remainder of you take your magazines out your fighting orders...'

A GPMG (general purpose machine-gun) gunner asks how much 7.62mm linked ammunition he should take: 'GPMG, you grab 300 rounds, yeah? No problems.'

With all the other weight they are carrying, the ammunition has to be carefully distributed. Each man carries six loaded magazines and an additional 200 rounds. The LSW teams carry linked ammunition too, some of which they farm out to other members of the section. Everything is to be tucked away into webbing and bergens, ready for use when needed.

That evening in the briefing room at Wyke Regis camp, the training staff prepare to give Orders for the Final Exercise. A Commando raid is a painstakingly planned operation in which every last piece of information is presented to the men in the clearest possible way. Each phase must be planned, then memorized by the troop and rehearsed, so that when they get ashore and the inevitable confusion sets in, they are able to carry on with the job. The corporals are colouring in diagrams, chalking names on to outlines of the rigid raiders, drawing the diagrams from which Orders will be given.

With Sergeant Barnett, troop commander Lieutenant Gillies mulls over the problem of the numbers of bodies, the boats and his landing plan. Barnett is slender, fair-haired (although it's hard to tell as he's got a recruit-style crewcut) and is straightforward and informal, but bites if provoked. Lieutenant Archie Gillies is a thoughtful, dark-haired Scot – kindly, but determined to maintain standards. They change the boat loading and landing plans around, trying to keep the sections together. The object of the exercise is not to carry out a perfect landing (although they hope that will prove to be the case), but to test the men within their sections – which entails keeping sections together with one of the Diamonds in charge. ('Diamonds' are the best recruits, given responsibility and the chance to shine.) Corporal Dave Layton complains that Chamberlain's name is too long for the space on the board.

Responsible for planning the whole operation, Lieutenant Gillies writes the Orders he must deliver later that night. Having just been posted to CTC after two years with the Corps ski biathlon team, he hasn't done this for several years and feels very rusty – although it doesn't show. The coxswains arrive wearing dark green immersion suits and life-jackets. Lieutenant Gillies takes a few minutes to give them the outline of his plan: one boat initially, then a second wave of two raiders leaving Wyke Regis at 0345 hours. The third wave will be of four boats, loading the remainder of the troop, leaving Wyke at 0445.

Lieutenant Gillies checks their radios, call signs and frequencies. Communications will be vital to the exercise – as to the operation if it were real. They are to use PRC 351s, and need alternative frequencies in case communications go down. He is also concerned for the safety of the landing. The rocks of the Portland breakwater will be very slippery and he doesn't want any rushed unloading and accidents at the other end. They discuss the landing point in detail, whether there will be a ladder or flat area to climb on to. There will be night rehearsals at the slipway just before embarkation to get everybody used to the boats they are in, and to exactly what they are going to have to do.

The end wall of the briefing room is covered with the maps, diagrams and sketches the training team have been preparing. They discuss the format of the briefing, covering much of the end wall with blank sheets of paper to prevent people being distracted until the correct point of the briefing has been reached.

Meanwhile 638 Troop have been dossing down in a classroom. They've learned to take every opportunity for a few moments' rest whenever it presents itself. They pack their kit and dress ready for Orders, then Lieutenant Gillies enters the room to explain how the troop is to be rearranged for this raid. The usually cheerful Recruit Lobb has just woken up, and looks totally bemused and very tired – even though the exercise hasn't even started. Lieutenant Gillies comments, 'You look wide awake there, Lobb,' to general laughter.

Recruit Spink, a tall, round-headed Lancashire man, is to be temporarily demoted to section commander, with Lieutenant Gillies acting as troop commander. Having been in the Royal Marines only a few months, Spink could not plan and command this raid, so Lieutenant Gillies has taken over until the raid is completed. It will also be difficult for the recruit section commanders, who are trained only as Marines and not corporals. This point will be emphasized during the briefing.

Rather than anything more complicated, the training team are looking for a sense of aggression and enthusiasm, with people remaining alert throughout the exercise. Lieutenant Gillies will be particularly interested in seeing how the section commanders act when under pressure:

> 'It's too much to expect recruits to get it right on their own, so the training team will steer them throughout. This raid will take place across dangerous ground, so we operate within limits.
>
> Frankly, it's impossible for these exercises to be totally realistic.'

The main problems the recruits face in carrying out this operation are those vital military necessities: command and control.

> 'It all boils down to awareness ... If they fanny about on the rocks, they'll end up slipping. Somebody going along with their mind in neutral will end up doing something horrendous like firing on his own blokes in the darkness. On this ground, it's easily done, so we constantly emphasize the need to stay alert.'

Lieutenant Gillies wants to see everybody in 638 Troop pass this exercise, but whether that happens is up to each individual:

> 'It's my job to ensure that as many as possible get through. If they fail at this late stage of training, to an extent it's my fault. The usual reasons for failure are attitude and administration in the field – plus lack of enthusiasm.'

Although Lieutenant Gillies' job is to get the recruits up to standard, if they can't handle the exercise then there is no alternative but to do it again:

> 'They're not chucked out of the Corps, but back-trooped. We remedy the problem, then get them back for another chance. Failure has shaken people up in the past, and they've emerged in the end as strong recruits.'

Recruits Bauduin, Nicolson, Spink and Dobson, being the troop 'Diamonds', are the exercise section commanders. Realizing that preparation time is vital, they ask Lieutenant Gillies for permission to enter the briefing room and look over the maps, photographs and diagrams in advance of Orders. He waves them in, and they pore over the details until it's time for the full-scale briefing to start.

The room goes quiet as Lieutenant Gillies steps to the front:

> 'This is your test exercise, and is a pass or fail event. We're looking for a good effort all round, a bit of enthusiasm. It's not going to be easy, obviously, and some of you will find it more difficult than others. Having said all that, I do expect everyone to pass who's here, including the – the more feeble members ... We know who they are.
>
> 'Before we crack on, I'd like to say that this is the bread and butter of what we do. It's all very well having a kind of racing snake ... who can fly round all the Commando Tests, but if he's gibbering with cold in the field then he's not much use.
>
> 'There are times in the field when you're all wet, miserable, manky and threaders [threadbare]. But you've got to carry on with it. This is what separates you who are going to be Marines from the likes of the punter from *Blue Peter* who ambles round a 30-miler, then goes back to the bathroom and contemplates his blisters – and feels like a hero!
>
> 'The important thing for you guys is the build-up – the fact that you're not just doing the Commando Tests, but you've also

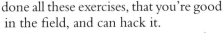

done all these exercises, that you're good in the field, and can hack it.

'Commando training is supposed to be hard, so expect it to be hard. During this exercise, as you're sitting miserably somewhere, think to yourself: "Well, I was kind of expecting it to be hard, anyway." It makes it a little bit easier at the time.

'And last thing to pack? Your sense of humour, as I'm sure Wilson will do.' The raid is but the first part of the Final Exercise – a 'warmer into the bank' which will certainly ensure that they are wet through from the very start. Lieutenant Gillies [pictured left] concentrates upon the raid, with a few non-exercise instructions:

'No-duff points: don't go near the round building at the end, and if anybody is injured, get on to the radio, then we'll send the medic across, and get you to HMS *Osprey*'s sickbay by raider asap.'

The forecast doesn't look good: strong to gale force winds, sea moderate to rough, with rain spreading from the west, clearing leaving showers. The troop note this prediction with stoicism. They have been lucky with the weather on their exercises thus far – having experienced very little truly wet weather. Their luck seems about to change.

Lieutenant Gillies gives meteorological details: moon states, rising and setting times, last light timings, high water at 0430. Some people are writing it all down, others are not. Lieutenant Gillies asks if they've got it all. Everybody nods.

Before he starts his formal Orders, Lieutenant Gillies talks them through the maps and diagrams, dispelling curiosity that might distract their attention later. He then follows the official Orders format: first giving details of the Ground, then detailing the Objective.

He divides the Objective into four areas, A to D. Information on the enemy is sketchy; they number around eight, and 638 Troop will have to find them. They are warned to expect all manner of obstacles, including barbed wire and trip flares. The enemy, having invaded England, have good morale and cannot be expected to give up. An overall battle picture is given involving the Paras as well as 3 Commando Brigade. Their raid is part of a 'bigger picture'.

Throughout all the detail of his briefing, Lieutenant Gillies stops to ask them questions, to check that everybody is listening. Next he gives the raid's mission very carefully: 'To destroy the enemy on and around the Objective, at grid . . .' repeating the sentence, including the grid reference, so there can be no mistake and everybody (including the poor note-takers) understands it. This clear definition of Mission is vital in case communications break down and somebody else has to take over, or in case everything goes totally wrong and a new plan has to be devised on the ground. Everybody notes the loading plan very carefully (lest they end up in the wrong boat), then Lieutenant Gillies launches into the detail of the raid itself – which is in six phases.

They will drop off from the raiders on to the breakwater, one section at a time, until the whole troop are safely ashore. 1 Section will then move forward along the breakwater and clear the hut. 2 Section will clear block B, then 3 Section move round the back on to the roof of hut A, to give covering fire for 4 Section to cover block C. 1 Section will then move through and clear the lower floors of the main building, 2 Section clearing the upper floors. 3 Section then move forward to clear the jetty area. Once the jetty is clear, they will summon the raiders and get away as fast as possible, which sounds fairly simple.

Lieutenant Gillies now breaks from the Orders format to get Bauduin to summarize the plan. Bauduin is stocky and dark, with a solid, square face and Mediterranean looks, and has been caught out. He explains that he's only taken notes for his section's particular part of the operation. It's vital that everybody understands all aspects of the operation, so Bauduin knows he's in the wrong. Lieutenant Gillies, however, reveals no irritation, turning instead to Spink, asking him to have a go. Everybody laughs nervously, hoping he won't ask them.

Spink goes deliberately through the whole plan until Lieutenant Gillies stops him. He then asks Nicolson to take over, which he does with equal confidence, pointing out the objectives on the diagram with his pencil. 'Good effort,' says Lieutenant Gillies. The remaining Diamond, Recruit Dobson, the stocky former Royal Engineers corporal (no relation to Sergeant Major Dobson on the All Arms Course), is called out, and details each of the sections' tasks up until the clearance of the jetty. Lieutenant Gillies then gives Bauduin another chance, to describe the tasks of each section in this last phase, which he does.

Lieutenant Gillies turns to radio communications, detailing how each section is to indicate their progress in each phase, so that the operation will not be held up or jeopardized by confusion. He then goes through 'Actions On', telling everybody exactly what they are to do in every eventuality. Many of these details are SOP (standard operating procedure), but he goes through them anyway: 'Actions on being mortared: spread out and take cover. Actions on flares: freeze until the flare burns out or hits the ground . . .'

He finishes up by asking 'Any questions?' They synchronize watches: 'Ten-O-three in 40 seconds.' Digital peeps fill the room.

They ask questions about the enemy: what are they wearing, for example. Lieutenant Gillies doesn't know: 'There's no int' – no intelligence.

Orders finish just before midnight. Time to get the kit ready and start night-time rehearsals. They walk each phase of the operation slowly, Lieutenant Gillies talking them through everything before making them rehearse again unprompted. Although these rehearsals are nothing like the real thing, they fix the sequence of events in everybody's minds, as well as allowing wrinkles in the plan to be detected and ironed out. After rehearsals they snatch a few moments' rest before it's time for the raid itself.

Loaded up and ready for action, 638 Troop file out of the Nissen huts and down the long hill to Wyke Regis slipway. The sections keep together, ready to climb into the rigid raiders at the correct time for the sea transit to Portland Fort. For 2, 3 and 4 Sections, there will be a wait while 1 Section lands and secures the ground.

The lighthouse's white beam flashes rhythmically across black water, reflecting off wave tops in the sheltered harbour. After an interminable wait in the cold, the main body load into the raiders and sit gripping the side rails as the coxswains manoeuvre their bobbing craft gently into arrowhead formation, opening the throttles with a gentleness absent from the daylight excursions in Poole Harbour.

Moving very fast initially, the four raiders thread their way from Portland Fleet, past the lines of street lights and under the road bridge into Portland Harbour. As they weave between brightly lit warships at anchor, authoritative pipes to the dog watch carry a long way on the still night air: 'D'you hear there, Officer of the Watch speaking' ... and they imagine warm matelots in cosy deck spaces, keeping themselves awake with hot mugs of strong, sweet coffee.

As the raiders approach the far end of the breakwater, they slow to walking pace, engines barely audible above the slap of waves against fibreglass hulls. Enormous, angular boulders loom above their heads, topped by a concrete walkway and wall to the seaward side. The coxswains nose the raiders gently into the seaweed, slightly increasing engine revs to keep the bows braced firmly against the slippery rocks. 1 Section beckon them in, having ensured there are no enemy in the area. 'Standby, action' – a hissed whisper of command, and the first men step carefully ashore on a perfect, tar-black night.

At the far end of the breakwater a log fire blazes, throwing dancing shadows against the square windows and stone staircases of the abandoned fort. A radio is playing somewhere, the enemy clearly blissfully unaware of what is about to be visited upon them from the sea...

The troop's objective is Portland Fort, a gaunt, imposing collection of buildings growing out of the enormous rocks that comprise the main breakwater at the mouth of Portland Harbour. With blank

The fort at the end of the Portland breakwater – an intelligence photograph of 638 Troop's objective for their night raid – as they will see it.

windows and square, sandstone buildings, it is a bleak, unfriendly place even in daylight. Ashore, the sections move carefully and silently down the breakwater towards their objective, visible only against the far-off street lights of the naval base.

The enemy catch sight of the leading section and open up. Sporadic firing breaks out and section commander Bauduin gets a grip of his men. They start clearing the first building, keeping in touch with each other through constant shouting. The explosions start, deafeningly loud, their flashes destroying night vision, leaving a disorienting imprint on the retina for several minutes. The eerie moan of the lighthouse's siren sounds every 15 seconds – a lonely, ethereal sound. The trip flares burn hard, throwing buildings and the outlines of enemy into sharp relief. The men try to keep one eye shut tight to preserve their night vision.

Lieutenant Gillies steps in as troop commander to control the operation. He uses a combination of radio and his voice, at times sending runners forward to find out what is happening. Bursts of gunfire and explosions indicate the men's progress. Lieutenant Gillies orders suppressive fire from the other sections as the blocks are cleared. This fire is vital to maintain the momentum of the attack. It is very confusing. Flares light up the sky, hanging under small parachutes, casting a peculiar shifting orange light until they fizzle out into the sea. As the sections close on each block, the fire and shouting intensify, rounded off with a series of explosions. The section commanders are getting a grip, aided by the instructors.

Contact with the enemy now well and truly made, Lieutenant Gillies moves up the very front ready to control the final phase of the raid, the attack on the jetty. Crouching inside block C, he controls 4 Section directly by voice, while ordering 2 and 3 Sections ('one-two charlie and one-three charlie') by radio to give covering fire. 4 Section throw grenades, then follow the explosions inside the building, shining torches and firing. Recruit Spink shouts them through:

'Keep away from the window . . . Room clear – everyone in!

Get into a fire position . . . I say again building D is clear . . .

Roger, I'll move back to the landing area. OK, everyone,

standby to move out on my order . . . Move now!'

At this critical stage, Lieutenant Gillies desperately needs information, requesting sitreps (situation reports) from the sections over the radio. Comms are less than ideal, and he has to give orders without knowing whether the sections can hear him. Despite this, however, he presses on: 'I want to know what's going on up there. Tell Dobson as soon as he's clear to send a runner back to me.'

Recruit Bauduin's section are out in the open, swanning around on open rocks – which are also dangerously slippery. Several men fall heavily. Lieutenant Gillies tells Bauduin to get a grip: 'Right, Bauduin, prepare to move forward and clear block B. Move now! And get one-one charlie to clear the other block. Come on, Bauduin, get a move on, and remember you are moving past 2 Section.'

Bauduin seems a little sluggish, a touch confused by what is happening. He gets his section moving: 'Right, get into your pairs and get ready to move. First pair, standby and go! Get a move on. And the next two – go! Get in there now! Go on.'

Grenade explosions light up the buildings, followed by the sharp, echoing rattle of automatic fire. The section commanders are shouting, urging the pairs on, each pair shouting to each other, reporting what they are finding in the rooms.

'Grenade! Get in there now! Move!'

Flares hiss as they launch towards the enemy, still more grenades and the rattle of automatic fire. The voices are growing harsh with urgency, hoarse with tiredness. Any hesitation or slackness cannot be tolerated. Even though the grenades are only thunderflashes, they pack a big enough punch to be treated with respect. Then suddenly out of the confusion, it is clear that they have secured the jetty and the raid is successful.

'Bauduin, get your ammo and casualty states ready for me – all right?'

Lieutenant Gillies is keeping close behind Bauduin's section. He wonders if Bauduin is a bit miffed at receiving all this attention: 'You've not got a sad on now, have you, Bauduin? Cheered up? Good man.'

Lieutenant Gillies calls up the raiders on his 351: 'Request pick-up as soon as possible. Like now! Over.'

He is pleased. The raid has gone almost exactly to time, but radio comms have also gone as he had expected – badly. He can't get through to the boats: 'You're unworkable, I say again unworkable. If you got that message, move in now and give me a call as you come in.'

He continues as before, hoping they will have heard his message, already working out his options:

'If I don't get any joy with comms, we'll have to send runners to the sections or shout. The only problem now is with the boats. During the op there could have been probs with the rear sections. Comms are always the problem with these operations.'

The sections check in with casualty and ammo states, going firm in the jetty area. The raiders can be seen motoring quietly in towards the harbour. The sky is beginning to brighten. Lieutenant Gillies orders 4 Section into the first boat, seven men into one boat, six into the next. A third boat arrives and Lieutenant Gillies organizes the extraction, ensuring that sections don't get split up. Inevitably in the gloom, somebody ends up on the wrong boat. Tiredness is beginning to tell and the loading plan goes to rats. Lieutenant Gillies resorts to runners to get the section back to the jetty.

'Ensure that seven blokes go into each raider – quick as you can now! Where is 2 Section? And get 3 Section down here right now!'

The raiders reverse away from the wall then, turning inland, accelerate off into the harbour, carrying the troop back towards Wyke Regis and the 4-ton lorries waiting to take them inland from the coast, to the muddy and very wet forests below the high ground of Dartmoor – and the next phase of the exercise.

CHAPTER THREE

AMBUSH

By the time 638 Troop arrive at the drop-off point in the rigid raiders, it is fully light – a grey, cold and miserable day. Two 4-ton lorries are waiting to carry them inland from Portland, towards the high moorland of Dartmoor, the traditional training ground for generations of Commando soldiers.

Lieutenant Gillies reflects on how the Portland raid went:

'I was a bit concerned that the orders might have been too complicated for them. However, they went through the whole thing during rehearsals later that evening at Wyke Regis, walking through the process of off-loading from the raiders and so on, which paid dividends. In the end, the raid was fairly well ordered . . .

'I had problems initially communicating with 1 Section – the point section. Then for some reason, these problems recurred later in the attack, so I used a runner . . . After the initial contact the troop seemed to lose momentum, which picked up again once we actually got into the actual blocks of buildings.

'It's difficult to say now how they've done against the pass/fail bench mark, 'cos obviously I didn't see too much of individuals during the attack. I'll have a chat with the training team about it. But as far as I could see there was enough enthusiasm and control for the blokes to pass.'

Recruit Potts, a tall 20-year-old who used to make quiches in a food factory, twisted his ankle getting out of the raider. Lieutenant Gillies is in no doubt as to the seriousness of such an injury so early in the exercise: 'I think he's going to be all right, though. The medic's seen him and he's got a sprained ankle but hopefully he'll be able to crack on ... although it might well come back to haunt him later on in the exercise.'

The Royal Navy medic is immediately on hand to treat Potts but, far from showing sympathy, shouts at him. He explains:

'One second Potts was waving all over the place, then when I started to shout at him, he suddenly perked up and took notice. It's basically just a sprained ankle. I mean – he survives the breakwater phase and then as we dived off the landing craft at the end, it was all seaweed and he decides to slip over and twist his ankle. These things happen.'

The Royal Navy medic, overweight and obviously not a Commando, is doing his best to be as macho as he believes everybody else to be:

'Most of the recruits ... knowing we're medics ... try to get off the exercise, get pampered ... to take you for a ride. The best thing is not to let them, otherwise you spend most of your time running round after them.'

These comments must be taken with a pinch of salt, and certainly do not apply to Recruit Potts. Most aspiring Commandos would do anything to remain on the exercise (and on the course), under-playing injuries rather than drawing attention to them. The medic probably doesn't know that Potts already has an injured knee from the tunnels of the Endurance course. Potts is no shirker; he used to be a section commander, but had his tape taken away because he failed to exercise enough authority on his fellows.

The troop sit back to back on two rows of metal seats in the centre of each lorry, bergens piled untidily at their feet. Only a flapping canvas canopy protects them from the elements, so although sitting at the end beside the tailboard gives the best view of the world outside, it's warmer to be in the middle.

With the usual grinding of gears, the lorries head north, through suburban streets, past rows of shops where early-morning workers are buying cigarettes and newspapers, then on to the dual carriageway. Everyone huddles together, the slipstream sucking away every last vestige of warmth. Some sleep – or at least appear to be sleeping, heads slumped forward, jolted by every movement of the hard-sprung military vehicle. They get cheerful waves from a group of uniformed sixth-form girls, who draw only weak smiles of appreciation from the two coldest men sitting by the tailboard.

The lorries roar and grind through small villages and narrow lanes, climbing steadily upwards from sea level. Nobody has a clue where they are – nor do they care. Outside the flapping canvas the Devon countryside unfolds: rolling hills, small mixed arable farms, and ridge lines topped by woodland. From a warm tourist coach it would look picturesque. From a CTC 4-tonner it looks like heavy going – saturated clay underfoot, steep inclines and very wet vegetation. Lunch before a roaring pub fire would do nicely – but nobody is crazy enough to imagine such a prospect.

Suddenly, as the lorries slow to take a bend at the top of a hill, automatic gunfire breaks out – very loud and close at hand. The training staff are playing their first joker of the exercise – realizing that on this long, cold journey, the troop have switched off.

The troop's response is slow and initially uncoordinated, everybody confused and disorientated. People have their webbing off, and weapons are on the floor – a scene of non-tactical disorganization. At first nobody thinks to let down the tailgate of the lorries, so people have to jump the full 8 feet to the ground. There is uncertainty over where the enemy are, until more firing reveals their position – firing which effectively wipes out the troop.

638 Troop lay down covering fire having been ambushed during their lorry move from Portland to Dartmoor.

Spink and the section commanders get a grip, returning fire, then assaulting the enemy position – by which time the enemy have bugged out (left quickly).

The troop find themselves in deciduous woodland, far away from any habitation. Having cleared the surrounding area, ensuring the enemy have gone, they go into all-round defence, preparing to occupy a harbour position from which to launch further operations.

Recruit Potts is nursing his raid injury, the twisted ankle. The medic is pessimistic about his chances:

> 'Everybody says they'll carry on but we'll see when we start doing the yomps. I've been on this exercise quite a few times now – and some of the yomps are quite vicious.
>
> 'I think I'll be taking him off on one of the yomps . . . I can guarantee that I'll be hanging back with him as the rest of the sections go on, 'cos he won't keep up. They'll have full combat gear on, and in this sort of weather, it's gruelling.
>
> 'When someone's got an injury, the weather plays on his other parts. He'll also be down – not feeling like really fighting, so he's got to battle psychologically as well as physically . . .'

Potts seems philosophical: 'You have to carry on if you get injured in a war, so . . .'

The medic confirms Potts's situation: 'He's battling now.'

The bergens are heavy, and already several of the other men are limping. They saddle up and move off quietly, each man raising two arms to indicate 'file' formation to the men following, deeper into the woods along a very wet track, dead leaves squishing underfoot.

Lieutenant Gillies:

> 'The problem is that they finished the raid on a bit of a high. They relaxed a bit, then dozed off in the transport . . . they were sleepyheads . . . just needing a bit of a waking up. The ambush was designed to do just that, plus put on a bit of pressure.
>
> 'I was actually playing enemy, so I didn't see enough of how they reacted. There was certainly a lull before they actually started to get themselves together and return fire. It seemed to go quite well after that.'

One of the training team, Corporal Dave Layton, was lurking in the bushes and saw it all:

> 'Their anti-ambush drills were not good, which was hardly surprising as inside the trucks their equipment was not ready for action. So to start with, they had all the wrong kit. However, once they got organized it was better, but we did have to shake them up a bit, to motivate them and get them going.'

Dave Layton is tall, athletically built, with a sharp, sardonic sense of humour. Although he readily uses this against the recruits, his apparent cynicism is superficial:

'I expected them to be chaotic, but if it were for real their casualties would have been high – which is unacceptable. It's vital they do it properly, which we insist upon.

'Each of these blokes is being trained to be a Royal Marine – and we leave him to get on and do the job. If he makes a mistake he'll learn from it. We're trying to get blokes who think for themselves, rather than needing someone shouting at them to do things.

'We teach them to think two levels above their own level – as a Marine working to the corporal's level, in the same way that corporals are trained to think up to troop officer level. This enables them to anticipate what's going to happen, so we don't need to tell them every little thing. During the attack their control was good ... section commanders seemed to be taking charge. They needed a bit of prompting, but they always do. But we do tend to nit-pick a little bit – but then you've got to.'

Although Corporal Layton would never admit it to the recruits, he's very much on their side.

While the troop are recceing their harbour area prior to actually occupying it, the training staff have set up camp in an extraordinarily muddy clearing. Two 4-ton 'Q' store trucks are parked back to back, from which emanates the cheerful hissing of a Calor gas cooker – rough domesticity in stark contrast to the grimly tactical scene in the troop's prospective harbour area.

Each recruit troop does this (and every other exercise in the syllabus) just once. Their training teams, however, spend many nights of the year supervising such exercises. The instructors sleep on camp beds in 9-by-9 tents, eating meals from metal plates cooked off the back of the quartermaster's 4-tonner. To the recruits, this would sound like heaven. However, for staff supervising this same exercise for the second time in each year, any sense of privilege has long since worn off. Sharing the recruits' privations would not only be unnecessary for the instructors, but distract both parties from the task of teaching and learning.

After sorting things out after the ambush and getting the troop moving towards their new harbour area, it's tea time at the training staff's camp. Lieutenant Gillies, Sergeant Nick Barnett and Corporal 'Mac' MacDonald are poring over the map, planning the next phase of the exercise. The 'enemy' are there too, fully trained Royal Marines from a special troop at CTC. Dressed in chest webbing and black woollen hats, they are telling war stories about this and other ambushes they have carried out on various past troops of hapless recruits, tales that if overheard would make the uninitiated think they were out and out terrorists.

The 'enemy' troop live strange lives, used for a wide variety of jobs, usually at anti-social times, but with a degree of freedom from supervision that has led to a number of them adopting their own combat 'uniforms' – all-black suits, with balaclavas to identify them as the enemy. Unlike Hollywood extras, however, there are times when accustomed autonomy leads them to not quite do things as exactly as they should.

Away from the training staff admin area, much deeper into the woods, the troop have selected their harbour position and moved in. Patrols have cleared the surrounding area and sentries have been posted. Those men not on sentry duty are cooking food, cleaning weapons and getting some sleep. In the centre of the position a shelter with 4-foot-high walls has been built from green ponchos, to minimize the showing of light during Lieutenant Gillies's Orders for the next phase. Recruits Dobson and McKenzie have been making a ground model from twigs, leaves and military equipment – from which the details of the Orders will be described.

It's now early evening and pitch dark, the closely-planted coniferous trees steadily dripping water on to a thick ground cover of wet pine needles. Inside the light screen, Orders are about to start, the troop wearing waterproofs and camouflaged combat helmets, sitting on their webbing. A single hurricane lamp is burning, casting a homely glow over an otherwise cold and rather strange scene. From outside the light of the shelter, the woods are dark and gloomy.

Sergeant Nick Barnett and Corporal Dave Layton are poking around the troop position, investigating the recruits' kit. Some men have left their bergens unpacked, equipment lying around getting wet. In Royal Marine terminology this kit has been 'left loafing', a misdemeanour. People must look after their equipment. If it rains heavily, clothes and sleeping bags not properly packed are likely to get wet – a disaster on Dartmoor. But much more importantly, as during the lorry ambush, unless equipment is correctly stowed people can't respond swiftly to enemy attack. Time is wasted, invaluable kit gets lost in the confusion, the enemy taking easy lives.

The phrase 'admin vortex' is frequently used by training staff. Certain members of the troop are notably bad: their kit and uniforms frequently in disarray, reliable outward signs of inner disorganization, indicating failure to cope with the pressure of weather, tiredness and the demands of the job. Unless these individuals sharpen up, they will fail the exercise, either because poor personal administration leads to their becoming unduly wet and developing cold exposure or trench foot, or because they become a liability to the rest of the troop – something the training staff will not tolerate.

Barnett and Layton go quietly through the troop's position, shining hooded torches at each shell scrape, noting names. Some have left sleeping bags zipped inside waterproof bivvy bags, or sleeping mats unfolded; others mess tins and rations lying loosely under ponchos –

muddy rainwater gathering in puddles that will soon tip on to already rain-soaked bergens.

Back behind the light screen, Lieutenant Gillies's Orders have started, this time for a deliberate troop ambush on a known enemy supply route. The section commanders are at the front, peering at the model, notebooks at the ready. To help them visualize the plan, each section is sitting in the order in which they will occupy the ambush.

The most critical timing for this operation is first light – 0654 hours. By that time, everybody must have been in position, still and quiet, for several hours if the ambush is to have any chance of success. Ambushes of this sort can continue for many days provided administration is good and they are not detected. On exercises, however, first light is the usual time for springing ambushes. From information supplied by the back-troopers, the troop expect the Dartmoor phase of the exercise to start some time tomorrow, so although nobody is laying bets they hope the enemy will not delay coming. There is a considerable difference between lying still all one night, and lying still for some or most of the next day too – particularly when it's raining.

The ambush site is in the forest, just before a turning point where the main track splits into several smaller paths. The wide part of the track will be the 'killing ground', the main 'killer group' lying hidden in trees on a steep bank 12 feet above. Smaller 'cut-off groups' armed with LSWs (Light Support Weapon – 5.56mm machine-gun) will be positioned to either side to prevent the enemy from escaping.

As at every 'O' group, Lieutenant Gillies checks they are listening by asking questions throughout. Using the model, he details the routes to and from the ambush very carefully, and the 'RV' (rendezvous) drill in case (in the darkness) anybody gets separated from the troop and loses his way.

Recruit Spink is troop commander, and after Orders have finished he gets his sections organized for pulling out of the harbour area towards the ambush site. The sooner they are there and ready, the better. They line up at the edge of the harbour area, wearing warm clothing and waterproofs, ready for the slow, quiet move to the ambush site. At the front, Spink checks the compass bearing and they set off, grey figures vanishing into a wet and gloomy night.

The move to the ambush site takes some time. At regular intervals, or whenever anybody hears something, the troop go into all-round defence, lying in fire positions, listening for the tell-tale sounds of enemy following. Readily identifiable points are designated RVs, the term 'RV' passed by signal down the line from Spink at the front. If they were to be 'bumped' by the enemy, or in the event of somebody becoming separated from the rest, the RV becomes the gathering point, where a head-count would establish who was still missing. Eventually, the signal 'Final RV' comes down the line, indicating that

the ambush site is not too far away. (They have already memorized the ERV, 'Emergency Rendezvous', a point to which people gather if the ambush goes wrong and the troop have to split up, which Lt Gillies gave them in his Orders.)

The sections lie in the final RV for what seems an eternity, waiting while Spink [pictured left] goes forward and recces the ambush fire positions. A runner brings each section forward. When everybody is in place, lines of cord are laid between the killer group and the cut-offs – to enable the troops to signal the arrival of the enemy. With everything in place, Spink declares the ambush set, and they settle into a long, cold wait for something that might never happen.

Staying awake gets to be an almost superhuman effort, especially when it is cold and the night is particularly dark. When there is nothing to see, a tired brain invents things, waking dreams of sometimes bizarre sights, as a way of compensating for lack of sleep. Munching chocolate provides surges of instant body heat, and a degree of temporary comfort that breaks up the boredom into bearable slices of time. No amount of warm clothing can prevent people freezing in ambush sites, but even so, individuals fall asleep – to be nudged when snoring gives them away. The instructors take turns to creep into the rear of the position to check that people are still alert, and the long night seems interminable.

The next day wet and miserable weather continues, dawn arriving as a grey and gloomy lightening behind dull clouds – with an unpromising additional touch of orange to the east. The track is wet, moss squelching like sponge underfoot. Forestry vehicle wheel ruts have filled overnight with rainwater, the mud slippery and uneven.

A black uniformed enemy patrol are moving down their supply route, advancing carefully along the track in file, men to either side under the violet light of early dawn. The enemy walk carefully, trying hard not to make too much noise, scanning about them watchfully and cautiously, weapons at the ready. To the left, a steep bank with coniferous trees, to the right a slight clearing and piles of logs. The forest is silent, even the birds seeming reluctant to herald such a dank and dismal day.

A burst of automatic fire rips out, shattering the silence. Trip flares explode, then even heavier fire comes spitting out of the undergrowth. The enemy have been blown away, knocked lifeless into the bushes like ninepins. A voice from the tree line – troop commander Spink – bellows: 'Stop! Watch and shoot. Watch and shoot.'

Silence falls, curling wreaths of gun smoke picked out in silver by the growing light, drifting from the killer group's position down the chalk bank on to the track. The training team are here too (having followed the enemy), crouching beside the track, watching the troop carefully, ensuring that the correct drills are carried out. The enemy lie dead, spreadeagled over the log piles.

After two long minutes of total silence, waiting to ensure that no enemy remain alive, the voice shouts: 'Stop! Searchers move out.'

Two figures, Potts and Anfield, move carefully from the undergrowth to the rear of the ambush, shouting, 'Coming through!' to their colleagues in the cut-off groups. As they walk along the track to check the enemy dead, Spink tells Potts to keep talking to him: 'There's one lying on the logs at the end of this pile.'

The two searchers are very exposed. Spink reminds Potts to keep one man in the rear, giving cover: 'Pottsie – keep one foot on the ground at all times, OK?'

They search the enemy dead, one man covering. Two more men join them.

'How many have you got down there – three?'

They roll the bodies over.

'Two enemy here.'

Spink is watchful and concerned: 'Put a couple into each of them,' he calls. Playing dead is not allowed by the Geneva Conventions.

Four shots ring out.

'Two clear.'

They go through the bodies' pockets and equipment.

'Enemy clear.'

'One down here.'

'Come on, as quick as you can.'

'Clear.'

Spink is sitting overlooking the ambush site – and growing anxious. It's taking too long for his liking.

'Get what you can from them then move back in through the other cut-off.'

'Clear! Come on, let's go!'

'Keep one foot on the ground. And move back the way you came.'

Another burst of fire rips from the bushes. One enemy was overlooked. Bursts of fire from all four.

'What was that, Pottsie?'

'One enemy in the ditch,' comes the terse reply.

'Is he dead?'

'He is now.'

'Move back into the position and tell me when you're in.'

They move quickly back into the undergrowth and scramble up the steep shale bank, rejoining the others. Spink shouts, 'Withdraw.' In their sections, the troop move out, jogging quickly uphill away from the ambush site. The enemy may be following and nobody wants to hang around any longer than necessary. They gather in the communication cord as they go, heavily laden figures panting steadily upward through the trees.

The ambush site is silent, with only the sound of a solitary crow.

Sergeant Nick Barnett was pleased with the ambush:

'From the enemy side, this ambush was a complete success. The element of surprise was there. The guys were vigilant. They were awake. And as the enemy went through a big surge of firepower went down, that obviously would have taken out most of them. The searchers then went out and searched the enemy. They did miss one, but got the rest, and weapons and maps were taken.

'At its most basic, we're looking for command. Young Spink – he's only 17 years old – took command of the fire group. He sent out his searchers and controlled them. We're looking for good drills on the ground, and for guys that can react immediately to contact.

'They've only done about four ambushes during training, and are young lads, so obviously they are going to make mistakes. But we use those mistakes as the basis of constructive criticism, so they can work on it – and improve.

'As Royal Marines, the ambush is a very important operation for us, demoralizing the enemy being the name of the game.'

The troop return to their harbour area, moving quietly back in through dripping trees. They are helmeted, making silent hand signals, heavy in the weatherproofs and warm clothing that kept them going during the dark hours of waiting.

'Make sure your people get wets.'

The training staff are waiting, prompting the recruit section commanders, ensuring that the troop gets sorted out and ready for the next action with as little delay as possible. The priorities are military, but in these weather conditions care must be taken to keep people going.

Corporal Dave Layton has a quick word with Spink: 'Get your clearance patrols out, everybody in all-round defence. Then when you've completed that, get people making wets, checking their feet and getting the bivvies down.'

The patrols go out, clearing around the harbour area, checking that no enemy have come in while they've been away doing the ambush. They've already dug shallow shell scrapes, which they've camouflaged with brushwood and fern. Everybody takes cover, watching their arcs.

638 Troop returning from the ambush.

If Spink is relieved that the ambush is over, he doesn't show it. He seems unaffected by any of the pressure piled upon him by the training staff, or from being troop commander. When asked about the ambush, he thought the initial firepower went down quite well, but that the troop needed to gel together better – due to only 12 'originals' remaining. He didn't feel too much pressure himself, and thought that 'the guys did most of the right things. People can nod off when tired – getting cold and wrapping [giving up]. But it's not that bad.'

He's already learned that paying attention to detail is the most vital part of military planning, especially when people are tired: 'You've got to put the final touches to things – like communications.'

Lieutenant Gillies is not so sanguine about the ambush, and gets the troop together for a serious bollocking: 'Initially it went smoothly – with good control from the section commanders and troop commander Spink. However, where it fell apart was in your basic professionalism and individual skills.'

He goes through the whole thing, stage by stage:

'OK ... the move out along the tracks, led by 2 Section – no

real problems. Then we got bunching. As soon as it got a bit
dark on these forest tracks, people started to get scared. It's
human nature I suppose. It gets a little bit dark, you lose the
guy ahead of you, so you started to close up your front and it
ended up a big gaggle with no spacing whatsoever, specially
when we came to obstacles . . .

'Going up the bank to cut through the wood, I stood and
watched a whole queue of at least five, six, seven people back
to back, standing up when they should have been in a fire
position. There was no effort at all to use the skills that you
have been taught. You know whenever you stop you should
either get down in a kneeling position at least, or where suitable
you should be lying down on the deck in a fire position, your
weapon ready to use. It fell apart there on the move out. You
basically were wrapping on me.

'Then we recced and moved into the FRV, then into the
ambush position itself. No problems there. Quiet and well
controlled.

'Then once we were in there, virtually to a man, the whole
troop wrapped on me. The corporals visited you at various
times throughout the night and I reckon 80 per cent of you at
any one time were asleep – which is just not on. You know it's
wrong. Laziness, switching off, lack of professionalism and lack
of individual skills.

'In about four weeks' time, hopefully you'll all be in units
where they won't put up with that sort of thing. It's up to you
then. You won't have training teams to kick you up the butt.
It's up to you, yourselves. Have a bit of pride and do what's
been taught, on your own, without pushing and prompting from
anyone else. Your units won't put up with it, and we won't put
up with it here.

'Basically, you got cold and miserable – as I warned you would
do. You knew you were going to be cold and miserable, and
that's when it counts. You got cold and miserable – and you
wrapped. It all got a bit too much for some of you.

'The springing of the ambush itself went well initially –
good weight of fire – no unfortunate pregnant pauses which
we would have had if you all changed your magazines together,
so that went well. However, you knew from the Orders that
the enemy's strength was four to eight men. In the killing
group itself, you only caught three out of the five men who
were in the patrol.

'Basically, the ambush was sprung early. Not a major problem.
It's not laziness, just something that happened. However, in
future make sure that you don't spring the ambush early. You've

got cut-offs either side, you've got a good width to the ambush – it's not a problem – make sure you get the whole patrol in there before you hit them. That way you don't have problems with enemy who haven't been killed off.

'The searchers went through, didn't notice that there were still enemy around, and they would have been wasted. Again the right-hand cut-off – One One Delta – didn't notice that there was an enemy taking cover in the ditch. Observation is vital.

'The withdrawal and FRV; the cut-offs came in, moved out through the HQ section and all the sections moved off up the hill. That was quite good. Slight pauses. But on the whole it was a good swift move up the hill, back up to the FRV.

'No problems in the FRV. Troop sergeant Wilson did his head count. A brief pause there and we moved off.

'On the way back, control went smoothly enough. Once again though, individuals continued to wrap. There were people with waterproofs unzipped at the bottom – basically walking around like a bag of shit. Again, it's up to yourselves. Make sure your kit's together, that you are ready to crack on with the next task, whatever it may be. If you've got bits of kit hanging off you and suddenly you get bumped, you get your weapons tangled, you can't operate properly.

'Going back to the ambush, people were caught with their helmets off – totally inexcusable, as is falling asleep. Weapons were off your body – you'd taken the slings off, weapons basically ditched by your side . . . no use to anyone. These weapons are designed for the sling to be on you at all times, in any fire position.

'It's a test exercise. It's up to you guys to pass. You've got to prove to us you've learned what's been taught to you over the 26 weeks you've been in training. It's up to you to prove to us that you're good enough in four weeks' time to go and join one of the Commando units.

'The watchword from now on in is "professionalism" and it's down to you to sort your shit out and do as you've been taught. You know what you've to do.

(*Left*) A recruit listens to Lieutenant Gillies's assessment of 638 Troop's ambush.

Basically, it's just laziness not doing it. OK. Any questions?'
Sergeant Nick Barnett takes over:

'A couple of points on admin. Some of you may be under the
illusion that troop sergeant is a big fat boy sat in the bottom of
his fire trench worrying only about bullets and beans? It's not
true – as Wilson knows. Where is he? Busy job, isn't it?'

Because Wilson is only a recruit working with his equals, nobody is
helping him. Aged 17, he's the youngest man in the troop, and has
impressed the training team, who consider him 'Commando Medal
Potential'. He's a 'good egg all-round, and in a couple of years' time
will be a serious monster – really horrible!'

'You guys must assist him. At the moment you're not pulling
your weight. Wilson is working above himself – a young lad
getting in amongst the troop – getting things done. However,
you are not working for him. When he wants a working party
he wants it then and there. When he wants rations unloaded, he
wants them unloaded when he says, not when you think it's
necessary, all right?

'Stores: Wilson's got to go around and make sure he knows
where all the stores are. If you've got empty ammunition boxes
loafing by your bivvy, he doesn't know where they are. So when
the re-supply wagon comes down, or the dead letter box is sent
off, because he doesn't actually know where those stores are,
they get left behind. There were empty jerry cans left by the
positions last night. And empty ammunition boxes. They must
be pre-loaded at HQ's position, so he knows exactly where
they are, and can get rid of them.

'Ammunition states: I came down this morning and Wilson
didn't know how many rounds the troop actually had. The
section 2IC's job is to go in amongst the section with a piece
of paper – asking how many magazines you require. Then get
that across to the troop sergeant as quickly as possible.

'Wilson's got a hundred and one other things to do when he's
in Troop HQ, plus making sure Troop HQ's working when the
troop commander's away. He can't go around to your position
and get these things. In future all 2IC's will come in and say,
"I want X number of rounds", and their orders will be written
down on a piece of paper. Yes? Understood? Good.

'Individual admin: kit has been left loafing around the bivvy
positions. We went round last night and checked. A couple of
guys have been put on warning as a result. A bivvy bag and a
sleeping-bag were out, but not under the cover of the poncho.
With the Dartmoor phase coming up, your sleeping-bag is your
lifeline. It's got to be kept dry. The troop sergeant hasn't got
time to go around making sure that you've packed your kit.

Recruit Snazel being told the error of his ways by Troop Commander Lieutenant Gillies.

'I came down this morning to find numerous people ditching rations, soup packs, biscuits ... We're out on the moor over the next phase. You may not get a re-supply when you think you're due one, so always make sure you've got a reserve amount of rations in your fighting order.

'I've given you more water than you've been due, so why not get a wet on? If you're stopped, get down, get a wet on, get some warm fluid into the body. Obviously the weather's not too bad today. Last week there were hailstones and a couple of inches of snow. Start thinking about personal admin.

'Right, any questions for me on the troop sergeant's task? The orbat [order of battle] will change. The next troop sergeant will be nominated when we go into the next phase. Let's start working for him, making his job a little bit easier. Enough said.'

Lieutenant Gillies takes Spink to one side: 'Good effort. You controlled the ambush well ... and the withdrawal was good too.'

Recruit Snazel, however, is in trouble. Corporal Layton found him asleep, so to teach him a lesson took his weapon. On waking, Snazel then took somebody else's weapon – a futile and foolish action that could only get him into more trouble, an indication perhaps of tiredness rather than dishonesty. Lieutenant Gillies turns to Snazel, whose gaunt face seems a touch too impassive.

'OK, you fell asleep, which was inexcusable, but it's one of those things that happens. You take a bollocking for it, you take it square on the shoulders.

'But I find it hard to believe that when you found you didn't have your own weapon, you took someone else's? That's basically you stitching up your oppo. He's one of the guys you've got to work with. Can you imagine what would happen to you in a unit if you did that?'

Snazel is anxious to put his side of the story:

'Yes, Sir. That's why I realized and went and told Corporal Layton straight away.'

'But you didn't do that, though.'

'I did, Sir.'

'Don't come the biscuit with me. Corporal Layton was giving Smith a hard time for not having his weapon.'

'Yes, Sir.'

'And that's how Corporal Layton found out that you had Smith's weapon. So don't come the biscuit. Corporal Layton checked the weapon number and found that Smith's weapon was with you.'

'Sir.'

'And it was with you because you'd taken it from him . . . I can't believe you did that, frankly. You must have known that you hadn't left your weapon where you picked up Smith's weapon. You knew the score. Can you imagine what would happen to you in a unit if you did that?'

The question hangs in the air:

'You're on a warning, which means that from now on you're going to be watched. Put it behind you. Let's have a good effort from now on. But I'm going to be watching you, because this is basic lack of integrity.'

'I know. It was totally out of order, Sir.'

'OK. As long as you realize you went wrong. Put it behind you. Crack on.'

CHAPTER FOUR

638 TROOP – DARTMOOR

638 Troop are having a tough time on Dartmoor. The weather is appalling. After the ambush in the woods, although their harbour area was wet, it had been well sheltered and they'd stayed reasonably dry. They then moved by 4-tonner on to Dartmoor proper, and started an 'advance to contact', during which the weather seriously worsened. Relentless, driving, north-west winds are now sweeping over the Bristol Channel to scour the desolate uplands. Trees survive only in well-sheltered valleys so there is precious little shelter for the troop up here, save the stone remnants of ancient encampments.

Being a 'fair weather troop', unused on their exercises thus far to rain and the misery of being wet, this has come as somewhat of a shock to many people – particularly those like Recruits Smith AD and Pyott whose poor personal admin meant their kit was wet before anybody else's. Having experienced bad weather on Army exercises, Recruit Dobson wasn't too bothered; nor was Recruit Nicolson, from the Isle of Skye and therefore a man for all seasons and weather conditions.

Advancing to contact involves walking in formation, the troop's three sections moving one up, two behind, with troop headquarters in the middle, spread out across a 200-metre triangle of moorland, advancing towards a suspected enemy position on one of the tors. In such open country where cover is hard to find, and where any movement is visible for miles, it's vital to spread out so that only a few people will be hit should the enemy open fire.

Each section is moving in arrowhead formation, which presents the enemy with people spread both laterally and in depth across a large piece of ground, with the smallest number closest to him in range.

Having one section in front and two in the rear keeps the majority of the troop back, from where they are free to attack the enemy. Nicolson's section is in front, 'on the point'. Once the enemy open fire and reveal their hand, everybody will take cover. Camouflage and fieldcraft skills enable the troop to go to ground and effectively vanish. If they are in the correct formation when this happens, reorganizing, firing back, then mounting an attack will be very much easier. Troop commander Spink will extract his two rear sections, leaving the point section to return fire until he puts in a troop attack.

The first moments of coming under fire (and people's reaction in these moments) are critical. A real battlefield is full of explosions and projectiles coming from all directions, from small arms but also from mortar rounds and artillery shells. The noise is very great and, particularly when it starts suddenly, disorientating and shocking. Combatants always experience a strong and understandable temptation to take cover and stay there.

If, however, people reacted to every single shot or explosion by going to ground, advances would grind to a halt, attacks turning into disaster. Troops are trained to keep moving forward until they come under 'effective enemy fire' – defined as fire that causes injury to themselves or to others close by. This moment can be surprisingly hard to judge. When people come under effective enemy fire, especially for the first time in a real war, the reality of what is happening can take precious time to sink in. They can be confused, hesitating for vital moments – in which they may suffer unnecessary casualties.

In these critical moments, military training takes over, saving men's lives – which is why 638 Troop are today plodding across Dartmoor in the driving rain. They've learned all the drills and practised them on other exercises. If however they are to be trusted to do all this in a real war, with high explosive and lethal metal flying around their ears, they'd better be able to do it now – when the worst that can happen is to get wet. (In fact, as they are already soaked, it shouldn't really matter.)

At the first crackle of enemy machine-gun fire, having ascertained that it is effective, the point section take cover, while Spink uses his radio to find out where Nicolson, the point section commander, thinks the enemy are. It looks like playing soldiers but, under such appalling conditions, carrying out the drills properly is very difficult. In war, however, the drills must be so well learned that they take over the men's thoughts and actions, for a moment turning individuals into automata – a life-saving reflex action.

When you come under effective enemy fire, the drill is: 'Dash, down, crawl, observe, sights, fire.'

Nicolson's section dash forward and sideways for several metres before getting 'Down' into a fire position. The enemy had them in his sights, but now has to readjust his aim, and, with the rain running off his weapon optics, isn't sure exactly where they have gone to ground. The section then crawl to new fire positions to further unsight any enemy who may have seen exactly where they dropped.

In war, it is likely that each part of the drill will be closely followed by a burst of machine-gun fire directed at fire positions men have just vacated. Carried out promptly, the drill saves lives. When an enemy opens fire, the smoke of each burst and the vibration of his weapon temporarily obscure the target, which may be as far as 1000 metres away. It takes time for rounds to travel over that sort of distance, by which time the target can have moved a few metres out of the firing zone. It takes time for the enemy to work out whether his rounds have hit anything, and, if not, where his quarry might have gone.

Once in a good fire position, the drill tells you to 'Observe', peering from behind cover to catch sight of the enemy. If he's over-oiled his barrel, there might be a tell-tale wisp of gunsmoke, or the glint of sun on binocular lenses. Once you've located him, the 'Sights' part reminds you to work out how far he is away in order to adjust your weapon sights. When taking accurate shots under such tense and desperate circumstances, there's no point in giving away your position by firing with incorrectly set sights. Set at too low a range, your rounds will hit the ground in front of the target; set too high, they go over his head. Normal battle range is 300 metres, to which everybody sets their weapon sights before starting any kind of advance to contact.

After firing a couple of aimed shots, the drill is to crawl away to another fire position, observe, adjust sights if required and fire once more. By this stage, each individual will have recovered from the shock of being shot at, and be thinking for himself once more, the drills having carried him through the initial danger – hopefully in one piece.

Advancing to contact across Dartmoor in November is wet, windy and very cold. Diving for cover in rain-soaked heather, then crawling to fire positions in response to the rattle of blank ammunition seems rather ridiculous, especially when you are tired and freezing already. The maxim 'Train Hard, Fight Easy' is the reason why – which at this precise moment is scant comfort to 638 Troop.

Nicolson's section are giving covering fire to keep the enemy's heads down while Spink organizes the rest of the troop for a right-flanking attack, using the cover of a small gully. He gives very quick orders to section commanders Dobson and Bauduin, then leads the troop round to the base of the gully. They file up until parallel with the enemy position, forming an assault line, each man some 10 metres from the next. Over the radio, Spink orders Nicolson to give rapid covering fire, and the troop assault forward, running as hard as they can from the cover of the gully, before the enemy realize what is happening.

The bad weather is an advantage now – 'good infantry weather' – the rain and mist a screen from which they emerge to overrun the enemy's two-trench position. They kick his weapons aside, running through the positions, pausing only to grenade the trenches. Spink establishes all-round defence then details Bauduin's section to return to search the bodies and the rest of the position. As they reorganize, acting troop sergeant Wilson goes round the sections finding out how much ammunition they've got left, and whether they've suffered any casualties. Despite Sergeant Barnett's talk after the first ambush, Wilson still doesn't get sensible answers from the sections – who are so wet that notional casualty returns seem somewhat of a waste of time.

The training team take careful note.

Exercise Highland Anvil started on Tuesday. By the time the enemy on the tor had been sorted out, it was late afternoon on Friday and everybody was soaked through. After sorting out the casualty and ammunition returns – and getting another carefully worded lecture from Sergeant Barnett – Spink is given the grid reference of their next rendezvous, a farm which they will attack.

638 Troop covering ground rapidly on a rare stretch of road during the final Commando Test – the 30-miler – a forced march (but jogging much of the way).

They yomp north for several hours, initially into rapidly gathering darkness, then through a wet and miserable night, finally arriving east of the farm hill well into the small hours. This first serious yomp goes badly wrong, as tiredness and general misery get the better of some individuals. Recruit Johnson, the son of an RM Captain, becomes the unwitting architect of great confusion by losing sight of the man in front of him, causing those behind to become separated from the rest of the troop. Blond, cheerful Corporal MacDonald comes forward and sorts it out, giving Johnson a formal warning for what he considers verges on insubordination: 'He was blaming other blokes for the split, so I gave him a warning. Rather than accept it, he wanted to know why? So I left him – gobbing off...'

Johnson was already finding the weather difficult to cope with, wearing his waterproofs all the time rather than only when raining (so perspiring inside his clothing), and not paying careful attention to his feet.

Age, as in youthful immaturity, also plays a part. Only 17 years old, Smith AD is also finding it hard. Attention had focused upon him from the start of the exercise, when Lieutenant Gillies picked him up for not taking notes during Orders. Amazingly, when asked to recall the radio frequency for that operation, he had given the correct answer. Snazel had taken his weapon in the harbour area – which was obviously not his fault – and through not taking the trouble to put on his waterproofs whenever it rains, he's allowed his combat jacket to get wet. He is also an 'admin vortex', his kit rarely properly packed. It's becoming clear that either he can't look after himself, or in this harsh and unforgiving environment is losing the motivation necessary to survive – although he's been given a 'chuck-up' (praise) for carrying the heavy LMG (light machine-gun). That night is particularly wet, and in the LUP (laying-up position), Smith AD leaves his socks loafing and gets himself even wetter.

The next morning, Lieutenant Gillies gives Orders for the observation of the farm in preparation for a deliberate attack later in the day. Nicolson is chosen to command the observation team – of Prater, stocky Anfield and the tall Kelly ND – who spend until last light that day observing the objective, returning after dark to give a detailed report on everything they've seen. Armed with their information, Lieutenant Gillies gives his Orders for the attack, using yet another ground model – which, as all the other models thus far, is very poorly made by the troop. They should be getting better, however ... As Corporal Layton tells them: 'This model looks like a compost heap, and you've used weird things for the features: a shovel for a river, a stick for Black Tor...'

The attack takes place in appalling weather later that evening. Bauduin doing a good job as troop commander

The next phase of the exercise is a long and testing yomp from the farm to another tor. The troop are in bits – exhausted, wet, with some individuals quite clearly wishing they were somewhere else. A number have wrapped – given up. Others – notably the married man Mc-Kenzie, who seems always able to laugh or tell a joke – are doing well. However, the training team can see that as the weather shows no sign of abating, the yomp risks becoming a disaster, which apart from being irresponsible and dangerous, would be of no training value. The decision is made therefore, to go 'non-tactical' for 12 hours, to give everybody some chance of recovery and getting dry.

Having been wearing soaked boots for over five days, people's feet are white, wrinkled and painful to walk upon – the onset of trench foot, a serious cold-weather injury akin to frostbite. A day of warmth, foot powder and dry socks should make all the difference.

The recently attacked farm opens up its hay barn as a dormitory, the farmer very kindly drying off everybody's kit in his dairy, even providing fresh milk, boiling water and that greatest of exercise luxuries – bread.

Getting started again the next day is hard. Five people are picked up for having rusty weapons, Smith AD and Johnson (who are both on warnings) and Holmes included. Already being closely watched, Smith AD, who suffered hypothermia on his first attempt at the Final Exercise, has not made the most of the respite, and when it's time to go is far from ready. He gets pissed off, and Bauduin has to pack his bergen for him.

The long yomp from the farm proves to be too much for the other Smith – MR (a back-trooper due to an ankle injury) – who had seemed to be doing all right. To the instructor's surprise, he develops a knee injury and wraps with only 10 kilometres to go to the final harbour position. Former electrician Nield (who almost quit the Corps after breaking a leg) develops a muscle or tendon problem in one leg and drops out, then Anfield falls behind and is pulled off the yomp by the medic as he fails to keep up with the rest. Potts is soldiering on, despite the ankle injury he sustained at Portland. Another back-trooper, Anfield has already suffered medical problems on field exercises, but under very different weather conditions:

> 'During the summer, on long-distance physical events, I was
> going down with dehydration and heat exhaustion. I was taken
> out of training while they did medical investigations. In the end
> they decided I could carry on with training.'

Anfield is put into the back of the safety wagon, and the survivors complete the yomp and establish yet another harbour area. From there, they recce a site for a vehicle ambush, then after dark, they move in to occupy the ambush site.

They lie in the ambush all night. At 0800 an 'enemy' truck drives through carrying supplies. The ambush is sprung, the truck captured, then pressed into service to carry the troop from the moor down into more hospitable elevations by the sea, near to where captured documents reveal the enemy to have their main headquarters. The troop occupy an LUP one tactical bound away from this HQ, their final objective – a Napoleonic fort located on a hill overlooking a Cornish river estuary.

Reconnaissance of the final objective takes place that afternoon, with Orders at 2200 hours that night – for an attack at first light the next day, Tuesday, a full week after the start of the exercise. As they prepare to make their final attack of the exercise, the troop are very tired, gearing up themselves for one last final effort.

Although it's cold, for the first time in days the sky is clear – and it isn't raining. The enemy, their shouts echoing against the darkness of early morning, have lit large fires within the ramparts of the neglected fort. Light flickers across 300 yards of scrubby grass. One complete side of the fort consists of large rooms with doors and windows, in which the enemy are resting. Flights of stone steps go up 50 feet to the ramparts, which are wide enough to drive a vehicle along, with iron handrails on the inside and stone buttresses on the outside.

Outside the fort, its 20-foot-wide moat is bridged to the main entrance, only part of it filled with brackish-looking water of uncertain

An intelligence photo of rooms in the Napoleonic fort that 638 Troop must grenade and fight through on the final attack of their Final Exercise.

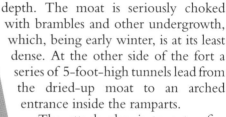

depth. The moat is seriously choked with brambles and other undergrowth, which, being early winter, is at its least dense. At the other side of the fort a series of 5-foot-high tunnels lead from the dried-up moat to an arched entrance inside the ramparts.

The attack plan is to get a fire support section up on to the ramparts to one side, while the other two sections infiltrate through the tunnels into the other end of the fort. When these two sections are detected inside the fort, or when everybody is in position ready to begin clearing the enemy positions, the fire support section will open fire from the ramparts, covering the whole open area inside the fort. The assaulting sections will then clear each of the rooms along the side of the fort. The Diamonds are taking turns to command the troop. Dobson is in the hot seat for this final attack.

The first part of the plan requires immediate modification as the helicopter supposed to fly the fire support section to rope down into woods to the north of the fort is cancelled due to bad weather. All three sections set off on foot from the harbour area at 0300 hours for the long walk along the river estuary, then up the steep wooded hillside to the fort itself. The irrepressible McKenzie [pictured above] receives a sudden shock in the darkness when he walks into a cattle strength electric fence. He is thrown to the ground and can't work out what is happening. When he realizes, he finds the whole thing so funny he can hardly stifle his laughter.

The fire support section, led by Recruit Dobson, separate off from the main body and cut away into the darkness across the fields to make their own careful approach towards the eastern side of the objective where the ML's have set up a wire ladder. They scramble down the steep sides of the moat, struggling through thick undergrowth on its dried-up bottom.

At the foot of the massive stone walls, McKenzie and Hilton (a former longbow maker) search for the foot of the ladder. It looks secure, but nevertheless Hilton carefully pulls on it until he is satisfied that all is well. Robin Hood would have been proud of him.

McKenzie motions Farrimond and Sullivan forward. They sling their weapons and, using the rope, Sullivan climbs steadily up the ladder, his left foot hooked around for better stability, the rungs hard into his instep and boot heels. At the top, he pops his head over the breast cautiously, ensuring he is not being observed, then slithers over and on to the ground, unslinging his weapon. As each man arrives at the top, some carrying LSWs, they spread out in all-round defence. McKenzie, left alone at the bottom, ties the rope on to the carrying handles of several boxes of link 5.56mm magazines for the LSWs, before then climbing the rope himself.

Down below, in the darkness of the centre of the fort, one of the enemy walks by accident through one of his own trip flares, a bang and surge of light that cause Dobson's section to freeze. Then once the trip flare has died down, his fire support section move along the ramparts to place their GPMGs into fire positions beside the railings, from which they can cover the whole of the fort's interior. They keep very low in order to avoid being skylined against the grey glimmerings of dawn.

Meanwhile the main assault group are infiltrating the old fort from the other direction, through its gun crew tunnels. For some reason 2 Section's commander, Recruit Lobb, despite the overwhelming need for speed and surprise, goes into a huddle with his section, to give further instructions and redistribute thunderflashes – tasks that should have been completed back in the harbour area. Like everybody, Lobb is tired and hadn't fully thought it through:

'It was my first command appointment, and unlike the raid at Portland when we had maps and photos, we didn't know what to expect in the fort. At the end of the tunnels, once I realized the set-up in the fort, we had to have a quick sort-out.'

The enemy are alerted by mutterings from the tunnel, and open fire, cutting short Lobb's impromptu briefing.

General firing breaks out in the darkness of the tunnel entrance, trip flares go off and schermulys (hand-launched flares) are fired. The assault group enter the open area inside the fort and assault the first building in the line along the left-hand side of the fort's long, seaward-facing rampart. To their right, Dobson's men give heavy covering fire from the ramparts. Smoke quickly swathes the fort's square interior, automatic fire echoing around its walls.

The thunderflashes throw violent bursts of harsh white light against the crumbling masonry, their explosions reverberating around the massive stone walls. Flares arc skywards, falling back down to burn on the ground with plumes of smoke. The noise seems to rise and fall, the explosions together, then heavy eruptions of gunfire, a lull, then more gunfire, with the cries of the section commanders controlling fire and urging their men on: 'Watch your muzzle clearance. Grenade! Get in some cover then. Get in that building now!'

Instructors' voices become more apparent, pointing out enemy the sections have missed, demanding that they get on with the job:'Come

on, get into that fucking building. Anybody ...! Watch your back ...
don't just fucking stand in the doorway then ... Right, on the top –
Enemy!'

Several thunderflashes arc upward at the enemy, one of whom tries
to duck both ways but is caught in the middle of several large
explosions. There is laughter. Amazingly he picks up a fizzing thun-
derflash and throws it back down on to the attackers. Things are
beginning to get a touch out of control. Despite being well and truly
shot, the enemy are refusing to die, which is starting to annoy the
recruits, who don't know when to stop attacking one position and
turn their attention to another. Having been irritated at the confusion
in the tunnel, Corporal Dave Bateman is also getting annoyed with
Lobb's 2 Section: 'Right, get up here. Now! And clear these fucking
bastards out of here – move!'

Lobb gets a grip of his section: 'Next building along ... Grenade!
On this side ... get in here now ...'

The enemy are running about on the tops of the ramparts like
Hollywood Indians, contrary to Lieutenant Gillies's orders, which the
troop are still obeying – causing additional and unrealistic confusion.
In Lobb's words, 'After the enemy went up on to the ramparts, it all
went to pot.' At the other side of the fort, Lieutenant Gillies is very
concerned about the evident disregarding of his instructions – but
more worried for the safety of the people now running up and down
the steep stone steps and along the crumbling ramparts 50 feet above:
'The enemy went to "rats", by going up on to the ramparts, not
dying, particularly the one in black wearing the chest webbing ... I
wanted them to stop it earlier.'

It's growing light and acrid cordite smoke is swirling around in the
cold, dank wind. One of the enemy has hidden himself in the gorse
at the top of the wall. Clearly something must be done about him.
Corporal Bateman gets 2 Section up to sort it out, but doesn't tell
them where the enemy is hiding:

'Have you cleared this end of the ramparts yet?' he asks.

'Yeah.'

'Then what about clearing this other end then? Get the section
along here now.'

'2 Section get along here now!'

The solitary enemy gunman opens fire, but the section just run past
him. Corporal Bateman realizes they are tired and confused ... 'Don't
just fucking run past him.' ... and has to get a grip. The enemy is
eventually killed, but 2 Section have had to be very bad-tempered
with each other in order to make it happen. They are tired, and
confused at being ordered on to the ramparts.

However, now secure on top of the ramparts, 2 Section quickly
redistribute ammo and reload magazines. Several are coughing, with

colds from Dartmoor but also because of the smoke. Some people are still down below, making Corporal Bateman increasingly more frustrated.

In confusion, men run up and down the steps several times, complaining at each other. Corporal Bateman shuts them up: 'Lobb is the section commander. Stop gobbing off and do what he says.'

They congregate downstairs, inside one of the cleared buildings. Lobb orders them all to load one magazine, then put it on their weapons. Corporal Bateman further prompts him: 'Give the troop commander a quick sitrep over the radio. Tell him what's happening, keep him in the picture ... The call signs are Delta 10 to Delta 1 charlie.'

Radio comms don't work, so the signaller goes outside and shouts to Bauduin in a big, loud voice: '2 Section cleared the top and spread out across this side.'

Afterwards, Lobb is characteristically philosophical about what at the time was a tense situation:

'The training team put you under extra pressure, but for real the pressure is going to be a lot worse than that. If you do it wrong people are going to die – as simple as that.

'I got stick from Corporal Bateman – as usual. He's all right, out of all the training team, probably the most mellow. They're always putting you under pressure, so all I could do was try to make some sense of the situation. Getting people organized in all the noise is really hard.

'I enjoy being section commander – sometimes. And sometimes it's a pain in the arse. You've just got to have a lot of confidence in yourself. Trouble is I'm too nice a guy!'

Dobson's fire section are ordered down from the ramparts, moving fast down the steps and into the centre of the fort, their wet webbing bouncing rhythmically as they jog. The instructors are applying pressure to the other sections to get ammo and casualty reports to troop sergeant Bauduin. Bauduin details Potts to go round each section and get the ammo reports in. People aren't responding, and Bauduin gets annoyed: 'I'm not bloody shouting to myself!'

Lieutenant Gillies arrives in the centre of the fort with the other instructors. They are discussing the exercise. Recruit Chamberlain has drawn attention to himself by revealing a fear of heights, having problems climbing a ladder during the attack.

Dobson reports that so far he has one casualty, Recruit Gault from 2 Section. Potts still hasn't returned, so troop sergeant's runner McKenzie is told to run round the sections and get the casualty and ammo reports himself. Then Lieutenant Gillies orders Endex, a whistle is blown and shouts of 'Endex, unload!' bring proceedings to a strangely abrupt and anti-climactic end.

People whistle and one man whoops. Lieutenant Gillies orders the troop to close in to the centre of the fort for an instant debrief. The instructors relax and chat among themselves about how it has gone. As the troop line up, the LSW gunners fire off their last bursts of ammo. The troop forms a single line to have their weapons cleared by an instructor:

'With your weapons pointing in a safe direction, unload!

'For inspection, port arms. I warn you that it is a court martial offence to knowingly take away any blank rounds or pyrotechnics from this training area. When the instructor comes to you, make this declaration: I have no live rounds or empty cases in my possession . . .

'Clear, and ease springs.

'De-ammo into the right-hand man's helmet. Make sure you keep the 7.62 and 5.56 separate.'

They flip the rounds into their helmets, throwing in unused boxes too. A sudden muffled hissing noise reveals that Lobb has set off a red smoke grenade in his webbing. As the smoke envelops him he runs in circles across the grass, arms outstretched like aircraft wings. The others sing the RAF Dam Busters' theme tune and laugh. Corporal MacDonald takes the webbing off him and tries to extract the hot canister before the pouch gets burned or too badly stained.

Solidly built Chamberlain (his large head earning the nicknames Meathead and Haybox Head) has lost his helmet while running down a steep hill during the attack. Lieutenant Gillies saw where it fell and asks Nicolson to go with him to find it. Losing a helmet would cost Chamberlain a lot of money. Nicolson however has an injured leg, so Tobin goes off with Chamberlain.

Lieutenant Gillies:

'It ground to a halt towards the end, although that was partly because I'd briefed them to stay on the lower floors whereas the enemy tended to work their own routine. We had sections chasing around a bit towards the end but I think overall it went well: good weight of fire, stacks of aggression as they cleared down the buildings. A bit slow coming down this side initially, but there are quite a few buildings to clear, so it's just one of those things. Overall, it went well.

'I was looking for aggression from the blokes, and an awareness of what's going on around them – during the move in, as well as in the assault and the re-org. At the end of an exercise, there is a tendency to switch off, so we wanted to see that they were still switched on right up to the end.

'Because recruits are not trained as section commanders, although they are put in charge of a section we can't really expect them to control the whole thing adequately. The training team is there to chivvy them along a bit and give guidance so that the whole thing doesn't go completely awry.

'In terms of their performance over the whole exercise, I think they've gone in waves. There've been times when they've done really well, there've been times when they've been appalling.

'On all their exercises up to now they've had dry weather until the last day, and most exercises have been completely dry. On this exercise, the weather's been absolutely dreadful and I think that's taken its toll on them. They're a bit shocked at the severity of the weather on Dartmoor.

'Overall, they've done adequately. I don't think they've done particularly well, and there have been times when they've been pretty bad. One of the harbour positions in particular, up on Dartmoor, I told them to be ready to leave for nine o'clock. Got up there at nine o'clock – none of them ready. Half an hour later they'd just got their kit together. We went back to that position the next morning to find the place strewn with litter, tent pegs, bungies, the lot.

'It was a particularly bad day, and I think the weather had got to them, and they wrapped. They were starting to blame each other: "It wasn't me who had the radio"; and "We didn't get a radio check"; or "It wasn't me who had the LMG when it wasn't cleaned" ... so I think they went downhill there, but picked up again towards the end.

'Overall it was OK.

'We started off with 33, and took three off the yomp, partly through injury, fatigue or lack of ability to complete the yomp. We still have a final talk about it but I think we're looking at failing at least two for poor admin in the field and lack of effort ... perhaps failing five in total.

'I'm pleased with the way the majority of them survived the yomping, because with the weather it was pretty horrendous. Their kit was wet, making the bergens heavier, so they'd had to work that little bit harder. Just from a morale point of view, it's always much, much harder in the rain just to keep yourself going. I'm quite pleased to have so many left at the end.

'We've got 12 "originals" in the troop now, out of the total of 33, which at times was actually part of the motivation problem. Some of the 33 joined us only two weeks ago, so the guys didn't really get a chance to know them. There wasn't any acrimony, but it's still a factor ... Ideally you want a hundred per cent "originals", with a hundred per cent finishing at the end. But obviously it's an imperfect world and we have to make do with what we've got.

'It's our job to get them up to standard, but if they don't reach the standard, they either get back-trooped, or if they're just not capable of it, I'm afraid it's back to another troop or eventually Civvy Street.'

Corporal Dave Bateman was with Lobb's 2 Section as they came through the tunnel and assaulted the buildings down the far side of the fort:

'We had a 300-metre approach down in the tunnels and they were doing a lot of admin like passing out grenades and giving orders which the section commander should have done back in the harbour position. He was wasting time in the tunnels, causing a lot of noise . . . which annoyed me to start with.

'When you're clearing something like these buildings, you need a lot of speed and momentum. There was no talking between the guys, so nobody knew exactly what they were doing. They needed the section commander to take charge, to tell them where to go – 'cos they won't go unless he tells them. That's why I was giving him a hard time, to get that speed and momentum going.

'I'm quite pleased with my 2 Section. I've got five originals out of the actual eight. They respond quite well to a bit of pressure. If you have a go at them, it just takes the once, they take it in and start doing the job properly . . .

'I'm pretty confident that they'll be wearing Green Berets within a few weeks, no problems.'

638 Troop gathering brass – used cartridge cases – on their support weapons position on the ramparts of the fort.

McKenzie has been troop sergeant's runner throughout the final attack, working in its latter stages from on top of the ramparts. The troop had taken Sergeant Barnett's earlier comments to heart, making the troop sergeant's job a lot easier for Bauduin than it had been for Wilson at the start of the exercise. McKenzie has clearly not been affected by being electrocuted, and has come through the exercise well:

'When I first started I thought the Commando Tests were going to be really hard, but now I know that the hardest part is the test week itself. I think the actual tests are just to finish it off. To be honest, they aren't really that hard. It's the amount of weeks before that makes it hard, not the tests.

'I knew it was going to be hard. When I got here it was even harder than I'd thought, so I'm just glad to have got this far.

'I've thought about getting a Green Beret since I was 16. I got married when I was 20, and had two kids. I had a better job with a lot more money, but it was just something that I wanted to do. I applied for the Royal Marines when I was 21, going for it now while I still can!'

Recruit Dobson was troop commander for the final attack:

'I thought it went pretty well overall. Everybody was in position on time, then they put down a good weight of fire from up here on the ramparts, but then the assault sections went their own ways in the courtyard. It got a bit confusing once the smoke generators went off. We had to hold fire here 'cos we couldn't see anything, but apart from that it went pretty well.

'The plan was followed virtually to the letter apart from missing the odd pocket of enemy, then having to retrace their steps a bit.

'It was my first time as troop commander. Us four Diamonds have been taking a turn each throughout all the exercises. With all the smoke and rounds going off, and a lot of confusion, you try to concentrate on what you're doing rather than on what anybody else is doing. 2 Section got a bit bogged down over the other side towards the end. I haven't seen the section yet so I don't really know the reason.'

With the arrival of full daylight, the civilian Training Area Warden arrives to ensure that everything is left to his satisfaction. With Endex, all exercise reality stopped very abruptly, a total relaxation from being 'tactical' to peacetime, barracks routine. The Training Area Warden can make life difficult for the instructors if he decides to put in an adverse report, so for the next hour the recruits crawl through the grass all over the fort, picking up empty cases and ammo links. They form search lines, sweeping methodically across the open areas, while other groups concentrate on places where the LSWs were firing.

Recruit Anfield is walking around disconsolately, wearing his quilted 'Chairman Mao' trousers, without a combat jacket, looking dirty, fed-up – and very like a refugee. He failed to complete the yomp from the farm, which means he's failed the exercise. The significance of this is just sinking in – that he will have to leave the troop, join another, and go through the whole thing again with another bunch of strangers.

'The weather was very rough. Just like everyone else, I'm very tired, and disappointed in myself knowing that I didn't complete the exercise but . . . it's no fault of anyone else's. It was my fault – you know – I've obviously done something wrong along the way . . .

'I ended up with trench foot, so I'm going to have to do the exercise again. I'll just have to see where I went wrong and put it right.

'When your feet are cold and wet for a long time and you don't dry them out properly, they wrinkle – like when you're in the bath for a long time. But through yomping, they also get very sore and blistered, until in the end you just can't walk on them any more.

'You realize it's happening but it didn't stop raining at all for about the first four or five days, so there was no chance of drying your feet out properly to a state where they are actually going to get any better. Once you're on that downward slope with something like trench foot, there's just nothing you can do about it. But, as I say, like it's obviously something that I've done wrong, because out of 33 lads who went on the exercise, I was the only one who went down from it, so I can't really say it was anyone else's fault.'

He is very tired, speaking slowly, unshaven, sniffing with a cold, his eyes puffed up like a boxer after a fight.

'In the end, 'cos I couldn't keep up with the other lads on the last yomp, I was pulled off by the medic. I don't know whether I would have finished, but I was disappointed to be pulled off. I wanted to carry on – specially being so close to the end of the exercise.'

As Anfield [pictured right] clears up the remains of the enemy's wood fire, he drags half-burned, smouldering railway sleepers across the open ground to the gate, head down, obviously upset. Perhaps it's just the contrast between his misery and the others' evident happiness at finishing, but the rest of the troop appear to be keeping away from him. Anfield remains determined, and even positive: 'I'll get back-trooped now. I think I'll have to wait another month till next Final Ex. I'll just have to do it again and make sure I do it properly this time.'

Smith MR has also failed to complete the exercise:

'When it came to the yomp I didn't think I'd have any problems. Then the weather got really bad, windy and that, and it got dark. Then I fell over and found I'd torn a tendon in the back of my knee . . . I couldn't carry on . . . I felt gutted. Absolutely gutted.

'I'll have to wait until we get back to find out what happens next, but honestly I haven't really thought about it.

'I've had a recurring injury in my ankle, damaged ligaments from a yomp. Last time I thought, "Yeah, I'll be ready to go on the Final Exercise . . ." but it weren't ready and I went over. I was out of training for three months. My ankle's all right now . . . at least it was.'

Smith is clearly very upset, but determined to carry on and attempt the exercise yet again, although one suspects that the thought frightens him a little.

Recruit Jaftha fell behind on the second yomp, and had to be put into the wagon. He too feels gutted, saying that after nine months in Hunter Troop recovering from a serious fracture, his leg is still weak. This is hardly surprising as his entire lower leg is held together by a steel plate.

Jaftha is quietly spoken, cheerful but unassuming, running and walking with a slightly awkward gait that appears to be courtesy of the surgical ironwork in his leg. He expects to be returned to Hunter Troop for about a month, which because of the length of time he's already spent there makes him feel 'a bit cheesed off':

'Commando training is really tough once you get injured – a very different game. I've never considered quitting – but 16 months at CTC is a long time. I suppose if it looks as though my leg might not be able to take it, I might think of doing something else, but I'll probably carry on. You get used to the mental pressure, but injuries make it all much worse.'

A cooked breakfast arrives in insulated 'hayboxes', washed down with strong tea from 'Norwegian' containers. The troop queue up with mess tins for the 'full monty': bacon, sausages, fried eggs, fried bread, tomatoes and baked beans – no muesli served here! After the fort is declared clean, they load into the 4-tonners for the trip back to CTC.

After his session in the sickbay at CTC, Recruit Anfield is making his lonely way back across camp to the troop block. His bergen is huge and misshapen, a spade and thermal sleeping mat strapped on to the back – the whole lot covered in mud. He is wearing trainers and limping, and has trouble opening the entrance doors to get all his kit

Overwhelming quantities of fresh air and hard exercise, plus 'compo' rations, do wonders for the appetite.

through. The stairwell echoes with music played loudly from half a dozen sound systems in various rooms, its six flights muddy from the rest of the troop, who arrived three-quarters of an hour earlier.

In each of the bare rooms, groups of people sit wearing trainers, wet, filthy combat trousers and T-shirts, dismantling and cleaning their weapons. Large bottles of fizzy pop stand on the formica tables. In keeping with his former rank of Royal Engineers corporal, Recruit Dobson's room is a hive of activity and banter, whereas next door (a room of younger, less experienced people), the atmosphere by comparison seems lethargic and subdued.

Priorities are clear: clean the weapons first, have feet inspected by the instructors, then take a shower and clean everything else. The Deputy Commandant is due to inspect the block the next morning, which requires an early start to get everything absolutely immaculate. Life at CTC goes on as usual!

Corporal Layton arrives to inspect feet and discover if people have any other ailments, injuries or problems. He starts in Dobson's room, filing past the throng of people sitting on the plastic chairs by the window, stripping and cleaning weapons while listening to a cassette. Dobson takes his boots and socks off, probing carefully between his toes.

'You've got strange, deformed feet, Dobson!'

'It's me age, Corporal!'

Corporal Layton shakes his head in wonderment . . .

He turns to Kelly ND, who is lying back on a chair, his feet in the air: 'They're like hooves, Kelly! Not sore? They're not too bad. Show us your heels. How do you fasten your boots? Do you leave out a few lace holes in the middle? OK.'

Lee's feet are still very wet and wrinkled: 'I'll be back in an hour to see how yours dry off, OK? Wear flip-flops and use powder.'

Corporal Layton is as much instructing people how to look after themselves as he is inspecting their feet. Until men have actually experienced a long, hard exercise under arduous conditions, instructions on foot preservation and hygiene do not fully sink in. Some have clearly done as they were taught; others have either developed blisters or had problems through sheer bad luck – or because they didn't put as much effort as they should into looking after their feet.

Everybody's toenails are stained brown, while their soles are as white as snow and painfully wrinkled. Some toes are rubbed raw, with deep, red cracks in between the toes. Blisters have formed where skin has rubbed against boots.

Yomping, carrying equipment weighing 100 pounds, is far from just a question of being able to lift heavy weights, but an endurance event in which the state of each person's feet determines the extent of their pain. Everybody suffers some kind of pain – in the lower back, shoulders, knees – but after several days of being soaked, sensitive, painful feet bear the brunt of all the weight. The weave of wet socks can come to feel like a red-hot wire grid. Some have numb toes; others' are stinking – a combination of severe athlete's foot infection, immersion foot, blisters, and over a week without washing. A pair of new boots have damaged one person's toenails to the point where they will probably have to be removed in the sickbay.

Corporal Layton orders the wearing of flip-flops, to air their toes and dry them off. When dried out and well warmed, in good conditions their feet will heal fairly soon. But on the hill, with wet boots and soaked socks, it's impossible.

Weapons are stripped down and carefully cleaned, combination tools and cloths used to get into the nooks and crannies of the various metal parts. The weapons are very wet and in need of detailed attention. Once completely clean and dry, they are carefully oiled, with drops of rifle oil on a piece of 4-by-2 cleaning cloth. As large bottles of fizzy pop and crisps bought from the NAAFI are consumed, the conversation is of the next day's big event – the Deputy Commandant's inspection. Recruit Dobson knows exactly what to expect: 'The big cheese – Big Boss! There'll be kit flying out of the windows during that!'

638 Troop's Final Exercise may be over, but the beat goes on!

CHAPTER FIVE

THE **R**ECKONING

Having finished the Final Exercise, some members of 638 Troop are confident that they've passed, but others have serious (and in several cases very well-founded) doubts about whether they've passed. Several back-troopers have already experienced failure at this late stage – and are expecting further disappointment. Men like Anfield, Jaftha and Smith MR who failed to complete the exercise are reconciled to their fate, while others are still hoping.

The rest of the troop are on the final lap, the Commando Tests, yet another set of serious obstacles to be faced with determination – and overcome. Twenty-eight weeks of training have created a sort of momentum among the 'dirty dozen originals', and they are not about to fail now.

As ever, Jeff Lobb is smiling:

'I've not found anything easy, but I try to be quietly confident. We've done the tests already, on the day we know we'll pull it out. I'm not worried about the speed marching, because being with the troop helps you on.

'People ask what it's like, but unless you actually do it, you can't imagine it. It's relentless.

'I used to play bass guitar in a band. We did a gig for deaf people – really, they were all deaf. I now run the troop band, combs and tissue paper, mouth organs, improvised drums – by order of the training team.

'I want to be a Marine because they are the best – and make something of myself. I don't know whether it will be worth it. I hope so . . .'

638 Troop office is deep in conference, the door firmly shut to all comers. Lieutenant Gillies and Sergeant Barnett are seated behind their desks, with Corporals Bateman, Layton and MacDonald and PTI Eric Neilson on the chairs by the wall. Corporal MacDonald is being teased for talking like an officer, nicknamed 'Dominic Rupert'. The office is 10 by 12 feet wide, with windows on two sides, battered plastic blinds, two desks facing the door and rows of cheap tubular chairs along both side walls. The air is thick with cigarette smoke and steam from the kettle on the window ledge, while the plastic surfaces are stained with the circular brownings of coffee mugs.

Lieutenant Gillies must shortly go for a meeting with the OC of Chatham Company, Captain Leo Williams, who will decide which of 638 Troop will be permitted to progress within Commando Training Wing to do the Commando Tests.

Because Lieutenant Gillies has been in charge of running the exercise overall, he hasn't been able to monitor each of the different sections as closely as his corporals. Since starting their recruit training, each section has had the same corporal looking after them, who by the end of the Final Exercise knows exactly how each man has performed. Although Lieutenant Gillies will make his own decision as to what he says to Captain Williams, he needs as much information as possible from the corporals.

Their discussion of individuals is direct, clear and at times shockingly honest. In war, you have to able to trust the men around you; in the back of each instructor's mind is the question, 'Would I be prepared to go to war with this man?' The maintenance of standards is therefore the instructor's only consideration. Opinions are therefore very clearly stated.

Recruit Anfield is considered a liability. Lieutenant Gillies checks him against his list: 'He was withdrawn, wasn't he?'

Sergeant Barnett looks at his list: 'Yep. I've got nothing on him.'

The corporals, however, have very definite opinions:

'He's a liability. We can't afford to carry him.'

'If he can't look after himself now – he won't be able to do it in a unit.'

'He never even got to the first harbour position on the yomp – to the farm.'

'I took his weapon off him going up the hill. He wasn't bad, but then again he was going at snail's pace.'

'. . . and he got a warning for that, Mac [MacDonald] got him on that . . .'

Throughout the exercise, the corporals made notes on each man, to which they refer now: '. . . No helmet in the ambush; weapon to one side in the ambush; individual skills . . .'

Lieutenant Gillies intervenes:

'Hang on, hang on ... dodgy one. I'll take down the details ... no helmet in ambush?'

'Yeah, weapon to one side in ambush; he had his head down there.'

'Asleep as well?'

'Yeah.'

'He was unprofessional during the yomp. Basically he just sat down on his bergen when we stopped.'

'He had his head on his hand, didn't he?'

'Yeah.'

'He also wrapped when he was withdrawn, didn't he?'

'Yeah.'

'Fell asleep in the FRV and lost his section – that was on the move into the farm attack.'

'He turned up about two minutes into the assault.'

'Left his bergen cover in the harbour position. That was at the farm as well.'

'... dropped out during the yomp, we've got that. That was at Checkpoint One.'

'... it was only about 2k wasn't it? ... max.'

This litany of disaster sounds terrible. Anfield's alleged failings must however be seen against the exceptionally stringent code of standards to which the Royal Marines and Commando Forces operate. Unless the training team stick rigidly to these standards, without exceptions or favour, the rest of the CTC selection process will not work as it should. At this first level, the process is ruthless and very direct. However, behind their insistence on standards, each member of the training team sympathizes with the recruits and hopes that each will make the grade and pass out. In any case, everybody in the troop office remembers clearly the pain of their own recruit training.

Lieutenant Gillies carries on with the list:

'Dobson, no probs, doing well. Farrimond: newly joined, shining, better than Bauduin – more mature, and uses his voice better. We'll put him up to Diamond. Gault's TRC [Training Record Card] read badly, but I was impressed. I gave him the 320 [HF radio] and, although only a little bloke, he carried it all the way.

'Head is a bit grey, had yomping probs earlier and got it together. Hilton is solid – a "Kelly Mk 2" ... would do anything for you.

'Holmes is an admin nightmare – a fail. He can't look after himself. Weapon covered in rust, hadn't bothered with cleaning so it was verging on not working. Hadn't oiled it for 24 hours. Can't do Batco [a low-level radio code] or Voice Procedure. Didn't do a radio check. His sleeping bag was soaked but the bivvy bag was bone dry – he hadn't been using it! He wouldn't have lasted much longer.

'Baulduin. Yeah . . . no problems, I don't know what happened to him on that last yomp. He's not going to fail it but . . . he's a good bloke, did well as troop commander on the farm attack . . .'

Sergeant Barnett: 'Jaftha . . . withdrawn . . .'

Various voices come in with reactions:

'Tricky Dicky.'

'Another liability . . .'

Lieutenant Gillies:

'Is he a major liability, or is he just . . . so crippled?'

'He's weak . . .'

'What's his admin like – professionally? You tend to be overshadowed by the fact that he's such a biff when it comes to yomping and phyzz. There's no way that he's going to pass the commando tests . . .'

'At the end of the day, that's the job, isn't it . . .?'

Corporal Layton: 'I'm not saying he's disabled, but I think that those injuries have totally knackered his legs . . . I reckon because he's got pins in . . .'

Lieutenant Gillies: 'He's a decent enough bloke and it's not through lack of trying . . . apparently in his old troop, he was a really good bloke, getting on well with the blokes . . .'

'His TRC is really good . . .'

Lieutenant Gillies: 'We should give him a run.'

'Pardon?'

The corporals are incredulous at this suggestion: 'Give him a run at the commando tests?'

Corporal Layton: 'You can't, can you? He has not passed the Final Exercise . . . no way . . . it wouldn't be fair to the other guys . . .'

Lieutenant Gillies, firmly: 'We'll just have to see what Major Lear says.'

Corporal Bateman: 'Yeah, well, he's my section and he shouldn't be here . . .'

Lieutenant Gillies: 'Did we get Jaftha for anything else?'

Corporal Bateman: 'I picked him up in the ambush. He hadn't a clue who he was working with, and they were supposed to be working in pairs. Baulduin spoke up, and they worked in a three . . . It's the only thing we've got down for him.'

Gillies: 'Apart from the fact that he can't run and he can't yomp, and he's a physical biff . . . he's not a scrote though, is he?'

The corporals are clear that Jaftha should not continue:

'. . . and can't do the Tarzan course, and he won't jump into the net . . .'

'I think he'll hang himself on the tests, so if we keep him . . .'

'He won't get to the tests. He shouldn't get to the tests.'

'I don't think he should go any further.'

'Are we being pressurized or what? I think we're being pressurized to keep him going.'

'I think we should stick to our guns.'

Lieutenant Gillies: 'Yeah, I agree. I'll say we should get rid of him. It's not fair on the bloke . . .'

Everyone agrees:

'He's not fit, is he? And he's got to do the Tarzan course on Monday, drop off into that net . . .'

'He was pushed out of Hunter Troop too early . . . It's not fair on him . . .'

Lieutenant Gillies draws the discussion to a close: 'Right then, let's crack on! Johnson?'

'Admin vortex! Insubordination. He caused the split on the night yomp, plus left the radio kit on a wall. He wore waterproofs throughout the exercise. Didn't pass on messages, was hanging out on the yomp, rusty weapon, didn't look after his feet – and they were in bits. Left his notebook in a harbour position. There's lots more details . . . It's not as if any of these things were just a one off . . .'

'Kelly TJ – good strong lad. Offered to carry the gun . . .'

'Kelly ND – did well with a bad knee. Fell off the wall twice . . . a bit solid, but a good man to have in the unit.'

'Lee – young, but tries hard, and you can see the improvement. But he's an admin vortex.'

Lee recently received a 'Dear John' letter from his girlfriend, but coped. He made a poor start, but gets good marks for effort. He's good at PT.

Corporal Bateman:

'Lobb had a good exercise, and worked well as section commander. It's a shame we bust him. Could we make him up again? He's got a brilliant attitude. Hasn't quite got the command and control yet though. We really should give him another go as section commander.'

Lyons is deemed 'the ultimate grey man'. Corporal MacDonald however is happy with him: 'He is awesomely fit, and strong in the yomps.'

McKenzie is always laughing – even when electrocuted on the way to the fort. He's not thought to be Diamond material, but 'mega solid': 'Can be a bit slow at times; more "Commando Medal" type.'

In the next week, the training team will also have to discuss candidates for the various awards given at the King's Squad Pass-Out Parade, the King's Badge and the Commando Medal being the most prized. The shortlist already exists.

'Nicolson. Lost his notebook and got hamstring trouble.'

'That doesn't make you lose a notebook!'

'Strong . . . Good man.'

'Nield – withdrawn.'

'Did all right – until injuring himself.'

'Got to be a re-course.'

'His last TRC said he was a nightmare.'

'No. He's doing OK.'

'Potts – steady, always there, middle of the range, can get to feel a bit sorry for himself, can be a bit selfish . . .'

Despite the medic's dire predictions after the Portland raid, Potts' ankle injury has not held him back.

'Prater had bad admin when he joined. He seems OK now?'

'Schembri's personal admin can be poor: zips undone, drawcords missing on waterproofs. I've given him a chuck-up for good professional skills – his fire positions on the ambush . . .'

'Smith MR was doing all right, got a knee injury but wrapped and was withdrawn.'

'Strange that he came off when it got dark and everybody was miserable – but with only 10k to go? Is it bottle problems?'

'Smith AD. Where do we start?'

'Admin vortex. Cannot look after himself . . .'

'Blokes packed his bergen for him, Snazel proffed his weapon – but that's not his fault. Didn't take notes during orders . . .'

'But he did know the radio frequency when I asked him?'

'Let his combat jacket get soaked. But did well carrying the LMG . . .'

'No motivation, kit left all over the place. He got pissed off at the farm and Bauduin packed his bergen for him . . .'

'The blokes don't think much of him . . .'

'Snazel . . .'

Lieutenant Gillies: 'I can't believe he proffed that weapon . . .'

Sergeant Barnett: 'The doc says his feet were bad – admin again. He always looked as though he needed someone to tidy him up.'

Everybody chips in: 'I think he should go because of the weapon alone.'

Lieutenant Gillies:

'Still, after the bollocking he was trying very hard to impress . . .'

'What else could he do?'

'If he did that in a unit, he'd get filled in . . .'

'They don't realize what it's like in a unit . . .'

'He should get charged for that – at least!'

Lieutenant Gillies winds it up:

'I'm not sure that we can fail him on the exercise just for one incident. I'll speak with Captain Williams.'

'And now for Spink – the best man . . .'

'Him or Dobson for the King's Badge.'

'The Unflappable Man.'

'Top dog.'

Everybody is thinking about the King's Badge, and about the examining board that the King's Badge candidates (once chosen) will face when the Commando Tests are completed.

'You can't tell what the board will do . . .'

'I don't think it's right – people judging them who don't know them . . . they've no experience.'

Lieutenant Gillies moves briskly on to the next name before this theme can be developed any further.

'. . . He's just a Wendy . . .'

'Get him a Wren's uniform.'

'The way he looks and speaks you'd think he'd fail a cooking course.'

'I don't think he'll pass the Commando Tests.'

'But he didn't wrap . . .'

'I'll take wagers . . .'

The whole troop are judged dreadful at leaving things behind: 'Even Spink left that stuff sack behind at . . .'

The consensus is to fail Jaftha, Snazel, both Smiths, Johnson, Anfield and Holmes. Captain Williams is unlikely to be happy with this: 'They're going to have an explosion down at Chatham Company!'

Lieutenant Gillies:

'I'm not sure about Snazel. He should certainly be charged. We can't fail him from the ex for lacking integrity.'

'Had Jaftha been fit, he'd have passed – he's a good bloke. Anfield can't look after himself – got hypothermia, kept his goretex bottoms on most of the way through . . .'

They also decide to put the newly joined Farrimond up to Diamond, and Lobb to section commander.

'We have only four people for the King's Badge – Bauduin is too quiet – so we're left with Farrimond, Dobson, Spink and Nicolson.'

They then go through the whole exercise in detail, determining what was done, and by whom. Various points emerge: they bunched up at night, and were poor at passing messages. Dobson and Spink were good troop commanders.

Corporal Layton: 'In the morning, when the light came they weren't moving back into cover, staying out in the open like green bottles.'

Sergeant Barnett: 'What about good points – so we can leave them on a high.'

These are harder to determine. They made poor models, Chamberlain has a poor head for heights, Lobb was passing grenades around and giving instructions in the tunnel which should have been done back in the harbour position . . . Good points are hard to find, and in any case, the instructors prefer to talk about people: 'Big Kelly is a star . . .'

They like Kelly ND, who reacts personally to everything they say.

'I said after he'd not made the wall [on the assault course], "You're going to fail" – and he literally deflated in front of me!'

'He did the same when I bollocked him about leaving the radio on the wall . . .'

Kelly left a radio set on a wall after a stop on one of the yomps. He should be punished for this, but clearly nobody wants to charge him formally.

'He sort of deflates like a balloon in front of your eyes . . . He's a really good bloke.'

They decide to punish him in another way: 'Let's get him in and tell him he's failed.'

'Can we keep a straight face?'

'We can try.'

One of the recruits enters, to collect dirty coffee mugs:

'Get Kelly.'

'Which one?'

'ND.'

'Yes, Corporal.'

'Who's going to do it?'

'I couldn't keep a straight face.'

A knock on the door and Kelly [pictured below] enters in the pre-scribed fashion, saluting Lieutenant Gillies and standing ram-rod straight to attention: 'Sir, I am Kelly ND, number . . .'

'Thank you, Kelly. Stand at ease.'

Lieutenant Gillies tries to be serious, but nobody else can manage a straight face.

'Kelly, I've called you in here to tell you that you've failed the Final Exercise. You will be back-trooped and . . .' Kelly droops visibly from his six feet, jaw dropping open with horrified surprise, his worst fears suddenly coming to life. After the Final Exercise, he has been expecting some kind of punishment, admitting earlier that he was worried about forgetting the radio on the wall: 'Leaving that radio behind was an abysmal thing to do.'

At first he thinks the instructors' giggling and suppressed

laughter is amusement at his failure. He is far from being amused himself. Then he realizes that it's a joke, and reacts with stunned disbelief: 'You lot have got a really sick sense of humour.'

Corporal MacDonald is doubled up: 'We'd thought you'd have realized that by now.'

Even when reassured that he has definitely passed, Kelly says: 'I don't know what to say . . . I think I'll go and throw myself off the landing.'

They send him off to make the tea, he repeating that their sense of humour is sick.

The troop are summoned from their 'grots' into the stairwell, where Lieutenant Gillies gives them the exercise de-brief from the top of the landing.

'It was a fairly hard exercise weather-wise, which overall you did averagely. You went from doing things really well, to doing things appallingly. There was no middle ground. When the weather was bad, morale slumped and things went to rats. You lost motivation and wrapped. A lot of your personal admin needs to be squared away before you get to your units.

'You're not used to operating at night, which you haven't done much of. Personal skills and motivation went downhill when it got dark. You blamed each other and morale went downhill.

'On one occasion somebody came up on the radio and said that you were stranded on the other side of a stream. Although it was fast flowing, this stream was only a few feet deep, certainly not something to cause a bunch of Marines – or potential Marines – to be stranded on the other side!'

Everyone laughs.

'I don't want to know who it was, but the point is, when it gets dark and there's a little stream in your way, don't give up on it. It's part of the job, I'm afraid, to put up with things like this. It's the same with the rain and weather on the moor – you've just got to put up with it.

'When someone falls over on the moor, you don't have every single man in the troop stop for him. The next man asks if he's all right, then everyone walks around him. He gets out of the way, picks himself up and carries on. You don't have a whole troop of Marines stopped by one man falling over a clod of earth. That march down from the farm was criminally slow. I almost got exposure through standing around so much. It wasn't good enough.

'Noise. In a harbour position you should be tactical, but you don't suddenly go non-tactical on a march. You must also pass messages properly when on the march – it must ripple up and down the line in a matter of seconds, rather than by two minutes of shouting at each other.

'You know when you are doing things right, it's just a question of doing it. Don't leave kit lying around; leaving a radio in a harbour position is criminal. If you leave kit lying around in Northern Ireland, it could cost people their lives. I won't say any more on that . . .'

It's a cold morning, and outside the main gate the recruits of Hunter Troop are on parade wearing boots, denims, OG (olive green) shirts and webbing, their rifles slung ready for a 4-mile speed march. These are the graduates of Hunter Troop's regime, of PT and weight training in the gym, and light military work in the afternoon, men almost ready to rejoin training troops. The regime is steady and progressive, giving time to recover strength and mobility after injury, and to regain that peak of physical fitness that is vital if they are to avoid further injury and get Green Berets. The troop works in close conjunction with the sickbay, incorporating physiotherapy and specific training for each man's particular problem.

Remedial PT expert Sergeant 'Shiner' Wright describes the regime.

'Every morning they do one hour of general gym work plus a session in the swimming pool, then another hour in the gym specific to their injuries. We get over 80 per cent of them back to full fitness.

'The main problem, apart from the injury, is their friends passing out, leaving them behind. The atmosphere is much more relaxed than in a normal recruit troop.'

Discipline in Hunter Troop is much less formal than in a recruit troop, giving men breathing space to regain self-confidence that may have been dented by serious injury. Their injuries range from serious multiple fractures to muscle strains that prevent men from keeping up with the rest of their troop. Stress injuries like shin splints and the plethora of knee problems are very common – and require time and careful exercising to heal.

Hunter Troop is a very important part of CTC, of which the Royal Marines are justifiably proud. OC Commando Training Wing, Major Lear, sees it as a vital part of the Corps' responsibility for everybody who gets injured at Lympstone, regardless of whether they are likely to pass-out at the end: 'If we break somebody, we can't just throw him on to the scrap heap. We've got to get him back together again, then if possible get him through the course. Only 10 per cent

(*Right*) No soft option for the injured here. Hunter Troop recruits work hard in the gym to regain fitness after injury.

make it to Lympstone from the recruiting offices; so everyone here is special.'

Injuries are inevitable during Royal Marine recruit training, particularly when men are tired, their muscles strained and weary. The first weeks of Swedish PT in the gym succeed in building up each individual to a common level of strength, fitness and agility. Some people, however, are less resilient, and for others plain bad luck may result in injuries that make it impossible for them to continue. With five mornings a week spent doing circuit training in the gym, under the expert eyes of remedial PT staff, men progress quickly. Constant monitoring by sickbay staff and daily physiotherapy further speed things up. Daily swimming sessions work off muscle tensions and help strengthen without any potentially damaging loading of weakened joints. Afternoons are spent in military training and outdoor work, so that recruits do not forget too much of what they've already been taught.

Sergeant Wright has selected a squad of men whose injuries have healed, and whose fitness under the Hunter Troop regime has brought them close to being able to rejoin a recruit troop at the point when they were injured. This morning they will try a shortish speed march, eight of the twelve carrying full equipment, the others unladen.

This 4-mile speed march is the final test for men hoping to pass out of Hunter Troop, on an unpleasant wet morning, a cold wind encouraging everybody to get started. After warm-up exercises in the lee of the hockey pavilion, Sergeant Wright lines everybody up on the lane, ready to start:

'All of you are fit enough to pass this speed march. If you do, you can go back to training.

'Up to attention! That way turn! By the right, quick march! Left, right, left, right . . .'

The squad's right marker is an instructor wearing a Green Beret, combat shirt, and denims, boots and webbing like the recruits. Sergeant Wright runs wearing just his blue PTI's top. A Land Rover leads the way, its four-way flashers indicating the presence of the squad to oncoming traffic. Members of the squad in dayglo orange vests run at the front and rear, waving on the traffic, and a Land Rover ambulance follows immediately behind the squad.

After marching the first couple of hundred yards, they break into double time and run, breaking back down into quick time (marching) only for the hills. Recruit Glennon runs in the centre of the front rank, slender and ginger-haired, his webbing high around his chest rather than lower, around the waist, weapon and elbows resting upon his ammunition pouches. If he passes this run, he'll be joining 638 Troop for the Commando Tests.

'Step short up the hills . . . Well done, that's good . . . And step out when you get to the top, letting the downhill bit take you away . . . Open your legs and keep in step.'

When the leading Land Rover gets too close to the squad, its blue exhaust fumes catch in the recruits' throat. On the high-sided Devon lanes, there is room only for one vehicle to squeeze carefully past the squad. The traffic guides wave vehicles forward, after stopping cars from the other direction: 'Traffic rear. OK, hold the vehicle there. Let 'em through in the rear . . . Wave them on. Dig in, men.'

As the miles roll past, and despite the bitterly cold day, black strips of sweat break through the men's shirts, over their breast bones and down the small of their backs. A cloud of steam hangs over the squad, a combination of breath and perspiration. The rhythm of their pace is all-important, keeping the squad together, helping the miles to pass. Before climbing hills, they go from running to marching – at a brisk pace, arms swinging strongly to the side: 'Prepare to break into quick time . . . quick march!'

As they march over the crests of the hills, they revert to running, with the overall aim of covering each mile in 10 minutes. So 40 minutes later they reach the car park, move into open order and march the last few yards to the back of the hockey pavilion.

'Get your kit off, and as quick as you can get into the grandstand.'

Men are coughing. They do a quick warm down of stretching exercises then, after stripping off wet shirts stained black with sweat, put on dry vests and combat jackets. Glennon has done well, and so is passed fit to join 638 Troop. Sergeant Wright wishes him luck.

Glennon: 'I'm very happy to be getting back to training again. The training teaches us how to get a team working quickly, so I'm not too worried about not knowing anybody. I should fit in OK. I'm also not worried about the tests – I'll just stick at it and finish.'

It's early the next morning in Captain Leo Williams's office at Chatham Company HQ. Lieutenant Gillies has arrived for the critical meeting during which Captain Williams will decide who from 638 Troop will go forward to the Commando Tests. The company sergeant major is also present, with the company 2IC. Captain Williams sees each recruit troop at every stage of their training, and so knows far better than anybody the overall standard that must be maintained.

638 is Lieutenant Gillies's first recruit troop, and Captain Williams clearly understands the difference in perception between what he as OC requires, and the black and white attitude of the troop training team, who at times are too close to the action to be able to take a considered view (and who the Commandant considers 'are not a particularly experienced training team' either). Captain Williams explains how the system operates:

Sitting in judgement: Lieutenant Gillies, with Chatham Company Sergeant Major and second in command . . .

'It isn't us against you. We decide what is in the recruits' and our best interest, and whether they will make a Royal Marine. I've read through your list, and I can say before we start that none of the people you've listed will be leaving the corps.'
They get started immediately, discussing personalities: 'I see that Smith M R has been at C T C since May 1991 – over 12 months?'

It's up to Captain Williams to hand on those men he thinks have a chance of passing the Commando Tests. Clearly if he gets it wrong and too many men fail (through being poorly prepared), or too few men are put forward, then the O C Commando Training Wing, Major Lear, will become concerned.

Smith M R is aged 19, and Captain Williams has discussed him before when he was back-trooped to 638. Having been such a long time at C T C, Smith is in danger of developing an attitude problem: 'He took himself off the yomp?'

It was Smith A D 's second Final Exercise, having been back-trooped from 637 Troop. He's only 17. Lieutenant Gillies goes through the litany of misdemeanours:

'He let himself get soaked through at the harbour position, bad carriage of weapons, left socks lying around . . . asked others to pack his bergen and we were held up because of this. After 12 hours non-tac in the barn, he was one of five picked up for seriously rusty weapons. The farmer had dried out their kit for them . . . Smith still had bad rust, and was on a warning too. Lack of motivation . . .'

... face Captain Leo Williams, Chatham Company Commander, to discuss the future of the 638 Troop recruits.

'Is he a bit immature?' asks Williams. 'Has he got it in him to pass?'

'He made it to the end of the exercise, but he's a liability ...'
Recruit Holmes, another re-join. Lieutenant Gillies:

'This troop's had dry exercises every time, and this was the first time they'd had to sort it out. I think that once they get cold and wet, they wrap and stop doing things – hence Holmes not sleeping in his bivvy bag and having a soaked sleeping bag ...'
Captain Williams wants to know the exact details of what happened with each person, questioning the facts behind the judgements the training team have made – some of which are not actually theirs to make.

Recruit Anfield: good soldiering, but physical problems. 'When he was taken off his attitude was pathetic – he'd got the thousand-yard stare ... he'd withdrawn into himself.'

Captain Williams: 'I think this is the guy who heats up very quickly – who's had all the medical tests. I've seen him before. Let's discuss the next man, and go back to him later.'

Nield is in sickbay. An up-to-date medical report is required on him. He missed the Sunday yomp, but was all right until then. He is passed 'as long as he believes the physio' when the physio says he can pass.

Recruit Johnson: 'Another nightmare man. One of the five with rusty weapons after the 12 hours in the barn. He was there at the end, but hung back on the yomps. He has attitude and motivation problems, and I wouldn't like him to pass.'

Captain Williams asks questions about the troop-splitting incident and Johnson blaming other people and saying he wasn't actually there.

'Corporal MacDonald warned him, and he answered back. His feet were in bits – although he's had foot infections in the past. It didn't look as if he'd looked after his feet.'

Captain Williams: 'Did he do anything well on the exercise?'

'No particular chuck-ups, Sir.'

Jaftha: physically weak. Lieutenant Gillies thinks he came back from Hunter Troop too soon: 'A good lad but not strong enough. He had no chance of completing the long yomps. He is professionally OK and well motivated – he must be to persist!'

Captain Williams comments that nine months of repetitive physical training in Hunter Troop would wear anyone down: 'His physical capability will show up on the Commando Tests. If he's OK in the field then he's cracked the greatest problem we find with recruits.'

Lieutenant Gillies does not agree. They move on to the next name – Snazel: 'Carriage of weapons, waterproofs on all the time after being told . . .'

Lieutenant Gillies then tells the story of the stealing of the weapon:
'It's a bit of a strange one; in the first ambush [in the woods, in the pitch dark], Corporal Layton went down to check the troop's position. Snazel was rear protection and Corporal Layton found him asleep, his weapon resting on his thighs. Corporal Layton took the weapon and went down to check the cut-off positions, then came back and gave the weapon to the person he thought he'd taken it from – finding Smith, who hadn't got a weapon. When he handed the weapon back, this person went off to a different fire trench from the one in which he'd been caught sleeping, which Corporal Layton thought very strange. And Smith didn't say anything about having two weapons. In the end the weapon numbers were checked, and it was discovered that Snazel had taken Smith's weapon . . .'

Captain Williams is keen to establish how Snazel performed apart from the weapon incident. Lieutenant Gillies is worried about Snazel's character, while insisting that he shouldn't fail the Final Exercise because of the incident. Captain Williams believes that guys under all the pressure of training should be given a bit of leeway – and hints that the taking of Snazel's weapon put him under too much pressure.

They return to Smith MR. Although it is now known that he has a ligament injury, in asking to be taken off he is judged to have wrapped. Lieutenant Gillies is worried about Smith's attitude, 'because of having been in Hunter Troop for so long'. Captain Williams sees it differently: 'After being in the Corps for 18 months, can we honestly say he's not met the standard on the Final Exercise at this time?'

Lieutenant Gillies: 'He hasn't done all the serials.'

'Well, I'm going to pass him on the basis that he's got to do well on the Commando Tests to prove himself physically. I'm going to fail Smith AD, but investigate whether he should be back-trooped even further into the New Year.'

Lieutenant Gillies suggests however that Smith AD should go back on to a Final Exercise as soon as possible, on the grounds that further delay is unlikely to help him – and more likely to make him worse. Captain Williams agrees.

Holmes: 'Rusty weapon time and time again.'

'No two ways about him either, back-trooped until 6 December.'

Lieutenant Gillies: 'Anfield didn't complete the exercise but had done reasonably well until then – a less serious case of the Jafthas. His skills and motivation are all right.'

Captain Williams passes him, commenting that he needs a good firm word from Lieutenant Gillies.

In making the decision to keep these men going, Captain Williams understands how Lieutenant Gillies feels, having his recommendations overturned:

'It might upset your training team, me passing guys they think should fail through physical attributes. However, provided these people have got the motivation and soldiering skills, we will find out about their physical attributes during Commando Test week. They certainly won't pass that without actually doing the four Commando Tests within the time limits.'

Captain Williams is clear about Johnson: 'He's a fail. It's just one thing after another. He became a bit of a nightmare for you on this particular exercise, so we'll back-troop him to Hunter, to have another go on 6 December.'

Jaftha, Lieutenant Gillies: 'I'm happy to keep him although I don't think he's got a gnat's chance. I do worry how he will be affected though – especially if he fails badly. He came back too soon.'

Captain Williams: 'We can't say whether or not he's come back too early from Hunter. We've had others through with plates in their legs, and there's no reason why he can't do it. It's a question of motivation. It's what we all get paid for.'

Snazel: 'The sergeant major will sort it out unofficially, and he's not to be back-trooped.'

Business completed, Captain Williams finishes the discussion positively: 'Get the men motivated for the Commando Tests – so we can pass them all in one go.'

Back in the troop training office, on hearing that Anfield, Jaftha, Nield, Snazel and Smith MR are to be kept on, the instructors are incredulous. Corporal Layton says it stinks. Lieutenant Gillies struggles to be loyal to the hierarchy and the view that the men's physical fitness is tested by the Commando Course, while agreeing with his training team that there's a difference between field fitness and Commando Test fitness, and that both are important.

Corporal Layton is particularly upset:

> 'Next week they'll be Marines! How can he pass Anfield? He didn't even do half the exercise ... They're taking the piss. Oh fucking hell, take me back to 45 Commando. I wish I'd gone in there [to the meeting] – I'd be a Marine now!'

Layton doesn't mean to be as disrespectful as he sounds – which everybody understands. Sergeant Barnett neither looks at him, nor comments during any of his tirade. Lieutenant Gillies carries on being reasonable, supporting the hierarchy without backing down from his own views.

As far as Corporal Layton is concerned, the worst bit of news is that Jaftha has applied to join 45 Commando, Layton's own unit. It's not that Layton has anything against Jaftha as a bloke – in fact he quite likes him. Layton's fear is that if Jaftha fails to make the grade in 45, his mates will hold him responsible for sending them an inadequate Commando.

Life however goes on, and Lieutenant Gillies has to interview the various people affected by the decisions, giving them the bad news face to face. Each man knocks on the troop office door, enters, salutes, gives his name and number, standing to attention:

> 'Holmes, I'm afraid you've failed the exercise. There's no other way of saying it. You've let everybody down: rusty weapons, soaked sleeping bag, and in another few days you'd have been off the exercise anyway ... You go back to Hunter Troop, then join 640 Troop and do the ex again on 6 December.'

Ex-milkman Holmes had expected to fail because of poor admin, but hasn't changed his mind about the Marines: 'I'll dig out blind next time and pass in December. I need to learn how to operate the radio too. Getting a hard time is all part of the job. I've had a fair crack of the whip ...'

Smith AD marches in:

> 'Smith, you have failed the exercise. You've got bad admin and are a liability to your mates. I can't afford to send you to a unit as you are. Rusty weapon, lack of motivation ... It's not just a matter of getting to the end of the exercise – you've got to perform.'

Jaftha stays with the troop: 'Because your problem is only a physical weakness, you are being kept on. I'm not happy, but that's the way it is. It's not a chuck-up; you got through by the skin of your teeth.'

Anfield also stays in the troop: '... because you were putting in the effort. You've got a physical weakness, so you've got to dig out blind on the Commando Tests ... Consider yourself lucky to be still here, and put in a good effort.'

Nield stays with the troop – provided the physio agrees – because he was injured: 'You were not actually tested at end of the exercise, so from now on, 100 per cent effort is required from you. You've also got to keep having physiotherapy on your knee to keep it going.'

Nield is delighted, but very aware of the problems he faces: 'I expected to have to do the ex again. The endurance course will be hard on my knee – going through the tunnels. I'm chuffed – getting out of this place before Christmas!'

Tall Smith (MR) also stays with the troop, because his professional skills are up to the required standard. He is surprised, but despite the leg injury is confident about the speed march, though worried about the final test, a 30-mile forced march over rough ground: 'I didn't get much sleep last night worrying about it.'

Snazel did all right professionally so hasn't failed the exercise: 'You cannot afford to drop your mates in it, or take things. The sergeant major will see you this week.'

Snazel is relieved:

> 'I've been crapping myself since the exercise. The first two into the troop office were failed, which was a real downer for the rest of us waiting outside the door ... Haven't spoken to my mum and dad – and I need to let them know the date for our pass-out parade.'

Snazel confides that this isn't the first time he's thought of failing the course:

> 'After the first ten weeks I'd decided to quit, and was four days from going home. Then I changed my mind. Once it becomes your life, it's a lot easier. You haven't to take it personally when they have a go at you. The tests aren't hard; it's just yomping that mucks your feet up – and the 30-miler.'

Jaftha was expecting to fail again, and feels very relieved to be staying on:

> 'Being a back-trooper when they don't know you, makes it harder. They look more at you. Doing all the phyzz again would be hard. I'm afraid of the Tarzan course – particularly of the chasm where I broke my leg. I'll just have to go for it ... hopefully.'

Lieutenant Gillies saves the best until last. Recruit Farrimond is congratulated on his performance during the exercise, and made up to section commander. Recruit Lobb is also congratulated, regaining his section commander's tape.

Chatham Company HQ occupies a single-storey block, with a store, the clerks and sergeant major's office, a larger training office and the OC Captain Leo Williams's office – all opening off a rather battered central lobby. Notice boards line every wall: Daily Orders, instructions for just about everything, security regulations and advertisements for kit no longer needed (usually because the owners have been binned). One particular advertiser seems to be shaking off a clash of identities, offering for sale electric guitars as well as the usual bergens, insulated jackets and combat knives.

Smith AD and Holmes arrive to be told their future by Captain Williams. The company sergeant major looks them both up and down, then checks that Captain Williams is ready to see them. Smith marches in, salutes and is told to stand at ease.

'I don't agree with the reasons I've been back-squadded, Sir.' Captain Williams runs through the list of Smith's misdemeanours. Smith agrees that he did all the things detailed, his objections swiftly evaporating in the face of Captain Williams's logic. He is put on an 'OC's Warning', meaning that having used up his second chance, Smith has just the one life left; one more serious problem and he will be discharged from the Royal Marines. The interview finishes with Captain Williams saying he hopes Smith will pass.

Outside Chatham HQ block, Smith is fed up, but reconciled to doing it all again:

'It's quite a hard exercise, so it's hard to have to do it again. I failed the first one through hypothermia, but at least I finished this one.

'It was little things – poor harbour drills . . . not getting into fire positions when carrying a bergen – which is the last thing you want to do when you're knackered.

'I do feel a bit hard done by; I was still standing at the end and I've been failed, when others who didn't finish were passed . . .

'I'll crack it the third time, with a bit of luck and a lot of hard work.'

Captain Williams gives Holmes a serious bollocking for having a dirty weapon: 'It's the most important part of your kit, which could save somebody else's life as well as your own.'

Captain Williams puts him on a '2IC's Warning', which means he's got two lives left. Holmes marches out. Captain Williams explains:

'Each man gets three goes at the various criteria tests – of which the Final Exercise is one. Both these men have done the exercise before – Smith twice. We don't want to waste all that money and just chuck him out.

'The training staff don't see every troop that goes through – I do. These two men have passed a lot of other exercises over 28 weeks of training. They've already done the 12-mile load carry. The Commando Tests will show us if they are up to the required fitness. Even slight injuries can prevent people from completing an eight-day exercise on the moor.

'I'm looking at the man overall – tactics, soldiering skill . . . as well as his fitness. We rely totally on the training teams who are with them 24 hours a day, for 28 weeks. But my job, running recruit training, is to ensure that the standards remain constant.

'In any case, every recruit has passed the PRC [potential recruits course], proving to us that they have what it takes to succeed here. The only thing PRC can't test is the man's commitment, which takes 28 weeks to show through.'

Later that day, the sergeant major summons Snazel to his office, 'for a little chat'. Snazel admits to being asleep, and on discovering that his own weapon was missing, to taking another from the next shell scrape. He says he did it because of 'shock and panic'.

'I put this to you, son. Think about what would have happened if you'd done the same thing in a Commando unit.

'I'll leave it to your imagination, but think very carefully about what would happen to you in a Commando . . . if your weapon had been taken by the enemy, or you lost it on active service or in Northern Ireland . . .?

'You must tell somebody if you find that your rifle has gone missing – not take somebody else's . . . Can you think of a word for what you've done?'

'I don't know what you mean, Sir.'

'Can you give me one word for what you've done, a word that you could be accused of . . .?'

'Stealing, Sir.'

'I'll tell you what I think about this. I put this down to a careless decision . . . If you don't think about this and sort it out, you could end up with problems that in the future you may not be able to handle. Think hard about where this could go, and what could have happened to you.'

This interview is carried out quietly with many pauses, the reflective logic given added force by the definite feeling that just under the surface, at one hint of dishonesty, the company sergeant major is poised to rip out Snazel's throat. Snazel is dismissed. The sergeant major explains:

'I will let the stealing bit go, but investigate the fact of sleeping on duty – and may yet charge him. He will certainly be punished. Sleeping on sentry duty has serious implications, even for a recruit.

'He's very inexperienced, which is why he acted like he did. He will nevertheless continue the training, and will probably pass out.'

638 Troop are running past the bottom field for their last practice session on the Tarzan course. They are wearing woollen cap com-

forters, white PT shirts under combat jackets, OG trousers and combat high boots. Turning right at the 30-metre range, they pass the 30-foot wall and form up in front of PTI Corporal Eric Neilson. It's another cold morning, and recent rain has made the grass playing field particularly wet underfoot.

They take off their webbing, laying the rifles on top, ready for a warm-up session. With Corporal Neilson standing in front, they prepare to do the Tarzan course in the same fashion as a first-class rugby team before a match: running on the spot, knees up high, shoulder rolling, shadow boxing: 'Do it as if you mean it.'

Breast stroke:

> 'Stand by for an arm sprint . . . Go! Go Go! Then backstroke to
> the rear . . . and . . . Sprint! . . . and steady . . . Side bends in
> time with me . . . Nice and slow – to the top of your socks . . .
> In time with me, Wilson, you turkey – and you, Bailey! I know
> it's hard for you . . . Squat down keeping your back straight . . .
> arms all the way up . . .
>
> > 'Now run to the wall and back again at three-quarter pace . . .
> Go! I don't want to see the same faces in the rear . . .'

Eric Neilson runs through the usual litany of PTI banter while watching each man very carefully, noting how those with injuries are moving, ensuring that each man is warmed up, switched on and alert, which, in view of the nature of the next activity, is vital.

The Tarzan course is not merely a daunting prospect for the recruits, but with its height and the skills it demands is a hard and potentially dangerous obstacle course for even the most experienced and fully fit Commando. To get round within the time allowed requires total commitment and self-confidence, as well as strength, agility and the necessary skills. This is the troop's last practice run before the real thing next week. Accidents today would be truly tragic.

As 638 Troop run back towards him, Corporal Neilson notes that Jaftha, as ever, is towards the back of the pack, running with his usual slightly lop-sided gait. He seems withdrawn, clearly gearing himself up for the fourth obstacle – the chasm, where, last time he made the attempt, he fell, bouncing off the metal supports, smashing the bones of his lower leg into several jagged pieces.

CTC Medical Officer, Surgeon Lieutenant Andy Hughes:

> 'Recruit Jaftha fell off the Tarzan course and sustained a very
> nasty transverse fracture of the lower leg, breaking both his tibia
> and fibula, puncturing the skin. The wounds were immediately
> opened up by surgeons, who put in a 10-inch metal rod held
> top and bottom by big steel pins, to hold his leg together.
>
> 'The metal is still in there, and bone has now grown into the
> fracture site. We'll have to take it all out some time fairly soon,
> but at the moment that's what he's carrying around.

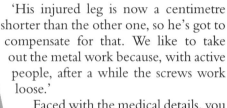

'His injured leg is now a centimetre shorter than the other one, so he's got to compensate for that. We like to take out the metal work because, with active people, after a while the screws work loose.'

Faced with the medical details, you are forced to wonder whether it wouldn't be more sensible for Jaftha [pictured left] to give up now and do something less strenuous, rather than risking further more serious injury, and the risk of being crippled.

'We wouldn't let him do it if there was a risk – and his leg is actually stronger now than a normal leg. Fractures are nice. They have an end point, and if you treat them right, the guy should make a complete recovery. If it ends up the same length and he gets full use back, it's all right. Overuse injuries are actually worse – shin splints and so on.

'On the medical side, our biggest problem at CTC is over-motivation. People will do everything in their power to carry on. We hold them back here for their own benefit, to protect them. Most injuries take time to heal – which people under training here don't feel they have. However, at the end, we want a fully functioning Marine. It's pointless us putting out a product that is flawed.'

After several months in hospital, a number of operations, including one in which a 10-inch metal rod was inserted into his leg to hold it together, then 8 months in Hunter Troop, Jaftha has so far not been able to force himself across the chasm, freezing with fear on the platform, unable to carry on. Having now passed the Final Exercise, to get his Green Beret he must break through his psychological barrier, and today is his last chance before the actual Commando Tests.

At the start of the course, a PTI tests the first obstacle, the death slide, adjusting the tension of the rope until everyone is satisfied. If too loose, people can get stuck suspended halfway down 40 feet from the ground; too tight and they fall too quickly, hitting the ground. Another PTI checks the rest of the course for frayed cables that rip men's hands, loose bolts or damaged ropes.

Wearing webbing with rifles slung across their backs, the first four men climb the ladder and wait, one at the top, one in the middle and one at the bottom, plus one on the brink ready to jump. The fastest from the last practice run go first today – as on the starting grid of a Grand Prix motor race. It's all done against the clock: 'Stand by ... Two, one, go!'

Each man carries a heavy rope loop which they wet with water from a barrel at the bottom of the ladder. Once at the top of the tower, this is placed over the slide rope and looped through their wrists. On the command 'Go!' each man leaps from the tower and slides rapidly down the rope, to instructions from the PTI: 'Knees up first to clear the net, then stretch!'

They drop off 3 feet above the ground, dropping the rope loop and sprinting away to the next obstacle, a net up to the rope traverses and crawls. Technique is everything here, especially the changeovers from one obstacle to the next – made some 50 feet above the ground.

Spink fails to swing on the suspending rope, from the ramp into the net, and has to go back and do it again: 'Turkey ... That's better. Now get on with it! Think about what you are doing.'

He's lost valuable time.

'Come on, Nicolson.'

The fastest men are racing each other for the best time. The penultimate obstacle in the woods is Jaftha's dreaded chasm: sprinting along a plank some 20 feet above the ground, jumping across an 8-foot gap into a climbing net, punching through it so as not to fall, climbing up and over the top, then down some 40 feet to the ground.

Breathing very hard now, they run out of the woods on to the playing field, 300 yards past the 30-foot wall, to the assault course and the first of the tunnels. Shots echo from the nearby 30-metre ranges. Like gophers they disappear into the ground, to scrabble through a series of pebble-lined drain pipes, then out, to the start of the assault course.

Without pause, they run hard at the 6-foot wall (a burst of energy is required to gain enough height to pull yourself over), then a 10-yard crawl under the net entanglements. Another burst of energy is required to get over the water jump, then a 10-yard hand traverse of the monkey bars over a large water tank. The ramp and 6-foot leap down is followed by a walk up scaffolding bars and a crawl across the regain rope, at which each man must successfully do a half regain before being allowed to continue. After crawling the rest of the rope and climbing down, they run crashing across the swing bridge, then 50 yards back up the hill, over a 6-foot metal frame then another 100 yards to the 30-foot wall, which they climb using a fixed rope.

By the time men reach the assault course, they are breathing very hard, lungs hurting and legs like jelly. Each obstacle requires a different technique, plus a special burst of effort at the critical moment. This is a sprint event, which creates physical pain through which you have to concentrate very hard to avoid making mistakes. It's very easy to get things wrong, losing time, getting wet and even more tired. Some men run at the 6-foot wall, hitting it hard without even leaving the ground, their legs having lost all spring, unable to summon the energy to pull themselves over. Others cannot hold the monkey bars, their hands incapable of grip.

A group of new recruits stands open-mouthed at the start of the assault course. Spink is running up the hill towards the 30-foot wall.

'Open your legs, pump your arms . . . Go!'

'You've got one minute to get to the top, Spink . . . Work hard and dig in!'

'Push it out faster. The last little bit. All the way in. Up and over. And jump down on to the rampart . . .'

'Spink! Corporal!'

'Well done.'

The ambulance revs up for a casualty at the zigzag wall, the young Wren medic racing on foot across the field, a medical pack on her back. Anfield has twisted his ankle outwards. A stretcher is required. He's loaded on, carted off to the sickbay. The others continue to run past. Prater fails to make it over the chasm net and is told to come back, having hurt his shoulder.

'It had better be a genuine injury.'

As the last man, Jaftha waits on the ladder thinking about the chasm. A slight figure, his black hair close-cropped in the US Marine Corps style, he enters the tower, puffing his cheeks with nerves. The PTI urges him to have confidence, then:

'Stand by . . . Go!'

'Stretch and swing back . . .'

'Work your hand free and drop off the rope.'

Throwing the rope loop to one side, Jaftha runs briskly through the trees to the metal ladder up to the first platform. Everything from now on is at least 20 feet above the ground. He swings across the rope into the net. Climbing up the net on its right-hand side, he reaches around the metal pole for the first traverse . . .

'Go hard! Let's go!'

He looks confident.

He gets on to the second traverse, then around the metal pole. Chest down on to the single rope crawl, then pull across on to the shackle, stand up by the post then on to the monkey crawl.

'Let's shift it, son!'

The company sergeant major is there, urging him on: 'Come on. You won't fall off that crawl . . . Move your hands and feet faster!'

On to the horizontal ladder up to another platform, then backwards on to the rope and slide down . . . taking a two-second breather on the way down. The next obstacle is the chasm, and you can see Jaftha thinking about it.

The moment of truth. Recruit Jaftha freezes at the chasm.

Walk then sprint along the beam, gathering yourself for the jump at the net . . . He's arrived at the chasm – and freezes, teetering at the edge, 12 feet above the ground.

The P T Is round on him: 'Look at me. You do want to do this . . .?'

The psyching-up takes place in private, two P T Is standing on the platform beside Jaftha, talking quietly to him:

'Walk back to the start of the plank, then sprint at the jump . . .
'Whatever the cost, get off the end of it . . .'

'Jump off into the net now! One! two, three, now!
'All these weeks and wasted effort – you haven't got time to mess about. You've done it before. Get into the net quickly – you won't fall . . .'

Jaftha stands at the edge, rocking backwards and forwards, puffing his cheeks in and out, psyching up to do the impossible.

'Close your eyes and do it.'

The P T Is stand beside him and do it with him. They are willing him. They really want him to do it. They also want to pick him up by the scruff of his neck and throw him off . . . they'd love to do that – but they don't. He's got to do it himself, on his own.

'Stand there and just jump into it – go on!'

By now, he can't make the pass time, so they try another tack.

'Take your kit off. You're not going away from here until you've done it.'

The PTIs place his webbing and rifle to one side of the platform.

'Go now! Go now! Go! Go!'

He rocks backwards and forwards in time to their shouting, doing everything but actually jumping, jerking strangely.

'There's no such thing as losing your bottle . . .'

He jumps into the net. He's given no time for thought. The PTIs help him out.

'Straight back up and do it again without even thinking. Please go off the end of the board, please . . . One, two, three . . .'

He jumps into the net again. Corporal Neilson: 'Ok, let him do it in his own time now.'

And he does it.

'Straight back up now, get your kit on and let's do it properly. We've done it now – cracked it!'

'Once you've got your kit on, just go! Fall into the net!'

He balances on the edge again, rocking backwards and forwards, puffing the cheeks, counting to himself. And then he does it.

'Right, get down, and come with me.'

Jaftha runs back up the start again, to try a timed run. The clock starts and he climbs the metal ladder to the top of the tower.

'Stand by, go!'

He reaches the bottom of the death slide, slips one hand out of the rope loop and runs once again for the first ladder. Across the rope crawl, then moves from the pole on to the monkey crawl. He flips across on to the wire ladder, bouncing as he walks up uphill hanging on to the two side ropes. Reaching the metal pole, he turns backwards and hooks his legs over the downhill rope slide, pressing his chest on to the rope and sliding down.

The next obstacle is the run along the plank, then the leap across the chasm into the net – at which he smashed up his right leg, and which up until now he has been unable to jump.

Eric Neilson settles him for his big effort: 'Come on now, when you get to the bottom of the rope, turn and run straight along the plank and jump straight off into the net – don't think about it, just do it!'

Anticipating this, Jaftha is already puffing his cheeks with nervous tension.

'Check [at the bottom of the rope]. Go. Walk to the end and jump off . . .'

Jaftha walks the length of the plank, then stops at the edge and winds himself backwards and forwards like a shot-putter building up momentum . . .

'Go! Go! Go!'

'No need to wait for the count of three. I'll throw you off myself – go, now, now!'

The hierarchy are out in force, keeping quiet as Jaftha shapes up to this enormous challenge. Then he jumps, punching through the net as he has been taught, pulling himself up the 15 feet to the top. The company sergeant major calls out: 'Well done, son, well done!'

Captain Williams immediately cuts through the relief that has swept across the watchers; Jaftha needs to get cracking if he is to get round the rest of the course within the time limit: 'Now get a move on, Jaftha!'

The company sergeant major agrees: 'Come on, son! The clock's ticking away now. Let's go.'

Eric Neilson continues to give instruction: 'Choose one of the vertical ropes and climb down. It's easier at the side . . . Go for the jump, swing across and jump away . . .'

He runs through the gates and plods into driving sleet towards the bottom field, passing the rest of the course as they line up beneath the 30-foot wall, having finished. Corporal Neilson decides to stop Jaftha there, allowing him to rejoin the rest of 638 Troop. Having fallen off the zig-zag wall, Anfield has been carted off to the sickbay, so his weapon and webbing are handed to the duty student to look after until they learn of his fate. In the cold men are coughing, their breath and body heat creating a cloud of steam over the entire troop.

Corporal Neilson: 'Well done, Jaftha – I don't know what for, but well done anyway. Get fell in.'

He urges them to get plenty of fluids and food down their necks in preparation for their first Commando Test, the endurance course, the next day.

'Who's Duty Bootie? Feel free to take them away any time today – unless you want to keep standing around in the rain.'

Duty student Spink uses the unofficial but very 'Royal Marines' word of command, 'That way turn', and is pulled up by Corporal Neilson: 'Let's do it properly, shall we? You haven't passed out yet – probably never will . . .'

Spink does it properly: 'Turn to the right in threes, right turn! Double march.'

'That's better. See you tomorrow, troop!'

'Bye-bye, see you,' shout the troop dutifully.

Lieutenant Gillies has been watching:

'Sullivan has had problems getting over the 6-foot wall, but should be all right on the day. Jaftha is over the chasm, so I feel confident about him. Jaftha's problem is that he expects to have a problem. You could see he'd given up, but the PTIs did a good job so hopefully he's cracked it.

'Anfield has injured his foot by not using a 2-footed landing off one of the 6-foot walls. It could be a broken ankle – he should have used the proper technique. After heat exhaustion, a cold weather injury, and now the ankle, he's a bit of a disaster area. I was surprised at Spink not doing so well, but he'll be O K on the day.'

At the sickbay, Recruit Anfield has a badly sprained but not broken ankle, and is hoping still to make the tests: 'It's a bit of a nightmare. I was running along the zigzag wall and fell off on to the side of my foot.'

The medic puts on cold compresses, and will X-ray the foot just to make sure: 'There's been many cases like this but they always get back on their feet again.'

Jaftha feels better for having mastered the chasm: 'I improvised, seemed to blank out a bit, but then I just leapt it. Something in your mind says not to do it. I don't feel bothered about it now.'

Having showered and changed after his 4-mile speed march test, Recruit Glennon has moved his gear over to B block. He knocks on the troop office door, marches in and formally joins 638 Troop, giving his name, rank and number to Sergeant Barnett. His initial Troop was 633, then 10 weeks ago, after cracking on with the Final Exercise, he damaged his left foot. After two weeks in Hunter, he's back on the road again.

'Good effort,' says Lieutenant Gillies.

Aged 18, from Lancashire, Glennon used to be a tiler, is single, and has no hobbies. He already knows Schembri, and will join Corporal MacDonald's section. He is confident that his foot is now strong, and Lieutenant Gillies urges him to make sure of passing.

Glennon already knows that he's to be posted to Scotland, to Comacchio Company. Lieutenant Gillies sees no problems with him: 'The word is that he's a good bloke – and really switched on. He was apparently made a Diamond, but decided he didn't want the responsibility and handed the tapes back in.'

Although 638 Troop are now set for the final leg of their journey, getting through the commando tests doesn't seem quite as straightforward as perhaps it seemed a few days ago.

Meanwhile, it's the second last day of All Arms Commando Course 4/92's Final Exercise on Dartmoor, and Sergeant Major Dobson's section are resting briefly by the side of a wet road. Their exercise started with a 12-mile cross-country load carry, minimum weight 55 pounds. From the start the weather was bad, and latterly it has been very bad indeed. Mountain rescue search parties have been out several times over the weekend looking for parties of civilian trekkers, and warnings have been broadcast on local and national television.

One man dropped out during the initial load carry, two at the end of the second serious yomp (during a wild and rain-lashed day), and a

All Arms 4/92 snatch a moment's rest during their Final Exercise on Dartmoor.
Sergeant Major Dobson and Lance Corporal Heaps look suitably relieved.

fourth on this last 10-mile yomp. Their kit is soaked, so everything is heavier than normal. They're carrying a lot of weight anyway, but the wet adds extra pounds plus dramatically increasing the chafing effect of bergen and webbing straps. The weight also puts additional stress on their feet; two people have had to quit because of weight exacerbating old injuries.

They've also had a mystery illness. Private Thomas failed to take off his wet clothing, instead put lots of clothes over the top. After getting into his sleeping bag, he suffered breathing problems and last night was taken to hospital.

> 'I had pain in my chest, and was scared about continuing. After a lot of blood tests, the next day they said it was a chest infection and filled me up with drugs.'

(Private Thomas made it back later.) There are 17 still on course. OC Captain Ray Pritchard: 'I'm pleased with their performance, particularly as they are still managing to put a bright, smiling face on it.'

Sergeant Major Dobson is in pain: his back, and the knee injury from abseiling two weeks ago. After a short rest stop, he orders them to saddle up – putting on the heavy bergens yet again. There is obvious and understandable reluctance from some, leaving their bergens on the ground until the last possible moment. Sergeant Major Dobson briefs everybody to go in single file and not bunch up. They cross a roaring river filled with rainwater, using a twin-arched stone bridge, then lean into the steep hill. Rainwater flows as a stream down the roadside, running over their sodden boots. They are moving slowly and painfully, placing each foot squarely, shoulders hunched against their heavy loads.

On the hard road, feet seem to expand outward when placed on the ground – and the weight comes on. Some men are hobbling with short, painful steps, while others keep a broad stride, using each leg steadily, to push them uphill. They lean forward, sometimes bending down to hitch up their bergens, standing for a moment head between legs to gain some relief. At each two-minute break, they flop backwards to rest their bergens on the turf and stone wall, to stand in the roadside stream constantly chewing food like squirrels.

Sergeant Major Dobson briefs everybody on the route, then off they go again, up yet another long hill, eating on the hoof. Dobson has his head well down, looking up periodically to see where he's going. Otherwise he walks head bent forward checking his map, trying to keep the weight from pulling him backward, absorbing the pain.

It's raining, a constant, heavy, miserable drizzle. The bergens are massive, sleeping mats and steel helmets strapped to the outsides. Sapper Roach is suffering from breathing problems, gasping and coughing. Dobson stops to sort him out, and after taking off his bergen, one of the training team arrives and takes over. Roach's kit is removed and the medic examines him.

They've got around four and a half kilometres to go – downhill now, then along the side of a river estuary. They drink water and eat, as the instructors make sure everybody is all right. Like overturned turtles unable to get back to their feet, they help each up from the wall and carry on. They chat as they march comparing loads, making jokes, talking about the coming weekend, keeping each other going by banter and escapist conversation.

Those with sore backs (everybody) stop, dip forward with heads between their knees, throwing their bergens high up on to their backs to relieve strained shoulders. Going downhill is almost as bad as going up ('worse' says one) – from strain on the knees. You can see they're carrying heavy weight; no longer plodding uphill, on the flat, between strides their knees seem somehow loose, as the weight comes off each leg, as it swings forward. Finally arriving at the harbour area, they have to climb over the MOD's barbed wire fence as nobody has brought a key for the padlocked gate.

Sergeant Major Dobson gets the course into all-round defence, amid gorse thickets overlooking the estuary. Yachts bob at anchor, shackles ringing against masts in the cold wind. He briefs them: no move before 2130, moving to their next location by Rigid Raider some time later that night, followed by attacking the same fort that 638 Troop laid waste a few weeks ago, at the end of their Final Exercise.

'The lads should just eat and drink until they've used up everything. We'll try to get a water replen. Anybody with ammo problems, come back to me. Good chuck-up for everybody on the yomp.'

They've all got very bad feet, most with some kind of immersion foot, which looks white and spongy and is clearly very painful. Life has come down to the basic essentials: 'The only thing we look forward to is eating – you've got to keep your calories up.'

Sapper Xavier is suffering, but he reckons he'll be all right: 'Feet, back in bits, webbing burns . . .'

It's important that friction burns don't become infected.

'Hideous amounts of weight . . . Can't do much about bad feet, blisters can be punctured then taped up. If you've got injuries, carrying the weight makes it worse.'

Royal Navy 'schoolie' Lt Linderman feels he has become worn down over the time. He sees the exercise as very much a test of character:

'The idea of the attack is to see whether after living so rough for a week, we can actually get it right.

'My wife probably thinks there's something wrong with me for wanting to do this kind of thing. I'm an instructor officer in the navy, and I have to do this course to work with the Commando Brigade. It doesn't really matter if I pass or fail because I can always do something else in the navy.

'Nobody is confident about passing this course – but you have to avoid injury. It's demanding and tiring, to the extent that it slows you down; at this stage anything you decide to do can take very much longer than normal.'

People's feet are branded white with the weave pattern of their socks imprinted on the upper surface, snow-white and puffy at the bottom. Xavier washes his, using his precious water, then dries and puts on clouds of foot powder, leaving them to air while he finds a clean, dry pair of socks. They eat boil-in-the-bag meatballs and pasta ('at least that's what it says on the packet . . .').

HQ section are busy making Sergeant Major Dobson's briefing model, while he writes his detailed Orders for the attack. His signaller has just finished cooking him some food and a brew. The section commanders will be arriving outside his basha in about 45 minutes for Orders, so he's not got much time to think it through. They're now in the last 24 hours of Final Exercise, the worst of it behind them, with just the fort attack to do. However, with the Commando Tests to come, getting a Green Beret seems an eternity away.

CHAPTER SIX

638 TROOP – COMMANDO TESTS

In charge of the Commando Training Wing is the bear-like Major Jon Lear, who, at well over 6 foot 4 inches and built square 'like a Pusser's locker with a head on top', is everybody's idea of a Commando. Despite ears that bear witness to years of second-row scrummaging and heavyweight boxing, Major Lear is friendly, cheerful, positive – and caring, particularly when it comes to deciding who is to be failed: 'You have to be a caring person to train these men. They all change a great deal within the time they spend here, so we've got to give them time to reach the standards.'

How the instructors behave is vital:

'It's a matter of communicating what is required – and care is also required in doing this, because youngsters can be more sensitive than older men.

'We give each man the basics, no more than that, ending up with a very good quality person, who then matures greatly in the real world, doing real world jobs in the units.

'There is also an element of self-selection within the system; some opt out at the 12-week point. Many of these then write back asking to return – and have to go through the whole thing again. Others can't handle the amount of information they have to absorb, so we have to ask them to leave.

'Only 20 per cent of the training is physical, the rest being mental. Mental toughness is very important. At the pass-out parades, the mums and dads see dramatic changes in their young men – the results of stretching them mentally, so they can think on their feet and make the right decisions.

'In my day there were a lot harder people joining the Corps. Our parents had served during the war, and we were more prepared. Today, young men wear trainers most of the time [developing weak feet], don't get milk every day, and competition at school is much less. But although they might not be as hard when they start, the tests are still the same – although in my day we didn't have to run over that horrible footbridge across the road. Also, today they have high-tech weapon systems to master.'

Economics have streamlined the process:

'It should cost about £150 a day to train each man, but at the moment, with less people going through, it costs around £300 per day, so we can't afford to get rid of trained people. The weeding out therefore happens earlier in the process, rather than later.'

The Final Exercise is very much a culmination of a whole series of field training exercises:

'The Final Exercise embraces the whole of training, during which we look at their capability to live in the field, their tactics as well as their stamina. Although they end up tired and run down, we find that having completed the Final Exercise, few people fail the tests.

'Constant feedback from the Commando units keeps us informed about our standards. They are happy with what they are getting from here. As to why we test them in the way that we do: the four commando tests are as they are because that's what they are and always have been – our heritage from Achnacarry.'

And so to 638 Troop's endurance course test. After they've marched the 4 miles out of camp on to the Common, the timed part of the test is a slog through more than 2 miles of tunnels, steep hills, streams, deep pools and rough tracks, followed by a 4-mile run back to camp. They carry webbing and weapons, starting in groups of three or four, keeping together until they have negotiated the water tunnel – which can only be done as a team. After the water tunnel, totally soaked through, it's every man for himself; a long haul through the woods, up several very steep hills and muddy cart tracks, before hitting the roads, and the long run back to CTC.

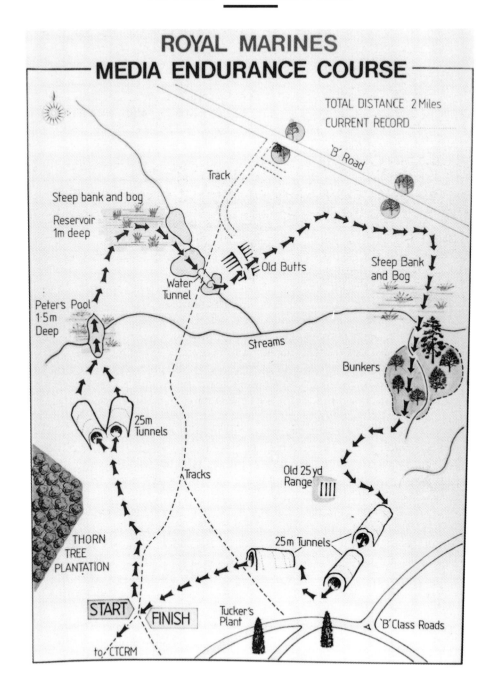

ROYAL MARINES
— MEDIA ENDURANCE COURSE —

TOTAL DISTANCE 2 Miles

CURRENT RECORD

'B' Road

Track

Steep bank and bog

Reservoir
1m deep

Old Butts

Steep Bank
and Bog

Water
Tunnel

Peters Pool
1·5m
Deep

Streams

Bunkers

25m
Tunnels

Tracks

Old 25 yd
Range

THORN
TREE
PLANTATION

25m Tunnels

START FINISH

Tucker's
Plant

'B'Class Roads

to CTCRM

(*Right*) OC Commando Training Wing Major Jon Lear. (*Above*) The obstacles
of the Endurance Course – less the 4–mile run back to camp, which members
of the media foolish enough to have a go on Press Days are spared.

As ever at the end of November it's cold, but with a watery sunshine that several local dog-walkers are enjoying as they share the woodland car park with the instructors' Land Rovers. Commando recruits are so much a part of life on the Common that none of these civilians bats an eyelid. Corporal Neilson is supervising the weighing of kit, using a set of brass scales suspended from a tree bough. One man is 3 pounds over and wants to get rid of the extra. Neilson berates him: 'If you are going to do it, 3 pounds extra isn't going to make any difference. So stop whining!'

Their webbing must weigh at least 22 pounds. Nicolson turns out to have 24 pounds, Glennon a massive 35 pounds – which he explains is extra water so he can drink in large quantities without worrying about being underweight at the end. McKenzie is told to finish in the first three: '. . . if you want to see your wife and children again'.

The staff bait the troop good-naturedly: 'Who's that with only 23 pounds? Little scrote!'

Men with fewer practice runs under their belts are carefully paired up with the more experienced who know the route. It is important not to get lost – the clock will not stop ticking.

The instructors synchronize watches and the first group set off running, down the hill to Peter's Pool for their first soaking, wading the 20 metres through its marshy depths, holding rifles in the air, forcing their way through the shoulder-high water, jogging as they come out the other side, muddy water pouring from their webbing, squirting from the eyeholes of their boots.

The endurance course runs through and around a large, steep-sided heather bowl, with deep marshy patches in its bottom. The small figures of the first group can be seen in the distance, trotting steadily along the tracks up its steep sides. Rain has washed down these rough paths, cutting deep into the soft, sandy soil, leaving large clumps of tussock grass, obstacles around which the men must jog. There are several sets of semi-dry tunnels to negotiate, long concrete tubes littered with pebbles that cut into elbows and knees, the change of pace exhausting. It is a steady, laborious plod, the four-man teams encouraging each other through the various obstacles until they reach the water tunnel.

At the water tunnel, two men stand on the other side ready to drag men out, while at the near end each man ducks down into the brown water, entering a completely submerged tunnel which they have to pull themselves through – a test of claustrophobia as well as nerve. When each has gone safely through, the group no longer needs to stay together. They are free to make best speed back to camp.

Recruit Jaftha is finding it very hard, unable to keep jogging, having to break into a laboured walk. After the water tunnel, his two oppos very soon leave him well behind.

Emerging from the water tunnel.

They force their way through another 20 metres of freezing cold, waist-deep water and into the woodland, then up a long hill via a relatively smooth vehicle track. Throughout the course, instructors are positioned beside some of the obstacles, but it would be easy to become disorientated and take the wrong route. Despite being totally soaked, the men are steaming with exertion, flopping into yet more stone-filled tunnels, murder to tired knees and elbows. The instructors run up the hills beside them shouting encouragement. Jaftha is very weary, doubling uphill only with slow, laborious paces.

Now they've completed the water obstacle course on the Common, the clock will not stop until they reach camp and the 30-metre range.

The first part of the route back is on woodland tracks, before reaching the road and the long downhill drag on tarmac back to Heartbreak Lane and camp.

They jog on rocky tracks cut into the gorse bushes, rifles slung across their backs. The mud increases in the woods, but the yellow leaves of autumn form a marginally better surface on which to run. Sergeant Barnett is running with McKenzie, Kelly and Smith. McKenzie reaches a downhill bit just before the crossing of the main road, opens his legs and pulls ahead. The others have no answer and let him get away. Nicolson catches up with the group, closing on McKenzie, who by the time they reach the road is several hundred metres ahead.

McKenzie is going like a train, Nicolson hot on his heels. The road is several miles of hills and dips, over which, having had a fifteen minute staggered start, the troop is spread. Stocky Chamberlain is one of the first home, bashing his solitary way along Heartbreak Lane, finally reaching the car park, threading through the cars and up the steps of the road bridge. The guards on gate duty stop all vehicle movement, raise the barrier and wave him through. He enters camp past the guard room and runs downhill towards the 30-metre ranges. Cars stop, and guests for today's pass-out parade watch open-mouthed as he bashes down the hill. Flag Officer Naval Aviation, an admiral in full ceremonial uniform, has arrived to take the salute, and is being greeted by the Commandant and his wife on the steps of CTCRM HQ. Chamberlain ignores them, getting his head down for the last few hundred metres of effort.

Recruit Glennon comes confidently through the main gate, chasing the more solidly built Chamberlain, his leg holding out well. More bedraggled figures trot through the gate, down the hill, turn right past the gym, then finally through 20 metres of mud to the 30-metre range for the last part of the test, getting 10 rounds into the target within the time allowed – without stoppages. There's no point in surviving something like an endurance course run, only to have your weapon fail to fire when you get to the other end. Men must take care of their weapons during the mud and knocks of the endurance course.

Taking cleaning kits from plastic bags in their pouches, they pull their weapons through – taking every second of the time available. Surprisingly, some men have failed to pack rifle oil, having to borrow some from better prepared (and generous) mates.

Recruit Glennon has completed the course in 69 minutes – his worst time of the four he has done so far. The pass time is 72 minutes.

'I never want to do that again – I hate it.'

Corporal Dave Bateman is in charge of the range:

> 'You will adopt the prone, unsupported position. There will be three exposures of five seconds, each indicated by a whistle blast. You will fire two rounds on each.

'Load, ready. Lying position down! Weapons to point down the range at all times, Test and adjust, watch and shoot, watch and shoot!'

The whistle blasts, and they concentrate on controlling breathing and squeezing off accurate shots. Some weapons jam, people muttering with frustration as they go through the clearance drills. They fail to get enough rounds off in the time, swearing with frustration as their scores slip away. Under this sort of pressure, the only solution is to blast off as many rounds as possible once you've got the stoppage cleared – provided the instructor doesn't spot you. You must achieve six hits to pass (from ten shots).

Sergeant Barnett congratulates Kelly ND as he finishes. On the parade ground, 100 metres away, the Royal Marines Band strike up – serenading the final runners as they plod along the road past the gym. Corporal MacDonald is running with Bailey, who will only just make it within the time.

Last one home is Jaftha, who arrives at the foot of the pedestrian bridge accompanied by a small entourage. Lieutenant Gillies runs with him as he half trots, half limps into camp, his ungainly stride tight with determination. His left leg seems to roll slightly – compensating for its weakness. He's a long way behind the rest of the troop – over five minutes. An improvement but ... He arrives at the 30-metre range. Corporal Bateman is getting a grip of the last detail: 'Come on, sort your lives out. Pull your weapon through. For inspection, port arms!'

Jaftha opens his ammunition pouch, extracting a magazine kept dry and clean through being wrapped in several plastic bags. He screws ear defenders in each ear, ready for his turn to fire. Unlike some of the others, he's got all the right gear, and his weapon cleaning is brisk and competent. He is limping heavily, walking to the firing point as if both legs are made of wood.

'There are six targets, and six of you. Line yourselves up, one to a target. Anyone firing on the wrong target will cause themselves and the man beside them to be disqualified. You are required to hit the target six times – any less and it's a big fat Freddie.'

Snazel hasn't listened to Corporal Bateman's instruction about targets. He fires on the target next door, Nield's. He is gutted to find no holes at all on his, until Corporal Bateman counts 20 holes in Nield's. Nield is very amused – especially after Corporal Bateman passes him: 'I fired 10 rounds and ended up with 20 holes – beat that!'

Because Snazel clearly did hit the target, Corporal Bateman orders him back to the butts to pick up ten more rounds and re-shoot – rather than making him re-run the whole course.

Corporal Bateman should not have allowed them both through. In theory they should have done the whole test again, which perhaps he might have insisted upon had Snazel and Nield not proved such good shots.

PTI Eric Neilson is very pleased with the results; only Jaftha has failed. Nield rates the endurance course as the hardest test, due to the effort required to negotiate the tunnels and the fact that it isn't done as part of a team.

'They're cold and wet, on their own and can get damaged in the tunnels. It's solid running for over an hour – plus the shooting at the end for them to get right.

'We had five marginal blokes, but they've all got through a couple of minutes under the time, lifted themselves up and come through. And people do fail the easy part – the shoot. Six out of ten is required, and they do it all again if they fail. Nerves can affect people as well as the tiredness, cold and mud.'

Jaftha seems hopelessly behind everybody else: 'He seems to have a problem with running. He's improving, but at the moment is a long way out.'

Lieutenant Gillies:

'He did keep going – but was too slow. The result is black and white.

'I think he'd be better off going back into the remedial system. It's not fair on him, nor on the rest of the troop. The 9-miler will be hard for him.'

Kelly ND has survived being told he'd failed the Final Exercise, and hasn't thrown himself off the troop's third-floor landing. He has however been attending sickbay, his knee swollen and painful. He first injured it after falling off a wall during the Final Exercise. On finishing (and passing) the endurance course, he complained of pain and went sick. The shock diagnosis is that he's got arthritis, and must rest. He's not prepared to do that, but is determined to continue and finish. It does however hurt.

'When I get going it's OK. I take painkillers every morning to keep it under control. I'm not overconfident – but I'm OK.'

The 9-miler (the next test) will be a painful experience for him, 90 minutes of knee-pounding along tarmac roads, carrying 22 pounds weight plus rifle. Kelly is now in survival mode – hanging in, making sure he finishes, but taking care to avoid anything that might make his knee any worse.

The next morning is frosty and bright. They step down from the coaches into a quiet, rural layby. As usual, before starting, the instructors weigh their webbing:

'22 pounds, OK – good lad.'

'Too light! Sneaky, go and find yourself a few pounds.'

Eric Neilson then takes them for the usual stretching exercises: working

Full Fighting Order with the main items unpacked. A long list of things must always be carried, and be clean and serviceable at all times. This is not always easy!

up comprehensively from the hamstrings, calves, to the shoulders and neck. Anfield is on parade, his foot feeling a lot better after his fall on the assault course. Although he was on crutches last night his injury seems only a sprain, so although the foot is swollen he hopes it will hold out.

Dobson and Wilson put on orange traffic marker tunics. Corporal Neilson gives last-minute instructions:

'Remain about an arm's distance from the man in front. Don't lag back because it makes it harder for those at the rear.

'Suck in the air and look at the countryside – it takes your minds off the speed march . . . In through the nose and out through the mouth.

'Keep the noise down, save your energy.'

Major Lear: 'Enjoy it, Troop! This will be the last time you see the Common until you come back on your Junior Command Course.'

In three ranks they set off, first crossing a main road, the cars flashing past. The first safety Land Rover crosses, then the traffic guide arrives, ready to stop the traffic to allow the troop across.

'Wilson?'

'All clear, Sir!'

'Swing the arms ... Hold the traffic rear.'

They are in two ranks now, thumping along, webbing bouncing in time with their boots. Sweat breaks through OG (olive green) shirts, steam rising from their shoulders, breath filling the narrow lane between the high hedgerows like a small cloud.

Jaftha is slipping back within the squad, and has arrived at the rear. Major Lear is helping him – a firm hand in the small of his back: 'Don't lean into me, Jaftha. I've done this speed march many times, you haven't. I want to see some Royal Marines spirit ... I want to enjoy this – and right now I'm not.'

Corporal Neilson keeps the rest of the troop concentrating on the job in hand: 'There's no need to talk. You need the air to breathe ...'

Cars pull over to the side of the road, on to the narrow grass verge, to let them pass. They step short going up the hills, sometimes breaking into quick time, marching briskly before doubling again. The 9-mile course has many hills, some steep, others gently rolling, sapping their energy. To keep each mile coming at exactly a 10-minute pace, Corporal Neilson has to keep them doubling for much of the time. It's relentless, and soon Glennon is having problems.

The instructors run at the back, keeping a sharp eye on the squad. Everybody runs shoulder to shoulder, exactly in step, boots smacking down into the footprints of the man in front. They are running as a single body of men, not as individuals. Getting out of step or altering the pace causes serious problems for everybody else, and for much of the way the narrow lanes do not allow any movement at either side of the squad. Men trying to fall back are pushed forward by their mates behind, or dragged along by their webbing straps.

As they approach the end of the march, beside a small group of houses at the bottom of a long hill, several people are having problems with the pace. Major Lear continues to be vocal from the rear: 'Only hundreds of yards to go, stick with it, Jaftha. I told you you'd enjoy it ... Mental determination, keep it there always ... cover off now, front to rear, look like Royal Marines now!'

They double into the hamlet, past the coaches, finishing outside a small sub-post office. They stand to attention, turning to the right in three ranks, then stand at ease – the steam rising. Dave Spink opens a packet of chocolate drops, which Dobson and Corporal Layton share. They've done it in 87 minutes – '3 minutes too fast'.

Prater was taken ill and has been put into the wagon. Two others needed encouragement to finish. Recruit Glennon tried to get into the wagon, but was kept going. Major Lear has lost his voice, but nevertheless tells Glennon what he thinks ...

'It's no good. I'm the one that decides what you do, not you.

You have got to give 120 per cent for the rest of these tests, do you understand?'

'Yes, Sir!'

'You and Jaftha change the cassette from "Can't Do" to "Can Do", but well done.

'Make sure that you eat and drink well over the weekend and on Monday – and I mean non-alcoholic drinks. And on the 30-miler on Tuesday make sure you keep yourselves hydrated at all times, which means you put the fluid down your throats, and you eat. You cannot do the 30-miler without a good meal the night before, a good breakfast and eating your bag ration on the way round. If you don't eat the bag ration you will flake out at the Cross.

'It's happened with me twice so far. You'll then have the wonderful experience of me putting six Twixes down your throat, your nostrils and your ears, then drinking four pints of water with sugar and salt in it. All of a sudden you jump to your feet and start moving. Make sure you eat and drink well. And let's hope it's a day like this!

'Anyway, well done this morning. A lot of hard work and effort. All right, Glennon? All right, Jaftha?'

'Yes, Sir!'

Major Lear looks at them both, then points to his head: 'It's all up here, that's all . . . thanks very much, Archie, S'arnt Barnett.'

'Thank you, Sir!'

Major Lear walks away, to the Land Rover that has come out from CTC to bring him back. Lieutenant Gillies walks to the front of the troop and quietly looks them up and down. Everybody relaxes.

'Does anybody know who said, "Does the body rule the mind, or the mind rule the body?"'

There is a reflective silence, then somebody says, 'Morrissey.' 'Right,' says Lieutenant Gillies, 'Morrissey from The Smiths, and, the Commandant who said so on your first day of training. Remember?' He smiles at them, then motions the duty student to march them back down the road to the coaches. They file quietly on board, reflective rather than relieved or animated.

After a short journey the coaches stop just inside the CTC main gate, and a Royal Marines Band drummer, side drum and bugle at the ready, steps forward. As the guard check the vehicle thoroughly for bombs, 638 Troop line up beside the road in three ranks. Sergeant Barnett takes charge: 'Head dress on, buttons done up. Turn to the left in threes, left turn! By the right, quick march!'

Led by the drummer, the troop march from the main gate to their block. From this moment they are no longer 638 Troop, but the King's Squad, yet another step in the graduated progression to becoming a fully fledged Royal Marine. Their whole training has been punctuated with milestones like this: passing the Potential Recruits Course, escaping from Induction Block to become 'proper' recruits, being issued with 'cap comforters' in week 24 after successfully passing the 6-mile speed march. None of the instructors says anything about keeping in step, keeping their heads up, or looking smart. As the King's Squad, that's up to them now. They slip into parade ground routine, swinging their arms to the taps and parradiddles of the drummer, mud, sweat and muscle pain forgotten. They begin to realize that maybe, possibly, they are turning into Royal Marines.

The side drum echoes off the concrete walls of the 'Q' stores complex. People look up from office windows as they pass. A gaggle of blue-bereted 'Nods' stand rigidly to attention until they have passed by, out of respect to a newly fledged King's Squad – the senior troop on camp.

Outside block B they receive their first word of command as the King's Squad:

'The King's Squad . . . Halt!

'Will advance, left turn!'

It's not however that much different, as they immediately discover: 'First man up the stairs get the training team kettle on. Safety stores to be returned now . . . then shout some more people back down here.'

It turns out that Prater had the runs last night, hence being too ill to finish the 9-miler. Lieutenant Gillies is sympathetic: 'It's bad luck. He's never had that problem before. He'll be OK for a re-run after the 30-miler.'

Anfield was apparently told by sickbay staff that he was not to attempt the 9-miler, which he chose to ignore:

'Anfield wanted to have a go, and I was surprised how well he did – very good news. Jaftha continues – he got round . . . "with a little help from his friends"!'

'As long as they crack the 30-miler, we can get them through the rest. It's a long way, but not a problem.'

Lieutenant Gillies inspects Anfield's feet: 'I thought you'd had it when I saw you on crutches last night. I was worried, so I phoned the physio to make sure you were all right.'

Anfield's ankle is tightly strapped, swollen underneath the binding. Lieutenant Gillies tells him to go up to the sickbay to be checked again: 'You don't want to be messed up permanently, just for the sake of a few weeks . . . good effort. Get a shower then I'll phone them up to expect you.'

The training staff gather in the troop office, voicing discontent over the results. Corporal MacDonald's voice has gone squeaky because of a cold; he sounded like a choirboy when shouting out the time on the march. He says Anfield and Kelly ND did very well. Corporal Layton, however, still feels that Anfield should have been back-squadded after the Final Exercise, and that Jaftha in fact failed the 9-miler – having been pushed round by Major Lear. Lieutenant Gillies sticks up for Jaftha, but says he and others are being pushed out too early from Hunter Troop ... 'We're becoming like a remedial troop.'

PTI Corporal Neilson shares their disquiet, feeling that the basic ethos of commando speed marching is being overlooked:

> 'In combat, speed marches are designed to take a body of men across any sort of ground – hilly, undulating, flat, whatever – in a given amount of time. The standard is ten minutes to the mile.
>
> 'At the end of a speed march, they must individually be fit to fight, and not become liabilities. They could have to do almost anything – an advance to contact, a section attack. At the end of the speed march, they should therefore be more or less as fit as they were when they started off. It shouldn't matter how long the speed march goes on.
>
> 'To me, today, certain members of that troop were not fit to fight after one mile, let alone after nine miles. And yet with, shall we say, "a guiding hand", managed to finish, but certainly were not fit to fight, and would have become a liability.'

Corporal Neilson agrees that people should not leave Hunter Troop too soon:

> 'Anybody can be made fit enough to do the actual Commando Tests. For some individuals, 30 weeks' preparation may not be long enough – because of injury, or because physiologically they may not be stable enough when they first join the Royal Marines. Such people need a helping hand in the remedial system. However as we saw today, to put them back into a troop is not only detrimental to them, but to the troop as well. Those two individuals, to me, should not have finished, and did not deserve to pass the 9-miler.
>
> 'Standards are a big thing. Are we lowering our standards or maintaining them? They say we are maintaining them, but to me, those two people certainly did not pass the 9-miler on their own.
>
> 'Glennon was in some distress at the end, so I've just talked with the sergeant who passed him fit from Hunter Troop. He believes him to be fit enough, and said he'd been working well in the remedial system. He certainly did well on the endurance course last week.
>
> 'Today, he'd fallen back a considerable distance, and we made him push back up into the troop again. Once he got back there he worked all right. He finished with a considerable amount of help – like Jaftha. Maybe through the Hunter Troop environment being different to a proper troop, putting him back straight into it made him suffer a bit.
>
> 'Every individual has his own determination level. Others like

Anfield and Kelly are carrying injuries, and finished looking good. Many good guys have come through here over the years carrying injuries, and have gritted their teeth, knuckled down and overcome it. A lot of it is wanting to pass; if you've got a bad injury, you overcome it, and become a good Marine at the end. To me, that's all part of the Commando Test.'

Across in Commando Training Wing, Major Lear sees things somewhat differently:

'Provided people with recurring medical problems are administratively sound, I'm happy for them to continue. However, if they can't look after themselves in the field, then I won't pass them. I think now the team would agree with me on this. I have seen many more troops through the system than they have.'

Major Lear nevertheless sympathizes with the training team:

'638 Troop are having to cope with much larger numbers than normal from Hunter Troop, plus their training team are mostly new to the job.

'You have to look at the overall man rather than highlighting what he does wrong. It's got to be very pragmatic and I do think we can be too dogmatic about it. Each man is a valuable asset, and matures on reaching a Commando unit. Everybody has strengths and weaknesses, but it's team work that gets people through, so you can't predict who will succeed and who might fail.'

Contrary to training team mutterings about keeping up numbers for the final parade and the First Sea Lord's benefit, Major Lear has no quota of 'pass-outs' to fulfil:

'I'm under no pressure from the Commandant to push people through – only to maintain standards. We've been asked to train 21 men per troop, and 28 are passing out with 638 Troop, which is great. If men make it to the end, they get a Green Beret, simple as that. Around 60 to 70 per cent get through from each troop, with around 40 per cent still in their original troop. Some troops have 80 to 84 per cent pass rates. One hundred per cent would be ideal.'

However, pass-rate percentages and all the other statistics of a training establishment are of little importance compared with the effect of the training process on the people passing through: 'By the end of training, they've acquired an inner confidence in themselves. And that's what we are looking for – confident young men.'

Having had a shower, Glennon feels bad. He doesn't want to quit, but his foot is killing him, and he admits to having trouble keeping going. He doesn't however think he's broken it again. The sudden change from Hunter Troop to the rigours of 638 Troop have clearly

ROYAL MARINES
TARZAN COURSE

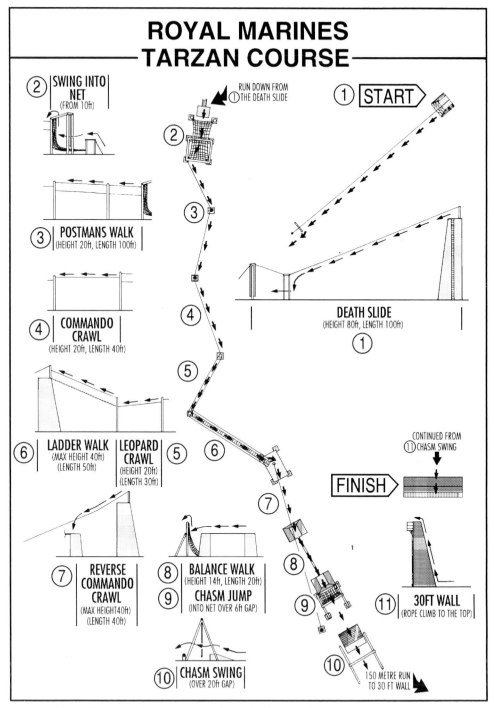

② **SWING INTO NET** (FROM 10ft)

RUN DOWN FROM ① THE DEATH SLIDE

① **START**

③ **POSTMANS WALK** (HEIGHT 20ft, LENGTH 100ft)

④ **COMMANDO CRAWL** (HEIGHT 20ft, LENGTH 40ft)

DEATH SLIDE (HEIGHT 80ft, LENGTH 100ft) ①

⑥ **LADDER WALK** (MAX HEIGHT 40ft) (LENGTH 50ft)

LEOPARD CRAWL ⑤ (HEIGHT 20ft) (LENGTH 30ft)

CONTINUED FROM ⑪ CHASM SWING

FINISH

⑦ **REVERSE COMMANDO CRAWL** (MAX HEIGHT 40ft) (LENGTH 40ft)

⑧ **BALANCE WALK** (HEIGHT 14ft, LENGTH 20ft)

⑨ **CHASM JUMP** (INTO NET OVER 6ft GAP)

⑪ **30FT WALL** (ROPE CLIMB TO THE TOP)

⑩ **CHASM SWING** (OVER 20ft GAP)

150 METRE RUN TO 30 FT WALL

Over 1 km in distance, the Tarzan course has to be done within 13 minutes.

affected him: 'We didn't do anything as hard in Hunter, so my foot felt all right. I'll get it strapped up and carry on. The 30-miler is just getting your head down and going for it . . .'

Glennon's got Sunday to recover, before the Tarzan assault course on the Monday, and the 30-miler on Tuesday. In fact the whole troop are feeling sore, particularly Nield with his leg, Kelly ND with his arthritic knee and Prater with a stomach bug, plus Jaftha, Glennon and Anfield. To survive the last two days of testing, they need all the rest and recuperation they can manage. The weekend flashes past . . .

Monday mornings seem particularly depressing at Lympstone after the relative calm of Sunday afternoon. This particular Monday has the added bite of really foul weather; rain is driving down, blown hard across the estuary, drenching and very cold.

638 Troop, the King's Squad, double to the bottom of the Tarzan course for their final test run. The warm-up session on the playing field has left them covered with mud, wet through before they've even started. Major Lear summarizes what is required: 'The Tarzan assault course is more mental, it being an individual effort against the clock. You really have to go for it wholeheartedly – 13 minutes' heart-thumping, blood-pumping work.'

The fastest men start first, to give them a clear run: Kelly TJ, Gault, Tobin . . . today's starting order determined by the finishing order last time. At the bottom of the death slide, a large board displays the fastest times, with the all-time record painted on permanently: '8 mins 6 seconds, 2Lt Pender'. Back in 1985, this was some achievement.

Corporal Neilson has a quick word: 'This is your last time on the course, 13 minutes the target. Go for it. Sprint hard between obstacles. Don't forget the basics on the assault course . . .'

The first three start climbing the ladder up the side of the tower. Kelly TJ loops his rope over both wrists and leans on the rope. The PTI looks at the watch: 'Make sure you've got a good, tight grip. Being wet, you'll be fast going down the rope.'

They start at one-minute intervals: 'Keep your hands warm . . .'

From the top of the tower you can see through the trees, and over the top of the buildings to the Exe estuary. Wind and rain are really driving across the bottom field.

'Thumbs in, ten seconds to go, enjoy it . . . stand by and go!

Stretch – good.'

The floor of the tower is wet with mud, and as each man slides away the rope bounces heavily up and down. It's very fast, the men continuing well under the restraining bar at the bottom, the instructors using a safety rope to stop them. On the bottom field the wet weather

(*Right*) Recruit Pyott on the death slide at the start of the Tarzan assault course.

is taking its toll. Men cannot grip the bars, slipping off, having to go slower, using extra care. The monkey bars particularly are a complete nightmare.

First down the death slide, Kelly TJ holds the troop record. After finishing the Tarzan course, he reaches the monkey bars, but almost at the end loses his grip and falls into the water. He clambers out and tries again, his now wet hands even less able to grip. He's shocked to discover that he simply can't hold onto the bars.

'Get your thumbs underneath . . . Pull yourself from one bar to the next . . .'

In he goes again.

'Got to crack it, Kelly, otherwise you're not going to pass . . .'

Kelly is losing heart, water running out of his boots, the time slipping away. After five watery failures, the best, fastest man in the troop realizes that he cannot do it, that he has failed. The Commando Tests suddenly take on a whole new meaning, and degree of difficulty . . . Kelly is ordered to run back to the start.

Recruit Spink is taking it very carefully, unwilling to risk falling in the wet. Having finished the line of obstacles on the bottom field, he runs up the hill past the 30-metre ranges and over the 6-foot bars towards the 30-foot wall. Nicolson is ahead of him and has ripped his trousers, pumping out the last few steps up the wall, pulling himself over the top, finishing with evident relief. The PTI keeps him on the platform for a few moments until he has recovered enough breath to climb down safely. Smith is hot on his heels: 'Stand up and use your legs to get up the wall. Both hands on the rope and you jump down at the top.'

'Smith, Sir!'

Smith MR finishes. Lieutenant Gillies is at the end talking to the men who've finished.

'Good lad!'

At the top of the course some are just starting the first obstacles, finding the wet equipment hard to negotiate. Men slip from the ropes on changeovers, hanging on grimly to avoid falling. They are forgetting the details of correct technique, slowing down to the point of increasing the risk of accident. Sullivan hesitates in climbing the chasm net, fails to jump for the rope over the log, then falls off the rope.

'That was pathetic, Sullivan. See me later,' shouts Sergeant Barnett.

Recruit Jaftha comes down the death slide and runs with determination for the ladder up to the first rope swing. He hits the net, climbing over the top and down to the double rope traverse. He reaches the pole and changes on to the 40-foot Commando crawl – made harder by the rope being soaked. Prater is hot on his heels, going well. Jaftha goes well over the baby crawl and changes over at the pole on to the uphill horizontal ladder.

'Pull hard with the arms. And get straight on to the rope.'

He slides down the rope, runs hesitantly across the plank towards the chasm, then fails to jump, standing jerking back and forwards – doing everything except jumping.

Prater arrives and jumps past him into the net. Jaftha is urged to follow, being talked to constantly by the P T I. He looks demoralized. The clock is ticking away – and then it is clear that even if he does jump, he has failed.

Sullivan has reached the first of the bottom field obstacles, and is having problems getting over the 6-foot wall. He seems unable to get any height into his jump, running at and then into the solid face of double thickness, London red, house bricks. He's short, stocky, dark-haired, a candidate for officer training. He has a brother in 45 Commando who regularly comes down to C T C and gives him a hard time. Time after time he runs into the wall, swearing and muttering with frustration, unable to get enough height to pull himself over the

The regains rope on the bottom field part of the Tarzan assault course.

top. His brother would not be impressed. Sullivan keeps doing it: walking back 15 metres, running, hitting the wall, scrabbling and straining, falling then walking back for another go.

Prater arrives blowing hard, and gets himself over – but only just – and must really motor to get in within the time limit.

Sullivan still continues running at the wall, hitting it, hanging with his elbows on to the top then flopping back to the ground, getting nowhere. He is finally taken off – his time elapsed.

Prater is dog-tired.

'Dry your hands off before the monkey bars.'

'Come on, get straight on with it. Grip, reach and swing – don't you give up! Don't hang there, move!'

Prater falls in the water, drags himself out and tries again. He looks defeated, hanging onto the bars, chest heaving, unable to grip, unable to let go with one hand in order to swing forward to the next bar, unable to move forward. He falls in again, swearing with frustration.

Despite already having failed, Jaftha has continued, reaching the half regain rope. Despite knowing he has nothing to gain, he is still putting in the effort. He struggles to use the correct technique – and, unlike several of the others, manages a perfect regain. He crawls to the end of the rope and sets off across the swing bridge uphill for the 6-foot bars. It's hard to keep running uphill, his jogging now painfully slow. Jaftha makes it over the second 6-foot wall, then runs up past the 30-metre range for the 6-foot bars, the last obstacle before the 30-foot wall.

It is however too late, his time ran out long ago. Before he starts the 30-foot wall, a PTI stops him. Sagging, he fishes his soaked cap comforter out of his ammunition pouch, adjusts it on his head and rejoins the troop – another failure.

It's a disaster. Fifteen people out of 31 have failed the Tarzan assault course, including the troop record holder – Kelly TJ. Prater has also failed the 9-miler, and Jaftha the endurance course. Getting through the Commando Tests is proving very much harder than any of the troop had imagined. Weather, tiredness and bad luck combine to drag down even the most able. Anfield on the other hand is still soldiering on, having been on crutches the night before the 9-miler.

After the Tarzan course, Dobson thinks he's done all right:

'... but it was hard. The 30-miler is just a matter of taping your feet up and going for it. A nice fine day will certainly be easier. The guys who failed the Tarzan course feel pretty sick, but there's plenty of time [before the parade] to get them through...'

Kelly ND thinks he's just scraped in; he had 40 seconds to go at the 6-foot wall.

'The Tarzan course was very hard. The monkey bars and half

regain were O K . . . the rain didn't bother me that much. It just took longer getting across the ropes.

'My knees are O K . . . I'm still taking the tablets! I'm confident . . . with the last test to go – there's nothing to lose, just go all-out.'

Kelly TJ – the troop Tarzan course record holder – is philosophical about failing:

'I really didn't want to fail it, just get it all over and done with and get me green lid on Wednesday. I'll do it next time – it's a piece of cake . . .

'I don't know what happened. After falling off the monkey bars once, I couldn't get past the second bar. I thought maybe the weather would give me problems there, but other people passed, so I don't want to blame the weather . . .

'I was pissed off big style running back up that hill knowing I'd failed. It's a real pain having to do things again to get your Commando flashes. Some people were really crying after the Tarzan course, failing really knocks your confidence . . . it's just lucky I'm not carrying any injury – like some of the others are.

'The Green Beret is very, very important to me. It's what I've been aiming for all this time. Today was just a little knock-back. I won't worry about it. I'll pick myself up and do it again. If other people can do it, so can I.

'People say that the 30-miler is all right, just like a walk . . . it's only 30 miles!'

Anfield is boosted by having passed the Tarzan assault course with a good time:

'I was fortunate. Last time I'd found the regains hard, but after some tuition from the P T Is, I did much better today. I didn't think about the conditions, but they do make the ropes sticky. It can have advantages as some things slip quicker. You don't notice it as you run round. It has however affected some of the others.

'The 9-miler was hard – specially the first 6 miles. It's because my feet are soft; they tend to rip quite easily. My feet are still sore, so I'll use plenty of tape, then get my head down and get on with it. I'm not letting the ankle stop me getting my Green Beret.'

Lobb failed the Tarzan course on the 6-foot wall, then came off the monkey bars into the water.

'Once you are in and wet, it's hard to get back. On my first go, I fell at the second last rung.

'My knees are sore from the endurance course, but I'm all right. I'm forgetting about it, and concentrating on the 30-miler. I know I can do the Tarzan course. I've done it before in the time. The weather's fucked it up for me. But well done to the lads who've passed it – a really good effort.

> 'The 30-miler will be all right – just limp round. It's only 30 miles . . .'

Recruit Prater was ill on the 9-miler and so failed, and has now failed the Tarzan course. Despite Sunday off, the illness is clearly still with him. After managing the 6-foot wall, he felt very tired then, like the others, couldn't grip the monkey bars, falling into the water: 'You can hear the P T I s shouting at you – which helps. But if you know you've failed, you do wonder at the point of them making you continue.'

Prater isn't letting any of it worry him, or if he is, he's not showing it: 'We'll get lots of scran, and loads of wets down us – then lots of Zs tonight, ready for tomorrow.'

Lieutenant Gillies is far from happy:

> 'It's pretty bad. They should be able to pass in any weather, even though bad weather does make it more difficult. Of the original "dirty dozen", ten passed – which is statistically significant. But the result depressed me, especially the number of back-troopers. We are not a remedial troop but a testing troop, so the back-troopers should do as well as everybody else.
>
> 'It's not that they are new to the troop – they've been here long enough for that not to be a factor. The fact is that they are not fit enough when they come to us.'

Corporal Eric Neilson expected the weather to cause failures, but, because all but two passed the practice run, is not worried. There will in any case be another run later in the week:

> 'You can't order the weather. Kelly will be O K – he's done it in the past, three minutes under the time so . . . I think today, the hanging around, and the tension of it all, plus the weather took it out of them. I'm sure they'll come good on Thursday.'

Corporal MacDonald had expected Lyons to pass, and is disappointed at the weather getting the better of his section:

> 'Bailey will be O K. Bauduin and Farrimond are major disappointments too. I've been a bit let down . . . Five in total have failed, but on the re-runs they'll be O K, although Bailey and Chamberlain will really have to pull it out of the bag . . .'

Corporal Layton didn't expect any of his three failures, but isn't worried about his section's prospects on Dartmoor:

> 'At this stage their endurance fitness is good. With the fast-running rivers, they're going to get wet anyway. But with a week and a half before the pass-out parade to get them through, they'll be all right. The 30-miler isn't a problem.'

Corporal Eric Neilson agrees:

> 'Eight hours is plenty of time to get round the 30-miler, unless the weather completely clags in, or you get somebody who is

injured and everybody slows down to help them. You quite
often get in without pushing the pace, at 7 hours 15 or 7 hours
30.

'It's a fast walk more than anything else, but it does hurt the
feet. Around 20 miles, rifle and webbing begin to dig in a little
bit. It's a case of getting second wind and carrying on. What
tends to let them down is their willpower to finish it.'

That night Lieutenant Gillies briefs the troop on the route for the 30-
miler, from a 20- by 30-foot topographical model of Dartmoor. He
emphasizes the finality of this last test, that '... apart from a bit of
scrambling on the drill square, that's it over ... then off to your units.'

The weather forecast is for rain – so nothing new. They go through
the details of the route, the overview showing each man the enormity
of it. Lieutenant Gillies asks how everybody is – relaxing the troop,
making them laugh. Kelly insists he hasn't got arthritis, at which
Lieutenant Gillies asks how long Kelly spent at medical school. It's
not a put down:

'But I, too, was surprised at the diagnosis. It's very important
for you all to get loads of water and sleep before tomorrow. Eat
heaps of pasta tonight and carry plenty of 'nutty' for the march.

'Carry a jumper tomorrow, but don't wear too much kit.
Start cold, you'll soon warm up.'

They then pack up the chairs, chatting happily. Lieutenant Gillies is a
good and relaxed mixer, drawing them to him easily, his interest warm
and obviously genuine:

'The 30-miler won't be easy for them – but it's the last test. You
don't have to be racing snake – 8 hours is just head down and
bottom up. But it's a long way. Bad weather will make it just a
bit more exciting.

'It would be nice if they were all getting commando flashes at
the end. But they won't – a downer for the re-runs standing by
on the flank. Still, on a decent day they'll pass the Tarzan course.'

That night in the barrack accommodation at the Dartmoor Training
Area's Okehampton Camp, the rotund R N medic checks everybody's
feet, taping them up, treating blisters, fitting pads. They sleep on iron-
framed double bunks one above the other, in a long, very bare shed
of a room. Outside the wind is howling and it is very dark. Neon strip
lights throw a harsh, bright glow, of which those who have already
gone to sleep seem completely unaware, cramming in the Zs even
though everybody else is talking and packing their kit.

Bailey has an infected knee, so the medic checks he isn't running a
temperature. Kelly's knees are checked out too, even though the medic
has no helpful advice about arthritis.

The next morning breakfast is at 0530, then, after cleaning out the
room and the ablutions, the sections make their way in the darkness

to the start beside the camp's bottom gate. The first section leave at 0700, the other two at 15-minute intervals, Corporal Layton's section going first. Sergeant Barnett understands that several of the section will be worrying not only about this 30-miler, but also about passing the Tarzan course – worries they do not need at this time:

> 'Those of you yet to do the Tarzan course – on a nice dry day we'll get you through, no problems. Thirty-miler now, stacks of effort, stacks of surge. If you're hanging out, hang in – get on someone's back if need be, and finish!
>
> 'End of the day, nice warm pasty at the Cross – good news, yeah?'

Corporal Layton sets off, walking briskly into pitch darkness, dawn seeming an age way. On mornings like this, daybreak will be but a gradual and greasy lightening of darkness, into a grey and gloomy day. The wind is still blowing hard but so far at least it isn't raining. They cross the stream using a narrow bridge, then follow the single-track road as it winds up the hill and out of sight.

Turning off the road on to the heather-covered moorland, section commander Dobson doing the map reading, they contour along the sides of hillsides to save height and energy, using ancient footpaths, following stone walls. Dipping down off the wind-blasted high ground, they pass woods, strung out along sheep paths through rough, thorny heather, tiny figures dwarfed by brooding, mist-shrouded hills, picking their way across rocky scree slopes.

Taking care that tired feet do not slip on wet rocks, they cross stone walls, running, half-walking, pushing along to keep up with the men in front. Captain Williams is there, walking with each section in turn, assessing each man as well as monitoring the instructors. Each section carries a safety bergen containing a shelter, sleeping bags, first aid kit, a cooker, brew kit and additional emergency rations – which they take turns to carry.

Jaftha is doing all right, his ungainly gait moving him along within the section, hanging in with everybody else. Anfield is pegging along too. They bunch at a gate beside a stream – an idyllic scene if you didn't have to move so fast. 'Last man shut the gate!' They hop from stone to stone in the stream – taking care not to get wet feet. (Wet boots and socks bring an even greater risk of blisters.) After climbing the side of an enormous hill they contour round to avoid going over the top, descending into wet fields. A small river meanders across this flat land, which they follow, heading towards a small group of houses.

Climbing a stile, they walk down the side of a road before crossing

(*Left*) Sorting out the navigation on the 30-miler; a member of the training team makes sure everybody knows the route.

Corporal MacDonald and his section of 638 Troop start the 30-miler.

a fine stone bridge across a raging river, then march up the road before turning into woods, and a car park where the 4-tonners, ambulance and safety Land Rovers are parked. Hot tea, sausage rolls and pasties are produced from Norwegian containers. Both staff and recruits pass round plastic mugs, ensuring that each gets a good wet and something to eat. 'Make the most of it,' shouts the CSM. They stuff food into mouths, washing it down with gulps of the hot, sweet tea, then after a quick check of their equipment it's off again along the road beside the wood, past a hamlet of houses, before crossing the river again and leaning into yet another steep hill.

Civilization is swiftly left behind on Dartmoor, away from the small roads and isolated groups of houses. The harshness of the terrain defeats even the ubiquitous sheep. The sections move swiftly through Iron Age ruins, sometimes on tracks, other times weaving between lumpy tussock grass. The men at the back have to trot to keep up with those at the front, who've got their heads down, swinging along.

At the 20-mile water stop, the RSM and Deputy Commandant join the troop – for the last telling miles of the march. As they gulp down hot tea, McKenzie gets his map and compass out to check how they are doing. Bauduin is clearly not well, quiet, having to make great efforts to keep up. Kelly's arthritic knee seems OK: 'So far so good, but I could do with some painkillers.'

Like some others on the training team, Corporal Layton admits to feeling a touch unwell himself – the product of not going to bed quite as early as the recruits: 'I felt all right to start with . . .'

It's the RSM's first day in post, and he sets about asking everybody questions, starting with the instructors. Lieutenant Gillies shows Snazel the route on his map: 'We've got just over 9 miles to go – and doing all right.'

The RSM descends on McKenzie. How big a quarter will he need to house his two children when he passes out and his family join him? Leaving the map, McKenzie answers questions: 'I see the wife about once a month . . . I've got two little girls . . . We live in Birmingham . . . I've never been in the mountains before coming to CTC, nor outside Birmingham.'

The RSM declares that 'the average infantryman receives only some six weeks' training, so imagine [compared to a Royal Marine who receives 27] how well trained he must be . . .' and 'The weather today is pretty good . . .'.

Corporal Layton looks at his watch, then gets them all going again. With the distraction of Deputy Commandant and RSM, they forget the safety bergen, leaving it beside one of the Land Rovers. Everybody waits while Nicolson runs back for it.

Following walls, over tors, they flog up hills, Corporal Layton keeping a constant check on Dobson's navigation. He knows how each man is doing, monitoring them all carefully from the rear. After 29 weeks, there's no need for him to say much. They all understand the need to keep going. The recruits themselves have slipped into the mindless overdrive that enables people to move fast while ignoring painful feet, shoulders and their injuries.

It's not however quite so easy to ignore the RSM, who is being jolly with everybody, chatting cheerfully, a veritable clinic of career advice. Having dropped his knapsack into a Land Rover, the RSM is now able to overtake and tuck himself behind people. He asks where they want to be posted, which Careers Office they first went to, the names of the NCOs they spoke to there . . . He asks for potted accounts of the training team NCOs' careers and aspirations . . . as they sweat up the last hills of the final test.

The RSM's on-the-hoof career interviews seem incongruous. But as the miles roll slowly and painfully past, the recruits realize that at long last they are being recognized as fully fledged members of the Royal Marines family. In Lieutenant Gillies's words: 'Apart from a bit of scrambling on the drill square, that's it over. Soon they will be Royal Marine Commandos.'

CHAPTER SEVEN

THE END OF THE ROAD

Since becoming the King's Squad, much water has passed under many bridges, 638 Troop having come a very long way in relatively little time. They first mustered at CTC on a bright spring morning in April 1992, coming together throughout the day, an awkward gathering of hesitant but resolute souls congregating from various parts of the country at Exeter St Davids railway station. Finding the Exmouth train had been easy, a simple matter of spotting the platform where other Royal Marines recruits were gathering, identities obvious from the heavy suitcases, tidy civilian clothes and worried faces. On the short train journey out of Exeter, through Topsham to Lympstone, they'd got talking, some having already met months earlier on Potential Recruits Courses.

The Exmouth line runs beside the River Exe estuary for almost a kilometre, the train slowing as the barbed wire and assault course of CTC's bottom field came into view. The station, right on the edge of the foreshore, has only just enough length for a small shelter and its name sign, the splendid 'Lympstone Commando'.

As fresh consignments of 638 troopers gathered their bags and stepped from the carriages into a bracing tang of ozone and fresh river mud, a reception committee in the immaculate form of a highly polished Corporal Williams was already there, standing to attention, pace stick tucked firmly under his left arm. They'd filed off the train, forming an uncertain crocodile on the platform, watching warily. As the train pulled away, their new lives had begun.

'I'm Corporal Williams, your drill instructor for the next five weeks. When you address me, you stand perfectly still with your

Welcome to Lympstone!

heels together, and you call me Corporal. Is that clear? Welcome to Lympstone!'

They'd filed from the station, past two armed sentries and through the barbed wire barrier into camp, up the steps past the River Exe NAAFI Club, along the main drag to the induction block. During the first two weeks, while learning the absolute basics of military life, they entered a kind of purdah, during which they were taught how to do absolutely everything Royal Marines style, starting off that evening with lessons in washing, shaving and taking a shower – with full and complete demonstrations from Corporal Williams.

The walls of induction block are lined with military posters, slogans, photos of the course and exercises, weapons, military vehicles, naval ships, helicopters . . . an exciting tableau of life in the Corps. Everything is highly regimented – beds, lockers, chairs and tables in parallel lines, floors highly polished, everything spotless. It was soon apparent that 638's first task would be to learn how to achieve this, then do it – for their first inspection early the next morning.

After a comprehensive checking of the documents they'd been told to bring with them, the dark-haired, paternal Corporal Jones carefully prepared them for formal attestation into the Corps, explaining their exact, legal commitment. The system of opt-out periods, and the length of time they had no option but to fulfil were particularly carefully explained. They were told about buying themselves out – at a price that increases as time goes by. The solemnity of this moment was heightened by the care with which the explanations were given.

Haircuts came that day too. After the agricultural use of electric clippers (all the way round and over the top) the troop suddenly looked the same – severely shorn, and knobbly. They also felt the same too, chilly around the ears, but with the beginnings of a collective sense of commitment – through everybody having no hair!

That evening, sitting bolt upright in the induction block's lecture room, fists clenched on thighs, freshly mown heads gleaming in the neon light, 638 Troop came together officially for the first time. The Company Commander of Portsmouth Company, Captain March, promised 30 hard weeks and 'the best and worst of times'.

He'd not been far wrong.

Captain March reminded them that they'd each already passed Potential Recruits Courses, and that therefore each of them had the potential to pass-out as Royal Marines. (In fact, of the 27 who started in April, only 12 would make it as far as the 30-miler.) He'd then described the wide variety of tasks that they might have to do as Royal Marines: as part of the UK's Rapid Reaction Force, plus the more diverse duties that come under the heading of military aid to the civilian powers, like emptying dustbins and fighting fires. He then talked to them about discipline, finishing up with: 'If you don't know how to behave, then pack your bags and leave. We don't want that kind of Marine.'

Each man then stated his name, and they'd repeated the Oath of Allegiance in unison:

'I swear by Almighty God that I will be faithful and bear true
allegiance to Her Majesty Queen Elizabeth the Second, her
heirs and successors, and that I will as in duty bound, honestly
and faithfully defend Her Majesty, her heirs and successors, in
person, Crown and dignity against all enemies, and will observe
and obey all orders of Her Majesty, her heirs and successors,
and of the Generals and Officers set over me. So help me God.'

Captain March: 'Let me be the first to congratulate you on joining the family of the Royal Marines, one of the finest corps of men in the whole world. Congratulations.'

He'd then made five very significant introductions – of each member of the training team, who, wearing 'lovats' service dress, stood up as their names were called out. Although everybody realized the significance of these people, nobody except former Royal Engineer Dobson had properly understood just how much power these five would command over every waking minute (and a good few sleeping moments too) of their lives.

Apart from his litany of hard work and dedication, Captain March also listed the benefits of 'giving all of your time, energies and efforts to becoming a Royal Marine':

'We give you a good career, good wages. We allow you to see the world. We let you work with some of the finest men in the world – the men of 3 Commando Brigade. When you get there you can be justifiably proud of your achievement.

'You'll get the chance to improve your education, and those that can improve their education will have a chance to become commissioned. Those who stay in the Corps will have assistance with housing. We are opening up a wide vista. We are offering you a good career.'

He also gave them a warning:

'As you know, after the first four weeks, you can leave any time you wish during the next three calendar months. This is called the "opt-out".

'Guard against the opt-out.'

He had looked seriously around the room, addressing each one of them:

'The opt-out will seem a short cut, the easy way. It is not. The best way, the correct way, is to keep your shoulder to the wheel. Stay with your troop. Get through training. Get your Green Beret. Get out into the Commando Brigade. Do not be seduced by the easy option of leaving the Corps because it's wet, it's cold and it's miserable. Fight it.

'You sit there now and think, "No, not me. I won't do that". But some of you will – particularly after leave. In training everybody feels crumbly round the edges after Christmas, so we don't let you opt out then. My office would be like the storming of the Winter Palace with people wanting to leave the Corps and go back home to Mum.

'Stick with it. We understand that you're going to be homesick, that everything is going to be strange. All of us in this room started where you're starting, several years ago. You can all get through training, so guard against the opt-out.

'Individually, you'll find it hard, and the only way you're going to achieve passing out is to do it as a team. You'll bond together, and 638 Troop will be one of the best troops here at CTC – won't it?'

They'd been briefed to respond to such questions.

'Yes, Sir!'

'And you'll all mix in and help each other, won't you?'

'Yes, Sir!'

'Because that is the way you'll get through training. By the end of this evening you should know the name and the home town of the guys either side of you. By the end of the week you should know the name and home town of every guy in the troop.

'Every time we look and see a large group going around, we shall say, "There's 638 Troop moving together", because that's how you'll get through – with a feeling of corporate effort.

'I shall be watching your progress through training . . .'

They'd spent 15 weeks in Portsmouth Company doing the basics, plus getting fit – in the gym, then outside on the assault courses. As Captain March had promised, the milestones of their progress were the field exercises: on the Common, 'a place you will come to know and love', starting off with a non-tactical, almost camping weekend, then, after being issued with their personal weapons, a progression of exercises to test their growing military knowledge, fitness and fieldcraft skills . . . Exercises 'Twosome', 'Hunter's Moon' . . .

Then 14 weeks ago they'd moved across to Chatham Company, where the soldiering had become more demanding, skills and tactics as opposed to fitness and the basics, culminating in this 30-miler, the end of a very long journey.

Back on Dartmoor, a short and rather dismal winter afternoon is drawing towards early darkness, with 638 Troop struggling against winds and occasional rain to cover their last four miles. In Corporal MacDonald's section Bauduin is ill, with diarrhoea and vomiting, stumbling miserably in the rear of the section – enduring a grim nightmare. After a long downhill leg from the tor, then a sharp uphill climb, he is some 50 yards behind, ashen-faced but hanging on, each step one yard closer to finishing.

While the rest of the section take a water break, Major Lear goes back down the hill to encourage Bauduin, who is feeling really terrible. Apart from watching him like hawks, there's nothing much the instructors can do – except ensure that he keeps taking water, and keeps going. He reaches the group and has a short break himself, after which he's pushed to the front. They're doing all right for time, but can't hang around for too long. It's clear that Bauduin's not interested in being encouraged, that he'll get on as fast as he is able regardless of what is shouted at him. He's withdrawn into himself, a problem not of motivation to finish, but of dehydration through vomiting, and potential cold exposure. Major Lear is far from happy: 'He will be there at the end – I promise,' he says grimly.

Corporal Ryder (the troop's Drill Instructor) stays back with Bauduin: 'You've got to keep replacing the fluid you are losing.'

All Arms 4/92 emerge from the fog during their 30-miler, a forced march across Dartmoor against the clock.

Corporal Ryder takes a water bottle from his webbing: 'Drink half of it – sip, don't gulp . . . get it down your head, more . . .'

Major Lear looks on anxiously: 'Only three miles to go, don't peg out on me. Up to the front now and let's get going.'

They set off again.

'Keep it closed up tight, gents.'

The sergeant major: 'When we get to the road it's only 2k – hang in, a bit more determination and you're there.'

They run downhill along a very wet sheep track, over soaked peat and water puddles, small streams, tripping on tussocks of heather and grass, people falling over, tripping up those close behind. They push the pace downhill, to make up time. Major Lear orders a two-minute break just before the road, then they run along the side of the road, keeping off the tarmac to avoid problems with traffic.

Major Lear shows them the finish. There is an end to it – although it still seems a very long way to go. Bauduin forces down more compulsory water. They take yet more chocolate bars and apples from their mortar pouches, then off yet again, with two miles to do and 35 minutes, so they're well within the limit. Corporal MacDonald tells them they're doing really well for time.

Finally reaching the tarmac road, they form two ranks and double the last mile, the hard surface absolute murder to their now battered feet. Bauduin stumbles along in the rear of the squad, encouraged by Major Lear and watched carefully by the medic, who has left the ambulance to trot beside the squad. As the road levels off after a gradual convex hill, in the distance they see the coaches parked at a small crossroads. The occasional car comes past, headlights already on, waved through by Corporal Layton at the front.

With 200 yards to go, they break into quick time (marching) and put on cap comforters, adjusting their dress and equipment, marching smartly.

'Heads up now, on parade.'

Left wheel into the car park, then a smart 'Halt!' and it's all over – except for the award of Commando flashes to those who've passed all the tests. Bauduin goes to the ambulance to be examined, and everybody else gets stuck into a tea urn and tray of pies and sticky buns. Jaftha arrives on his own, accompanied by Sergeant Barnett. His legs are moving at strange angles, but he's made it within the time.

'Someone get him a hot wet. Take his kit off him, and walk him round.'

Everybody is now in, all within the 8-hour time limit, so everybody has passed.

'Get your dry clothes on and get smartened up. The next item on the agenda is the presentation of Commando flashes.'

Bauduin's section did it in 7 hours 35 minutes. Corporal Mac-Donald thinks it a touch too fast:

'If you've got 8 hours, use the 8 hours.'

Corporal Layton, eating restorative pies and drinking large quantities of tea to assuage the effects of his late night, disagrees: 'No, do it as fast as you can!'

The training team surround Bauduin who has emerged from the ambulance. They say he can go back and do the last 10 miles if he wants – eliciting the first smile of the day from him.

Anfield obtained painkillers from the MA earlier in the march, but was all right. His legs and feet are very, very tired, but he feels it was mentally rather than physically hard: 'The hardest thing I've ever done in my life.'

Nield agrees: 'It were a lot harder than I expected – but I did enjoy the last three miles. I helped Jaftha which kept me going a bit. I'm very happy to have cracked it – after 19 months. Might even have a pint in the NAAFI tonight!'

Having finished, there are mixed reactions from the troop. Farrimond faces a re-run of the Tarzan course on Thursday: 'The

30-miler was easier than I'd thought – but then again it was very hard – very hard indeed.'

McKenzie: 'It's much harder than I'd thought – it wears you down.'
Glennon: 'I quite enjoyed it today. It was quite easy really.'
Lieutenant Gillies:

> 'It's not the hardest test, but it's just long – interminably long.
> It drags on and on. It's a good Commando Test – with a strong
> spiritual element to it.
>
> 'We've achieved a hundred per cent result, so as they say in
> football, the lads done well!'

They parade in the rain and gathering darkness by the roadside, headlamped cars sweeping past, at the end of a working day. Major Lear hands each his commando flashes and congratulates them, the Tarzan course failures looking on from the side. He asks them what they found hardest during the course, and what they found easiest. Spink reckons the Tarzan course the hardest of all, along with the Commando Test period: 'Induction was easy – just ironing, Sir!'

Young Wilson, however, reckons induction week and the ironing to have been the hardest. After nine months in Hunter Troop suffering from shin injuries and a fractured foot, Gault is just happy to have finished. Potts declares Exercise Twosome to have been the hardest – having (due possibly to some misdemeanour) been made to go for what he describes as 'a little walk'. Major Lear congratulates them all:

> 'With a 60 mph wind blowing the small ones over, you've all
> done very well today – although it's better than summer when
> you can drop like flies from the heat.
>
> 'Some of you have been in Hunter Troop for a long time.
> With around 50 per cent new faces, it makes 638 a very different
> troop to the normal. Well done!'

Now that the hard work is over, while 638 Troop, the King's Squad, prepare for their pass-out parade, a good deal of paper work must be done behind the scenes, to determine who will receive the various course prizes, the most important of which is the King's Badge. Throughout their various meetings, the training team have been mulling this over, and have put forward to Major Lear a list of people they think worthy of consideration for the King's Badge: Dobson, Spink and Nicolson. Major Lear is a King's Badge holder himself:

> 'I didn't realize what it was all about until the end of my course.
> I was competing with a former corporal in the Royal Green
> Jackets, then broke my ankle, recovered, then won the award in
> another troop.
>
> 'Whoever wins a King's Badge could well end up sitting in
> my chair some day – provided he has the necessary academic
> qualifications to become an officer. It's a very good first step up
> that ladder.'

After writing a Commando Training Wing assessment of each candidate, Major Lear forwards an enormous pile of paperwork to the board sergeant major, CSM Husband. That weekend the three board members, Major Hutchings, Lieutenant Jones and CSM Husband, make an initial assessment of the candidates from the plethora of reports written during their time at CTC, placing each in a provisional order of merit. By Monday, they agree that Spink is in the lead, followed by Dobson then Nicolson. In theory, provided Spink meets certain criteria, he will be awarded the King's Badge – but it doesn't always work out that way.

The Diamonds also go before the board to be assessed for seniority; in the Royal Navy, a few days can make a tremendous difference to a man's career opportunities. A good performance before the board can gain notional 'days' of service, and consideration for promotion ahead of their peers.

The men concerned are well briefed. Dobson, Nicolson and Spink are told what to expect by the Commando Training Wing CSM. He advises them to revise everything they have been taught. So while the rest of 638 Troop are relaxing, they spend the weekend poring over textbooks and lecture notes. It is serious stuff, vital for their careers, a golden opportunity to get the very best of flying starts in a very competitive race.

The final hurdle of the King's Badge board is the inspection and interview, a traditional and nerve-racking affair. Proceedings start with board chairman Major Hutchings inspecting the candidates in best blues. If a man isn't absolutely immaculate, he is unlikely to be given further serious consideration. Nicolson is told: 'One day you'll grow into that jacket.'

Dobson is wearing his Northern Ireland medal. McKenzie, Farrimond, Bauduin and Lobb stand in the rear rank, to win seniority. McKenzie is wearing pullover and lovat trousers, his blues being altered by the tailor, and is congratulated by Major Hutchings for taking trouble with his turnout.

The board members then convene in the attestation room, sitting in line behind a long table, facing the door. A single chair is placed in the centre of the room. They confirm the order of their grading – Spink, Dobson then Nicolson.

Spink stands to attention outside the door and is ushered in by Sergeant Major Husband. Major Hutchings takes over: 'Sit down and try to relax. You should enjoy this as much as we do.'

Spink is asked to talk about himself for a few minutes. He gives details of dates and schooling: at Keighley in Yorkshire, was in the Army Cadet Corps for several years as a corporal, competed at Bisley for his county, took a Duke of Edinburgh's Silver Award. His father was an engineer, his mother works, and his brother is at home after a work injury. Major Hutchings congratulates him on being a marksman.

CSM Husband then asks a set of basic military questions, on camouflage, the aims of patrolling, the names of the groupings in a linear ambush, and the principles of good shooting – which Spink answers perfectly. As usual, he is unflappable, answering detailed questions about subjects as diverse as section battle drills and nuclear, chemical and biological warfare; on the details of military organizations, and even the reason for the colour yellow on the Royal Marines flag (it was actually 'old gold', the colour of the facings of the uniforms worn by the Lord High Admiral's Regiment). He gets one thing wrong; the King's Badge is worn on the left upper arm and not on the shoulder, as a glance at CSM Husband's sleeve would have told him.

Major Hutchings then leads a general conversation; which was the best bit of training? On the tor doing cliff-climbing, and the bad weather on the Final Exercise was the worst. On careers in the Royal Marines. After a couple of years Spink sees himself going for a Junior Command Course and some qualifications – and a trade. He doesn't know if he's a career man or not. The interview is over; he stands up, salutes and leaves.

After Spink has left the room, they rate him: 'Quiet, with a streak of aggression under the surface – competent, mature, and knows his stuff. Sensible, level-headed.'

They agree formally that he's got all the qualities that a King's Badgeman must have.

Next is Dobson. Twenty-seven years old, Sunderland-born, he got no qualifications at school because he knew he was joining the Army and thus wasn't interested – which he has regretted ever since. Did quite a lot of canoeing and joined the Army Cadet Corps. He took a bronze Duke of Edinburgh's Award and was a corporal in the Army Cadets. He then joined the Royal Engineers, serving in Osnabrook and Iserlohn in Germany and Canada, then left at the seven-year point having completed a Northern Ireland tour – as a corporal.

By contrast with Spink, Dobson is a bit hesitant, using lots of 'Sirs', needing prompting from Major Hutchings. He couldn't settle into civilian life as a lorry driver, so decided to come back in, but the REs couldn't take him back because of Army cutbacks.

Dobson is trying to say the right things, and his two-minute talk about himself gets a bit laboured. During the military questions (which are exactly the same for each candidate), he needs prompting – not because he doesn't know the answers but because of nerves. Interview over, he leaves the room and they discuss his performance.

CSM Husband thought that given his background he'd have been less overawed by the board, but that he's clearly the right man in the right place. He's not thought to be as sharp as Spink, who's got the edge. It's clear that they are interviewing the candidates in order of merit, to confirm (or amend) that order.

Nicolson comes in and sits down. He left school at 16 and worked in his father's sports shop on the Isle of Skye. However, he wanted to do something more exciting ... He dries up a bit and has to be prompted. He does however look at where the CSM wears his King's Badge before answering that particular question. He's not sure that he enjoyed the phyzz, or being cold and wet, but has made a lot of really good friends. They rate him third, and note that he's had problems with military knowledge throughout the course. Spink is still top dog, and they call him back in. Major Hutchings breaks the news to him, and shakes his hand. Spink seems unmoved – as ever the unflappable man.

CSM Husband then follows Spink out of the room and in the corridor shakes his hand. He then quickly tells the other two what the board thought of them, before getting them before the board again to discuss their futures. They will all be made up to Marine First Class, which entails five months' seniority. Corporal MacDonald shakes Spink's hand, then Dobson and Nicolson shake hands too. Spink is clearly very pleased, but his well-balanced demeanour isn't affected. Dobson then asks the CSM if the board knows he is already a Marine First Class (by virtue of having been a corporal in the Army) and so has already got five months' seniority.

'Good point,' says the CSM. 'Looks like you've got an extra five months, but don't believe it until you see it in writing – you clever sod! But well done!'

Spink then has his photograph taken.

The King's Squad Pass-Out Parade is 638 Troop's final hurdle. The parade itself is straightforward: marching on behind the Royal Marines Band to await the arrival of the inspecting officer, presenting arms to him, being inspected and addressed by him, then marching past in slow and quick time before a leisurely lunch with mums, dads, wives and girlfriends.

However, in the middle of this, drill instructor Corporal Ryder has inserted a drill display, arms drill combined with what can only be described as 'formation display team' marching. Once started, there are no words of command, just John Williams's 'Fanfare to the Common Man' music to keep it all together, finishing with a dramatic climax and volley of rifle fire.

The display is fraught with opportunities for disaster. The day before the parade, on the Adjutant's rehearsal, using a tape recording of the Royal Marines Band playing the music, things do not go well. It's early morning with a bright, watery sun low on the horizon.

638 Troop, The King's Squad. (*Above*) during final rehearsal for their Pass-Out Parade. (*Right*) The Adjutant closely supervises as Recruit Spink practices receiving the King's Badge, with Sergeant Barnett and First Drill looking on from the left.

Lieutenant Gillies arrives to run through it with them. The atmosphere is very much end of term, which one can't help thinking will have to change if the parade is to be sharp enough. They do a complete run-through before a formal rehearsal for the Adjutant.

The Adjutant arrives, and after the drill display goes spare at the poor standard of their arms drill (which is far from slick and coordinated), commenting that it is 'Arse!' Corporal Ryder quietly defends 638 Troop, offering explanations which soon begin to sound like plati-tudes. The Adjutant and First Drill (the Warrant Officer Class One in charge of all parade ground matters throughout the Royal Marines) are unimpressed. After Corporal Ryder accepts that their criticisms are well founded, they all set about putting things right.

Although their method involves 'gingering up' 638 Troop, gal-vanizing them into extra sharpness and precision, the attitude of both the Adjutant and First Drill is very much that of getting it right so that the blokes will look good in front of families and friends – as opposed to insisting upon military perfection for its own rather esoteric purpose. Being a Royal Marine involves looking the part, whether in combat or on the parade ground. With the involvement of First Drill and the Adjutant, a new urgency takes over the troop.

Corporal Ryder: 'This is it, the last chance. *Faux pas* now and that's it.'

638 Troop go through their drill display routine again and again until the allotted time on the parade ground is up. The Adjutant orders an extra parade, early the next morning before their rehearsal proper with the Royal Marines Band. Half measures simply do not exist here; their drill will be either absolutely perfect, or 'Arse' – a disaster which will not be allowed to happen.

Lieutenant Gillies, who must lead 638 Troop throughout the parade, is having his own problems – with swinging his arms. The professional life of a Royal Marines officer is mostly spent in the field, yet at CTC parade-ground duties are a necessary evil – particularly because any and every error by members of the staff costs the perpetrator a bottle of port, which everybody else consumes. A port-tinted spotlight inevitably falls upon the troop commander, although the Adjutant and even First Drill have been known to purchase bottles.

The Adjutant has noticed that while marching carrying his sword, Lieutenant Gillies's other arm (the left), steadily but inexorably slips out of synchronization with his legs. After 30 or so paces, his left arm is moving in unison with his left leg – like a clockwork soldier gone wrong. Both the Adjutant and First Drill watch critically while Lieutenant Gillies marches up and down. Under their close and expert scrutiny, additional faults emerge: the offending arm is not straight enough, and the sword arm has a slight tendency to droop.

So while 638 Troop repeat their display routine, their troop commander is marching up and down trying to sort out his brain-to-body interface, while at the same time memorizing the orders he must shout on the morrow. Having returned only recently to military duties after two years of international ski-biathlon, Lieutenant Gillies had expected this first parade to be difficult – but reckoned without the additional worry of 'lazy arms'. So even though the hard work is supposed to be over, the pressure is yet again upon 638 Troop, the King's Squad, to deliver the goods.

All Arms 4/92, however, are still struggling through their Commando Tests. Doing the endurance course, the ever-cheerful Lance Corporal Thomson ripped his boots, then on the eve of the 9-miler ripped his shoulder. A REME craftsman, being aged 29 makes him more prone to injury than the younger men. He's been struggling, and the training team were pessimistic about his chances of getting even this far, predicting that he would fail the 9-mile speed march. He's taking painkillers and hoping for the best, particularly on the 30-miler. Being small, he finds many of the Tarzan course obstacles difficult, particularly walking across the jacob's ladder, where he has great problems reaching the upper ropes to support himself as he walks the horizontal rope ladder. To make up lost time, he has to go faster on the rest of the course — which apart from the 6-foot wall, he manages well.

'The worst thing about this course is once you pass something, you feel relieved for only a few minutes, before worrying about the next thing.'

The All Arms Course have their accommodation and offices in the former sickbay, below the Officers' Mess, well out of the way of the rest of camp — which particularly suits the instructors, who value their independence. Unfortunately, the sickbay poltergeist has struck, rendering eight of 4/92's 15 survivors ill with diarrhoea and vomiting. The sickbay has told them to starve themselves until they get rid of it — perfectly sound medically, but this is the day before the 30-miler. Captain Pritchard is most unhappy:

'I'll speak with sickbay, and give you all a time to report up there. Even without being ill, you need at least 10 or 15 pints of water in you today, to prevent getting dehydrated tomorrow. You'll need some pills to bung you up, so you can eat like horses.'

With the vague feeling that perhaps they are tempting providence, before the eight attend sickbay the whole course double across to the stores complex and draw their Green Berets.

Meanwhile, across on the Tarzan course, Private Thomas RAPC and REME's Lance Corporal Heaps, having failed their Tarzan course test, are having a re-run, along with Recruit Prater from 638 Troop (who failed a re-run that morning) and an injured Royal Marines young officer, Second Lieutenant Trickett. It's a nice dry day and everything goes smoothly. The whole world is there urging them on. Prater makes it with five seconds to spare.

'Why couldn't you have done that the first time, rather than the 15th!' shouts Corporal Eric Neilson from the bottom of the 30-foot wall. 'Get yourself sorted out. I'll have a beard by the time you get down those steps.'

Prater is clearly knackered. 'Fucking hell!' is all he can say between gasps as he gets back down to the ground. 'I thought I'd had it.'

One of Prater's mates from 638 Troop, dressed in parade uniform, comes down the hill during a break from drill rehearsals on the parade ground above, and shakes his hand. They walk off together, Prater very relieved.

Private Thomas and Lance Corporal Heaps scrape in too, as does

Second Lieutenant Trickett. They double off for some very serious eating and water drinking, in preparation for their 30-miler tomorrow.

Very early the next morning, after once more staying the night at Okehampton Camp, 4/92 start the 30-miler in the dark, setting compass bearings, leaving the road, vanishing into thick mist. The race is on. It grows light, they make their way jumping precariously and carefully across fast-flowing streams, jogging along sheep tracks. The instructors let them get on with it – as opposed to actually running with each squad as they do with the recruits.

Each section is nevertheless checked at the water stops. Sapper Xavier has found a map – which nobody owns up to having lost. Second Lieutenant Maddison has a painful foot – a hot spot that will develop into a blister, which requires taping up. He was nearly binned during the first week because of a foot injury. He washes a couple of painkillers down his throat, giving two to Sapper Rockey, who also has foot problems. They get loads of the quartermaster's wets down their throats, while they're still available.

Captain Pritchard is upset about poor map reading, which is putting them behind schedule: 'It's a crock so far – get it sorted out.'

Lance Corporal Heaps looks a bit vacant, Lieutenant Linderman is clearly out of his element but trying hard, while Sapper Xavier looks very strong, getting a grip like an NCO whenever a grip is needed. Lance Corporal Thomson looks good too.

They have to run to make up for lost time. Corporal Miles runs with them on this leg to ensure they don't go wrong again. They hit the tea stop in the woods and wolf down hot pasties, passing round mugs of hot sweet tea. CTC's commandant, Colonel Mike Taffinder, is running with them. He's clearly been following Sergeant Major Dobson's progress: 'Well Sergeant Major, remember I told you that the Commando Course is more mental than physical – what do you think?'

Sergeant Major Dobson seems to agree: 'Yes. But put it another way, warrant officers can't wrap – it's as simple as that!'

In fact Sergeant Major Dobson is still suffering pain in his ankle: 'It isn't easy but I'm using painkillers. It's not a stroll – but it's just the last thing...'

He hands the safety bergen over to Second Lieutenant Perkins. It's clear that in the stress of this last big effort some tempers are becoming a little frayed. He smiles ruefully: 'A couple of guys got a bit emotional, so I've had to get a grip. They thought they could just womble along which we can't – we've got to push on. Everybody's teddy bears are flying around a bit!'

Second Lieutenant Perkins gives the section a quick brief on the route: a couple of miles of hard work over a big hill, then a very long downhill flog. They've got around 90 minutes left to complete the remainder of the route. They scurry off up the track, through a gate and up on to open moor, tiny figures silhouetted against the sky. Then finally, after a long descent from a ridgeline and along a spur, they hit a small wood and a metal gate on to a lane.

The last mile or so is along a rough, rocky lane with solid, high sides, under scraggy trees. They run, treading carefully, unwilling to turn an ankle at this late stage. For the last mile they form two orderly ranks and run in step, joined by various people who have come from the units to which the men are to be posted – a traditional welcoming into the Commando Brigade. The last half-mile seems to last for ages. They see the 4-tonners in the distance and the pace quickens slightly. There's quite a crowd waiting. Colonel Taffinder has run on ahead of them, and claps each section as they arrive, giving each man a hearty 'Well done!' The spectators clap too.

'Seven hours 36 minutes!' announces Sergeant Swayne.

Lance Corporal Heaps and Sapper Xavier embrace each other. Sergeant Major Dobson's group make it in seven hours and 35 minutes. They collect their Green Berets from a baker's tray in the back of the 4-tonner. Referring to his cap comforter, Sapper Khanlarian says, 'You know what you can do with this now, don't you? Yeah, poke it!' The whole course then parade in a very muddy sheep field for the official presentation. No ceremony here! It's a bit like a school sports prizegiving, only in freezing rain with everybody limping. They form three ranks in the centre of the field, instructors in the rear rank.

Some of them have selected berets a size too small, which have shrunk so at the critical moment they can't get them on. Following the Commandant down the line, Captain Pritchard whips out his claspknife and does some instant tailoring – leaving Lance Corporal Hodgson (a cook going to the artillery regiment 29 Commando) aghast as his coveted Green Beret is slashed before he even gets to wear it. Khanlarian throws his cap comforter over his shoulder as he is presented with his beret. Sapper Xavier is particularly pleased; he is a postman, one of the few Postal and Courier Unit people to pass the Commando Course. Xavier is walking particularly stiffly, having had problems with his knees: 'It was the hardest thing in my life.'

Despite the worrying chest infection that hospitalized him on Final Exercise, Private Thomas has made it:

> 'Heaps had some trouble so I helped him along, and kept eating and drinking. You've got to keep eating and it boosts you back. You have to help each other along, both the older and the younger ones. I couldn't believe it was all over at the end!
>
> 'I'm not a different person, although I will be respected more for having a Green Beret, and feel a bit more at home in a Commando unit.'

Sapper Roach, like Khanlarian, is a Royal Engineer diver, so is well used

Corporal Hutcheon and Private Dredge wearing their Green Berets for the first time.

to being cold, wet and messed around, and declares that he will feel much better once he's 'on the wagon and on the way home'. Lieutenant Linderman found the 30-miler harder than he'd thought it could be:

> 'It went on for a very long time – longer than you'd think. The marching on the Final Ex was very hard too – probably the hardest. We thought we weren't going to make it – but then we realized we'd broken the back of it, and the 30-miler would be the final bit which we could all pass.'

Corporal Thomson:

> 'I'll never forget the course . . . very hard. You remember all the good points – the guys, and team work unlike anything you ever get in the Army, so strong it's unbelievable. Remembering the bad bits, although they are hard to remember now, will be good in future when things get cold and wet, knowing you've done it before. Things can't ever be worse. I know a lot more about myself now – having done more than I'd ever thought I was capable of doing.'

Sergeant Major Dobson:

> 'I thought I was off the course after injuring myself during the abseiling – it was so painful. With the help of pills I've been able to get through. You get to the stage where you'll do anything rather than go off the course, so you've got to be careful . . .
>
> 'Failure would have been terrible, but finishing is a bit of an anti-climax. I just want to get on with my job now.'

Before they disperse, Colonel Taffinder addresses them:

> 'Remember the high standards you have seen and experienced

The smiles of Sergeant Major Dobson and Lance Corporal Heaps show quiet pride in their achievement.

here at CTC. I ask you not to accept anything less in the future. The Green Beret is nothing to do with machismo or Captain Hurricane, but to do with that thing inside your heads that says "I will not give up". You know what that means, because you felt it today.

'Finally as new members of the Royal Marines club, remember we are a very proud organization and never, ever let us down. I'm sure you won't – but always remember what I've said.'

Next morning, enlivened by mist, cold morning air and the early start, braced by the sheer volume and beat of the Royal Marines Band, 638 Troop, the King's Squad, are doing very much better on the parade ground. First Drill then throws a spanner into the works, announcing a change to the parade routine; 638 Troop will have to march through the centre of the band. First Drill predicts: 'There will probably be the most almighty cock-up first time!'

Their drill display, however, continues to go badly. As the final and rather ragged volley rings out, First Drill asks Corporal Ryder: 'Have you got lots more rounds?'

The Adjutant advances on the front rank, coming up very close to their impassive faces, pointing his stick millimetres from the end of Sullivan's nose and bellowing: 'You are making more mistakes than everybody else put together. Sort yourself out!'

Corporal Ryder emphasizes the importance of following the band's drum beat: 'All you've got to remember is that the world's most expensive boogie box is playing behind you, and concentrate solely on the bass drummer – who by the time this is over will have muscles like Garth. Hit it in time with the bass drum . . .'

They do the display again. First Drill and the Adjutant watch like hawks. On the final volley, the Adjutant winces and looks away. Corporal Ryder orders 'Shoulder arms'. The Adjutant stalks forward, to find Recruit Head's magazine has fallen to pieces. While they fix it, First Drill takes them through the tricky manoeuvre of marching through the band.

However, in the end the Adjutant's final rehearsal is judged to have gone very much better, due to all their extra practice that morning. They then go through the whole thing over again inside the echoing drill shed – just in case it rains – using a different format, dodging the pillars, keeping in step with the echoes of the band.

Meanwhile, a traffic jam is developing outside camp. Parade guests are arriving, parking their cars, being checked through Security. A steady crocodile of family, friends, wives and girlfriends walk down from the Guard Room towards the River Exe and the Falklands Hall, dressed smartly as if for a wedding, Sunday hats in danger of being whipped away by the cold wind, overcoats a sensible formality. Some younger brothers are wearing their best trainers and baseball caps, looking (and no doubt feeling) a touch incongruous amid the crisply smart formality of the occasion.

Members of the Guard request everybody to move away from the main gate, on to the footpath. An exhausted figure, soaking wet and covered with mud, squelches through wearing full webbing, rifle slung over his shoulder. The guests step backwards out of his path, staring open-mouthed as more such figures make their painful way from the endurance course into camp, down the hill towards the 30-metre range. Even the trainer-shod younger brothers are silenced, suddenly realizing that these figures are the reality of CTC, its true purpose, and that the parade is by comparison a sideshow for their benefit.

This whole day belongs to 638 Troop, the King's Squad, to show families and friends around CTC, and to introduce them to the training staff, so that by the end everybody feels somehow a part of the Royal Marines. The first event is the Green Beret presentation, an unashamedly theatrical performance in the Falklands Hall. In a long, folksy ceremony the guests are introduced to each of 638's instructors, and see their men receive Green Berets, plus the various awards. Amusing anecdotes from the course are recounted by an avuncular Major Lear who, by the time they have coffee and walk across the parade ground, has made everybody feel very much at home.

Then the great event itself, the King's Squad Pass-Out Parade, with the First Sea Lord taking the salute. While the guests take their seats in the stands, 638 Troop are lined up on the road behind the drill shed, brushing each other down and talking quietly. Lieutenant Gillies stands with them. He appears to have put aside worries about marching, remembering the orders he must shout – and the price of port – seeming calm, relaxed and confident.

The Royal Marines Band are lined up too, shuffling through their sheets of music, unconcerned stagers with countless King's Squad parades behind them. Watery sunshine has broken through the earlier haze of River Exe mist, glinting brightly from the all-silver instruments of the band. The bass drummer's splendid tiger skin apron makes him look like a Zulu chief, a wonderful incongruity among immaculate, dark blue uniformity. The band's Director of Music arrives, unconsciously flexing his conductor's baton like a schoolmaster's miniature cane. The Bandmaster growls a word of command, transforming the gymnasium car park into the parade square annexe.

638 Troop are in three ranks, their troop commander out in front. Glancing at his wristwatch for the umpteenth time, with a smile of reassurance to the men behind, Lieutenant Gillies gives his first word of command. The troop come smartly to attention. Pitching his voice for the benefit of the band, Lieutenant Gillies orders: 'The King's Squad, by the right, quick march!'

638 Troop, The King's Squad in Open Order awaiting the First Sea Lord's inspection during their Pass-Out Parade. First Drill stands to the right.

638 Troop, The King's Squad – the survivors and the Training Team.
1 Prater, **2** Kelly TJ, **3** Lyons, **4** Hilton, **5** Bauduin, **6** Wilson, **7** McKenzie,
8 Glennon, **9** Spink, **10** Kelly ND, **11** Hamilton, **12** Gault, **13** Lobb,
14 Dobson, **15** Tobin, **16** Nicolson, **17** Smith, **18** Snazel, **19** Potts, **20** Pyott,
21 Farrimond, **22** Wheatley, **23** Anfield, **24** Head, **25** Lee, **26** Sullivan,
27 Bailey, **28** Nield, **29** Chamberlain, **30** Schembri.
(Training Team) **31** Cpl Ryder DL, **32** Cpl Bateman PW, **33** Sgt Barnett PW
(Tp Sgt), **34** Lt Gillies (Tp Officer), **35** Cpl Layton PW, **36** Cpl MacDonald,
37 Cpl Nielson PTI.

On his word, the Royal Marines Band strike up 'Her Majesties Jollies' and march forward onto the parade ground, creating the most enormous sense of instant swagger in spectators as well as among the troop. Old parade-ground maxims flash through their minds, the most useful being 'Right or wrong, stand still!' In other words, if you've made a mistake, don't worry, just stand firm and hope nobody has noticed. If you show enough brass-necked confidence, the chances are that nobody will. Whatever happens, they must do their best and get it right.

As the troop come round the corner of the drill shed, the guests crane their necks, hoping to identify their man. The troop wheel left and halt facing the stands, the band in three ranks behind, Lieutenant Gillies out in front. As the last cymbal crash fades across the estuary, they settle to await the arrival of the Adjutant and First Drill, the Deputy Commandant and his wife, then the commandant and inspecting officer and their wives. Seagulls wheel noisily overhead in a gentle but nevertheless bracing wind.

Lieutenant Gillies has stood the parade 'at ease', and stands with his sword resting on the tarmac in front of him, point downward. It's always tempting under these circumstances to rest the weight of your hands on the pommel of your sword. However, the point then slowly sinks into the tarmac. Swords can become inextricably stuck or, after undignified pulling, emerge plus a large lump of bitumen which can then not be removed, making sword drill embarrassing, difficult, ridiculous and – given the price of port – expensive.

The Adjutant emerges from the glass doors of the Officers' Mess and strides down the hill, spurs jingling – Lieutenant Gillies's signal to bring the parade to attention. The crowd stirs expectantly. First Drill comes over to meet the Adjutant, and they make their way to stand beside the saluting dais. Next the Deputy Commandant, escorting First Sea Lord's wife, the Commandant's wife and his own wife, stroll down the hill, to ringside seats.

First Sea Lord is not a man to keep people waiting for the sake of it. After a brief interval, he too emerges from the officers' mess, escorted by CTC's Commandant, Colonel Mike Taffinder. They walk briskly down the short hill to the saluting dais, taking their places. As First Sea Lord moves forward to the saluting position, Lieutenant Gillies orders 'General Salute'. The band strikes up 'Rule Britannia', the King's Squad present arms with a crash of rifle butts against forearms, and in graceful contrast their troop commander sweeps his sword up and down, bringing the pommel to his lips in salutation.

Despite being off to a good start, nobody is going to feel anything like comfortable until the drill display is over. First Sea Lord then steps out with the Commandant, Adjutant and Major Lear to inspect. He makes a point of talking with every man, congratulating them on their achievement, welcoming them to the Royal Navy. In his wake, the Adjutant has the occasional word, his attitude now one of total support, the harsh words of yesterday forgotten.

Time has come for the drill display. As Corporal Ryder takes over, Lieutenant Gillies steps off the parade ground, to become the most anxious of spectators. Everybody takes a deep breath, the band begins Williams's 'Olympic Fanfare and Theme', and 638 Troop are off.

Their display is a combination of marching and arms drill, both done at the same time. They split like a star into four groups, marching away from the centre, re-forming and marching through each other while performing various arms drill movements. As they discovered yesterday, the key to success is listening to the bass drummer's beat; the Zulu chieftain has put his drum on to the ground in order to hit it even harder. The display ends with the troop in three ranks facing the stands. As the music comes to its gradual climax, they raise their rifles to the sky, in the instant of the very last note fading away firing a sudden volley that echoes across camp, seagulls skidding and complaining with its shock.

A microphone is brought forward, and First Sea Lord addresses the troop, speaking to them, but also to their guests, making it clear how important 638 Troop are to the Royal Marines, the Royal Navy and the defence of the realm. When the man at the very top of the Navy speaks in such terms, everybody listens.

The rest as they say is a piece of cake: a march forward (an 'advance in review order') – 14 paces of the 'British Grenadiers' then halt. The Adjutant comes on riding his horse, a steady old trooper that behaves perfectly well provided the parade goes as it should and nobody wears red anywhere near him. The crime of being thrown could only be assuaged through the purchase of pipes rather than bottles of port, so the Adjutant is on his mettle.

They march past in slow and quick time, horse leading, band playing, sun shining. Some of the families become over-excited, and doubtless led by the baseball-hatted younger brothers shout out, trying to catch the eye of their 'boys' during the march past. They get absolutely no reaction. The King's Squad are not going to let themselves down at this late stage – not for anybody.

Finally they march off, to the smiles and congratulations of everybody, vanishing round the corner and past the drill shed. The band halts out of sight on the car park outside the gym, their final flourish echoing cheerfully across the estuary. Beside the ammunition compound, the engine of First Sea Lord's helicopter flashes up to rush him back to London for an important meeting. However, before he makes his farewells, he stops to talk with 638's training team, who have been standing to attention behind the podium throughout the parade.

Corporal Eric Neilson, having stood throughout the entire parade wearing only his flimsy PT instructor's rig, looks a touch pinched with cold. The others, smart in their full blues uniforms topped with white 'ice-cream man' peaked hats, look somehow younger than they seemed throughout training. Perhaps it's because they are now wearing exactly the same uniforms as 638 Troop – and we realize that underneath their manifest training and expertise, the teachers are the same age as at least some of their pupils.

First Sea Lord makes his farewells, and the assembled gaggle of parents, friends and family gather their belongings for the stroll back through camp to lunch. A troop of blue-bereted Nods are brought to attention and marched off, having been shown the final moments of the process they are just starting. The atmosphere is light-hearted and informal – until a single rifle shot echoes from the drill shed, followed closely by the guttural shouts of First Drill: 'Put that weapon into a plastic bag as evidence, and get it to the armoury for examination now!'

Firing any weapon accidentally is known in the Services as a 'negligent discharge'. Many people have been seriously injured, even killed, in such accidents, which are always the result of individuals failing to carry out correct weapon handling drills. 'NDs' are therefore serious offences, whether the ammunition used is blank or real.

The unfortunate perpetrator is frog-marched past the parents and families, a graphic reminder of what it means to be a trained soldier – and no longer a recruit. On concluding the parade, every member of 638 Troop achieves the status of fully trained Royal Marine. The tremendous cachet of that achievement carries with it an equally great responsibility for all their actions. A practical manifestation of this is about to be visited upon this individual (who will remain nameless), with the probable fine of a month's wages.

Having handed their weapons into the armoury and carried their number one dress hatboxes back to the accommodation, the King's Squad are now free to enjoy the rest of the day with their guests. Permitted to wear Green Berets with their blues on this one special day, they walk proudly round camp, showing their families the sights, telling them the stories. Lunch is preceded by quite a lot of drinks in the NAAFI.

While everybody else leaves their hats in the cloakroom, 638 continue to wear their Green Berets. Snazel's family tease him about his hair – or lack of it – and he resists their attempts to take his beret off. They wouldn't do that if they knew how important it was to him, and what he'd had to do to earn it. McKenzie's family have broken down en route, their hired minibus having packed up somewhere along the M5. Corporal Layton is concerned that McKenzie will have nobody to sit with at lunch and invites him to come and sit with the instructors. (In fact McKenzie's parents were later sent a video recording of the day by CTCRM, so at least they did 'see' the green beret presentation and passing out parade.)

Dimitri Bauduin is drinking pints, so has obviously recovered from the diarrhoea and vomiting. The training staff are installed in the centre of the room, chatting up parents, buying and accepting drinks, and congratulating each of the troop as they pass by towards the bar. Mrs Dobson gives Bob Dobson a big kiss. Still in uniform, he can't resist wiping off the lipstick. He's gagging for a drink, and as he pushes through to the bar, his wife hanging onto his arm, the training staff each shake his hand.

Once this lunch party finishes, 638 Troop disperse to the four corners of the Royal Marine world, never again to be together – unless they decide to have a reunion. Although a very happy moment, it's tinged with the sadness of something important and sustaining ending for ever.

Away from all the relief and happiness of the NAAFI bar, Recruit Jaftha is packing his kit prior to moving from B block back up the road into Hunter Troop – yet again. A new set of faces to get to know, more weeks and months of gym in the morning, map reading in the afternoon – with still that terrifying barrier of the Tarzan course chasm to overcome.

Depressing it may be, but having come so far, Jaftha is not about to give up now.

EPILOGUE

After Christmas leave 1993, many members of both 638 Troop and All Arms 4/92 found themselves drawing arctic warfare equipment and preparing for three months A&MWT training in Norway. As this has been a regular annual commitment for more than 20 years, 3 Commando Brigade have become Britain's arctic and mountain warfare experts. In this enormously demanding and extreme environment, everything they have learned at CTC must be combined with the very specialized skiing and survival techniques demanded by Commando operations in extreme cold.

Once he had completed his basic arctic and mountain warfare training, Sergeant Major Dobson ran the signals communications centre of 3 Commando Brigade Headquarters – in the process regaining the weight he had lost at CTC. Petty Officer Barrel, RTU'd after 6 weeks of the 4/92 All Arms course, returned for another go, passing in July 1993. He went back to MAOT (the Mobile Air Operations Team) at RNAS Yeovilton, providing ground support for 3 Commando Brigade Air Squadron (or 845 and 846 Naval Air Squadrons). He then went to Bosnia, where he worked with Seaking helicopters, and is currently in Baderfoss, Norway.

During the 1993 winter deployment, Lieutenants Kepple Compton and Lewis commanded Troops in Commando Logistic Regiment's Transport Squadron – running the fleets of lorries upon which the Brigade depends. At the end of their final arctic exercise Lt Lewis faced returning to CTC for another crack at the All Arms course – with determination. Promoted to Captain, Kepple Compton became second in command of Transport Squadron, and at the end of March 1994 is due to attend a Staff Course. Lt Lewis will take over from him, and is due to be promoted Captain in July 1994.

Recruit Jaftha had another bash at the endurance course, going round at the same time as All Arms 4/92. Despite a strong effort, he still failed to beat the 72-minute deadline. Corporal Dave Bateman, one of the Training Team members who earlier had urged 'binning' Jaftha, followed him round:

> 'Because of his injury, he's favouring the other leg, making his hips seize up so he can't run. If he tries it next week or the week after he still won't make it – but he won't give up. He's exactly the sort of man we want in the Royal Marines...'

Recruit Jaftha received his hard-earned Green Beret from Major Jon Lear in February 1993.

Formally binned from 638 Troop, Recruit Jaftha came back from Christmas leave into Hunter Troop, and after a few weeks training, cracked the chasm. Then on 19 February 1993, having passed all four Commando Tests, he was awarded his Green Beret, and passed out as a Royal Marine. He now serves at Royal Marines Poole, a member of Landing Craft Company – having heeded the plea by OC Captain Page that Landing Craft is the only truly and distinctly Royal Marine specialization.

After presenting Jaftha with his Green Beret, Major Jon Lear was posted to Arbroath in Scotland, to 45 Commando Group – as its second in command. He rings bells at two local churches (which have excellent eight-bell steeples), and has just finished making 10 gallons of home brewed beer, two gallons of wine and two batches of jam. Major Lear has found a good many members of 638 Troop already in Arbroath, including Corporal Dave Layton – whose first tour of duty back with 45 Commando took him out to the jungles of Belize.

Corporal Layton continues to train the Marines in his company, taking them well beyond the basics of the Commando Course, maintaining old skills as well as developing new ones – in the differing environments of jungle, arctic and Northern Ireland: 'My aspirations for the future are to stay in the Unit until I am called for a Senior

Marines Spink (left), Nicolson (above) and Wilson on exercise in Scotland, winter 1994, learning the type of skills useful for 45 Commando's training stint in Norway in 1995.

Command Course, hopefully moving from a company into Recce Troop to become a team commander for a future Northern Ireland tour. After that a move back to CTCRM looks inevitable although my real interest lies in the Commando and not in the training environment.'

Also in 45 Commando, Marine Dobson is in Anti-Tank Troop, having found the 6-month tour of Belize 'testing': 'The Corps is very much as I thought it would be due to having an insight from my earlier army career. My aims are to stay in the Corps and progress as far as possible in the short time available to me (due to having already spent 7 years in the Army).' Marines Wilson, Nicolson and Spink are also in 45 Commando – together in Yankee Company, and at time of writing are literally 'in communicado', yomping across the Scottish hills in the Kinloch Leven area, preparing for an arduous spring training exercise. With a Mediterranean amphibious deployment in spring and summer, there's not much time to pause – and a lot for them all to look forward to.

Marine Bauduin was posted to the Commando Logistic Regiment in Plymouth – finding himself working alongside the irrepressible McKenzie in the field surgical hospital of Medical Squadron.

In 1994, in a scaled-down Norway deployment, 42 Commando are to train and exercise in the northern Narvik/Harstad area – with several members of 638 Troop. The resiliant Lobb, Lee BW, Kelly TJ, Prater, Wheatley and Schembri are all now fully card-carrying members of 42, completing 'black-shod' training in the UK, then on 23 January, moving from their base in Plymouth, Devon, to Elvegardsmoen Camp in Bjerkvik to start basic arctic warfare training, building up to NATO exercises, before returning to UK in the second week of March.

638 Troop's Commander, Lt Archie Gillies made a sudden departure from CTC (nothing to do with his marching or sword drill), to Bosnia as a UN Observer. 4/92's Captain Rayson Pritchard is now OC Headquarters Squadron of the Commando Logistic Regiment, in Plymouth. Captain Leo Williams was promoted and runs the Royal Marines Cadets from the London Headquarters of the Sea Cadets. CTC's Commandant Colonel Mike Taffinder retired from the Royal Marines, and now works for the King George V Fund, a charity for former members of the Royal Navy (and Royal Marines).

Per mare, per terram ... Perhaps, provided you want it badly enough!

INDEX

Page references in *italics* indicate illustrations. Subheadings are in chronological order. The abbreviation OC means Officer Commanding.

Achnacarry (Scotland) 23
'admin vortex' 71
advance to contact, 638 Troop 82–5
ALJs (assault life-jackets) 50–1
All Arms Commando Course 4/92 13–17, *14–15*, 21–2
  helicopter training 17–21
  CQB training 24–7, *24*
  cliff-climbing 27–33, *30*
  river crossing 33–7, *34*
  BPT tests 37–42
  Final Exercise 129–32, *130*
  Commando Tests 22, *165*, 172–6
Allegiance, Oath of 162
ambushes
  on 638 Troop 67–9, *68*
  troop ambush by 638 Troop 72–81
  vehicle ambush by 638 Troop 87–8
amphibious boating 44
amphibious training, 638 Troop 47–55, *55*
Anfield, Recruit *97*, 98–9, 153
  Final Exercise 74, 86, 87, 96–8
  assessment and results after Final Exercise 102–3, 107, 115, 117, 118
  Tarzan course last practice 125, 128–9
  9-miler 140–1, 144, 146
  30-miler 157, 166
Arbroath 2, 187
assault course *see* Tarzan course
assault life-jackets (ALJs) 50–1

back-troopers 46
Bailey, Recruit 49, 139, 154, 155
Barnett, Sergeant Nick (Instructor) 56–7, 118, 143
  Final Exercise 70, 71, 75, 79–80
  conference after Final Exercise 102, 104, 106, 107
  endurance course 138, 139
  30-miler 157, 166
Barrel, Petty Officer 13, 26, 29, 33, 42, 186
basic fitness test 22

Bateman, Corporal Dave (Instructor) 186
  Final Exercise 91–2, 95
  conference after Final Exercise 102, 104, 105
  endurance course 138–9, *139*
battle physical training tests (BPT), All Arms 4/92 37–41
Bauduin, Recruit *45*, 154, 168, 185, 189
  Final Exercise 59, 61, 84, 87, 92
  raid on Portland Fort 63, 64–5
  assessment and results after Final Exercise 104, 107
  30-miler 158, 164–6
bergens (rucksacks) 18, 34–5, *34*
boat-training, 638 Troop 47–55, *55*
Boddy, Corporal (Instructor) 50–1, *52*
Boorn, Sergeant Pete (Instructor) 26
Booth, Bombardier Dick (Instructor) 17, 26
'Bootnecks' 16
BPT (battle physical training tests), All Arms 4/92 37–41

cap comforters 46
Chamberlain, Recruit 92, 93, 107, 138
character testing 17
cliff-climbing, All Arms 4/92 27–33
close-quarter battle, All Arms 4/92 24–7, *24*
combat fitness test 22
Commando Course Preparation Handbook 22
Commando Forces, formation 7–8, 16
Commando Tests 22, 47
Commando Tests, 638 Troop/King's Troop *see* 30-miler; 9-miler; endurance course; Tarzan course
Commando Tests, All Arms 4/92 *165*, 172–5
Commando Training Centre Royal Marines (CTCRM), Lympstone 13, 160, 186

Compton, Lieutenant Kepple *see* Kepple Compton, Lieutenant
CQB (close-quarter battle), All Arms 4/92 24–7, *24*
criteria tests 16

Dartmoor 22–3
  see also 30-miler; Final Exercise
death dive 29–33, *30*
'Diamonds' 57, 168
Diver, Chief Petty Officer 19, 20
Dobson, Recruit *45*, 99–100, 103, 152, 185, 188
  Final Exercise 59, 61, 71, 82, 84
  attack on fort 89, 90, 92, 96
  9-miler 141, 142
  30-miler 157, 159
  and the King's Badge 107, 167, 168, 169–70
Dobson, Sergeant Major 17, 176, 186
  cliff-climbing 29, 32–3
  tactical river crossing 35, 36
  Final Exercise 129, 130–1, *130*, 131–2
  30-miler 174, 175
dories *see* rigid raider assault craft
dunker training, helicopter, All Arms 4/92 19–21, *21*

endurance course 22, *135*, 186
  638 Troop 134–40, *137*
'enemy troops' 70–1
Exercise Highland Anvil *see* Final Exercise

4-mile speed march 112–13
Falklands War 8–11
Farrimond, Recruit 89–90, 154, 168
  assessment and results after Final Exercise 103, 107, 119
  30-miler 166–7
feet 87, 99–100
field training exercises 16
Final Exercise 22, 134
Final Exercise, 638 Troop 46–7, 56–9
  first briefing 59–62
  raid of Portland Fort 62–5, 66
  ambush on Troop 67–9, *68*

Final Exercise, 638 Troop – *cont*
troop ambush 70, 72–81
advance to contact 82–5
first yomp *85*, 86
the farm 86–7
long yomp 87
vehicle ambush 87–8
attack on Georgian fort 88–96
Final Exercise, All Arms 4/92
129–32, *130*
First Sea Lord 178, 182–3
fitness test, basic 22
Furness, ML Sergeant 29, 31, 33

Gault, Recruit 92, 103, 148, 167
Gillies, Lieutenant Archie (OC
638 Troop) *60*, 189
Final Exercise 57–9, 94–5
first briefing 59–62
raid on Portland Fort 63–5,
66
ambush 69
troop ambush 70, 72, 76–8,
80–1
the farm 86
attack on fort 91, 92–3, 93–4
conference after Final Exercise
102–110
meeting with Captain Williams
after Final Exercise 113–17,
114
interviews after Final Exercise
118–19
Tarzan course last practice 128–9
endurance course 139, 140
9-miler 143, 144
Tarzan course test run 150, 154
30-miler 155, 159, 167
Pass-Out Parade 171, 172, 179,
182, 183
Glennon, Recruit 112, 113, 129,
146, 148
endurance course 136, 138
9-miler 142–3, 145
30-miler 167
Gorrie, Corporal (Instructor) 16
Green Berets 8, 175, 178, 184

Hard, the (Poole) 44
Head, Recruit *45*, 103, 178
Heaps, Lance Corporal 173, 174,
175
Heley, Lieutenant 20–1
helicopter drills, All Arms 4/92
17–19
helicopter dunker training, All
Arms 4/92 19–21
Highland Anvil, Exercise *see* Final
Exercise, 638 Troop
Hilton, Recruit 49, 89, 103
Hodgson, Lance Corporal 175

Holmes, Recruit Michael 55, 87
assessment and results after Final
Exercise 103–4, 107, 115,
117, 118, 120
Hughes, Surgeon Lieutenant 16,
122–3
Hunter Troop 46, 110–13, *111*,
145–6, 186
Husband, CSM (King's Badge
Board) 168, 169, 170
Hutcheon, Lance Corporal 21,
29, 35, 35–6
Hutchings, Major (King's Badge
Board) 168, 169, 170

injuries 16
110, 112, *see also* Hunter Troop

Jaftha, Recruit *123*, 186, *187*
Final Exercise 98
Tarzan course last practice 122–
3, 125–8, *126*, 129
endurance course 136, 137,
139, 140
9-miler 142, 143, 144–5
Tarzan course test run 150–1,
152
30-miler 157, 166
Johnson, Recruit 86, 87, 105,
115–16, 117
Jones, Corporal (Instructor) 162
Jones, Lieutenant (King's Badge
Board) 168

Kelly, Recruit ND *45*, 100, 105,
108, 148
Final Exercise 86
joke played on 108–9
endurance course 138, 139, 140
9-miler 144, 146
Tarzan course test run 152–3
30-miler 158
Kelly, Recruit TJ 105, 189
Tarzan course test run 148, 150,
152, 153
Kepple Compton, Lieutenant 37,
38, 40–2, 186
Khanlarian, Sapper 36, 175
King's Badge 105, 107, 167–70
King's Squad *180–1*
638 Troop become King's
Squad 143–4
Tarzan course test run 148–54,
149, *151*
30-miler 154–9, *156*, *158*,
164–7
King's Badge 167–70
Pass-Out Parade
rehearsals 170–2, *171*, 177–8
Parade 178–9, 182–4
see also 638 Troop

kit, 'left loafing' 71

Landing Craft Branch 49, 187
Landing Craft exercises, 638
Troop 48–54, *55*
Layton, Corporal Dave
(Instructor) 99–100, 117–18,
154, 184, 187
Final Exercise 57, 69–70, 71,
75, 80–1, 86
conference after Final Exercise
102, 104, 107
9-miler 142, 144–5
30-miler 157, 158, 159, 166
LCUs (landing craft utility) 44
LCVPs (landing craft vehicle
personnel) 53–4
Lear, Major Jon (OC Commando
Training Wing) 133–4, *134*,
146, 148, 167, 178, 187
9-miler 141, 142–3
30-miler 164, 165, 166
and Hunter Troop 110, 146
and King's Badge 167–8
Lee, Recruit *45*, 100, 105, 189
Lewis, Lieutenant 37, 38, 40, 186
Linderman, Lieutenant 13, 26,
132
30-miler 174, 176
Lobb, Recruit *45*, 101, 168, 189
Final Exercise 58, 90, 91, 92, 95
assessment and results after Final
Exercise 105, 107, 119
Tarzan course test run 153–4
Lympstone, Commando Training
Centre Royal Marines
(CTCRM) 13, 160
Lyons, Recruit 54, 105, 154

MacDonald, Corporal
(Instructor) 116
Final Exercise 70, 86, 93
conference after Final Exercise
102, 105, 109
endurance course 139
9-miler 144
Tarzan course 154
30-miler 164, 166
McKenzie, Recruit *89*, 105, 168,
184, 189
Final Exercise 71, 87, 89–90,
92, 96
endurance course 136, 138
30-miler 158, 159, 167
Maddison, Second Lieutenant 174
March, Captain (Company
Commander Portsmouth
Company) 162–4
Miles, Corporal Tam (Instructor)
17, 21, 35, 37, 174

Morgan, Sergeant John (Instructor) 37, 38, *38*, 40, 41, 42–3
Mountain Leaders 27–8

9-miler 22
    638 Troop 140–3
'negligent discharge' 184
Neilson, Corporal Eric (Instructor) 102, 145–6, 173, 183
    Tarzan course last practice 122, 127, 128
    endurance course 136, 140
    9-miler 140, 141, 142
    Tarzan course test run 148, 154
    30-miler 154–5
Nicolson, Recruit *45*, 51, 106, 159, 188
    Final Exercise 59, 61, 82, 83, 84, 86, 93
    endurance course 136, 138
    Tarzan course test run 150
    and King's Badge 107, 167, 168, 170
Nield, Recruit 87, 148
    assessment and results of Final Exercise 106, 115, 119
    endurance course 139, 140
    30-miler 166
'Nods' 45
Norman, Captain 31, 35, 36

148 Commando Forward Observation Battery 44
Oath of Allegiance 162
Operation Corporate 8, 11
opt-out 163

Page, Captain (OC Landing Craft Company) 48–50, 187
Pass-Out Parade, King's Squad rehearsals 170–2, *171*, 177–8
    Parade 178–9, 182–4
Pelling, Corporal (Instructor) 33, 35, 37
'Percy Pongo' 13
Perkins, Lieutenant 33, 174
Poole, Royal Marines 44, 187
Portland Fort 62–3, *63*
Portsmouth Company 164
Potts, Recruit *45*, 106, 167
    Final exercise 66–7, 69, 74, 92
Prater, Recruit 50–1, 86, 93, 106, 148, 189
    Tarzan course last practice 125
    9-miler 142, 144
    Tarzan course test run 150–1, 152, 154
    Tarzan course re-run 173

Pritchard, Captain Rayson (OC All Arms 4/92) 25, 130, 175, 189
    BPT tests 38, 41–2
    30-miler 173, 174
Pyott, Recruit 82

RIBs (rigid inflatable boats) 44
rigid raider assault craft 44, 51, *51*, 52, 62
river crossing, tactical, All Arms 4/92 33–7, *34*
Roach, Sapper 131, 175–6
Rockey, Sapper 21, 174
roller haulage system (climbing) 28–9
Royal Marines *2*, 13, 16, 162
RTU (return to unit) 22
Ryder, Corporal (Instructor) 164–5
    Pass-Out Parade 170, *171*, 172, 177–8,
    183

638 Troop 44–5, *45*
    arrival at Lympstone 160–4, *161*
    commando boating training 47–54, *55*
    Final Exercise 56–96, *68*, *85*
    assessments and results after Final Exercise 101–10, 113–21
    Tarzan course last practice 121–9
    endurance course 134–40, *135*, *137*, 186
    9-miler 140–3
    become King's Squad 143–4
    see also King's Squad'
Schembri, Recruit Alain 52, 55–6, 106, 189
Seaking helicopters 17–19
Smith, Recruit AD
    Final Exercise 82, 86, 87
    assessment and results after Final Exercise 106, 107, 114–15, 117, 118, 120
Smith, Recruit MR
    Final Exercise 87, 98
    assessment and results after Final Exercise 106, 107, 114, 116–17, 119
    endurance course 138
    Tarzan course test run 150
Snazel, Recruit 54, *80*, 159, 184
    Final Exercise 80–1
    assessment and results after Final Exercise 106, 107, 116, 117, 119, 121
    endurance course 139

Spink, Recruit *45*, *73*, 167, 188
    Final Exercise 58, 59, 61, 64, 69
    troop ambush 72–3, 74–5, 76, 80
    advance to contact 83, 84–5
    assessment and results after Final Exercise 106–7
    Tarzan course last practice 124, 125, 128, 129
    9-miler 142
    Tarzan course test run 150
    and King's Badge 107, 167, 168, 168–9, 170, *171*
Sullivan, Recruit *45*, 89–90, 128, 150,   151–2
Swayne, Sergeant Nigel (Instructor) 37, 38, 43, 175
    CQB training 24, 25–6
swimming test, basic 22

30-miler 22
    All Arms 4/92 174
    King's Squad 154–9, *156*, *158*, 164–7
12-mile load carry 22
Taffinder, Colonel Mike (CTC Commandant) 174, 175, 176–7, 182, 189
Tarzan course 22, *147*
    638 Troop/King's Squad last practice 121–9
    test run 148–54, *149*, *151*
    All Arms 4/92 173
Taylor, Flight Lieutenant 13
Teers, Corporal 52–3
Thomas, Private 33, 130, 173, 175
Thomson, Lance Corporal 172–3, 174, 176
Tobin, Recruit 93, 148
Training Area Warden 96
Trickett, Second Lieutenant 173

weapons 100, 138
Williams, Captain Leo (OC Chatham Company) 113–17, *115*, 120–1, 128, 157, 189
Williams, Corporal (Instructor) 160–1
Wilson, Recruit *2*, *45*, 78, 79, 85, 141, 167, 188
Wright, Sergeant 'Shiner' 110, 112, 113

Xavier, Sapper 37, 38, 40–1, 42, 132
    30-miler 174, 175

Yeovilton, Royal Naval Air Station 17
yomping *85*, 86, 100